THE
AMORALISTS
& OTHER TALES

THE
AMORALISTS
& OTHER TALES:
collected stories by
Cyrus Colter

THUNDER'S
MOUTH
PRESS

NEW YORK

Published in the United States by

THUNDER'S MOUTH PRESS,

93–99 Greene Street, New York, N.Y. 10012

Cover design by Loretta Li

Grateful acknowledgement is made to the
New York State Council on the Arts and
the National Endowment for the Arts
for financial assistance with
the publication of this work.
Some of these stories have appeared
in the following magazines:
*Black World, Chicago Review,
New Letters* and *The University Review.*

Library of Congress Cataloging-in-Publication Data

Colter, Cyrus.

The amoralists & other tales : collected stories /
by Cyrus Colter.—1st ed.

p.   cm—(Contemporary fiction series)

ISBN 0-938410-67-9 : $19.95.

ISBN 0-938410-65-2 (pbk.) : $9.95

I. Title. II. Title: Amoralists & other tales.
III. Series.

PS3553.O477A6   1988

813'.54—dc19   88-9749   CIP

FIRST EDITION

Manufactured in the United States of America

Distributed by Consortium Book Sales

213 E. 4th Street

St. Paul, Minnesota 55101

612-221-9035

Contents

For IMOGENE

THE
AMORALISTS
& OTHER TALES

A Man in the House

Verna bent over the old-fashioned bath tub—the kind with legs, and the white enamel worn thin in places—to turn the faucet and start the hot water running. But the motions she was going through were mechanical, for her vivid, purposeful mind ranged elsewhere: it had just occurred to her she was beginning to like Chicago. Her unconscious psyche had toyed with the idea for days; now *she* was adopting it. But the reasons were not at all clear to her, and she was aware of faint misgivings about probing them too far. She was seventeen now, and spent most of her time in a ritualistic reverie about herself, her current projects, and the small, but earnest world she moved in—and she considered herself the center of that world. But this self-love—actually, unrecognized by her—was almost always hidden behind a tender-maiden exterior. That was her uniqueness; except, possibly, for an odd, brown, virginal beauty—a source of great anxiety to her widowed mother.

Steam was billowing up out of the tub now, and she started a jet of cold water into the hot. It was almost eight weeks since she had left her mother and sister, Cindy, for the summer, and, although at first she had been homesick, she seldom ever missed them now; and whenever she did, it was with the slightest tincture of guilt—she did not know why. She knew her mother had fretted about every boy she dated down in Memphis, and she thought this silly, for she had never been attracted to any of them, and, as far as she knew, had never acted like it. Yet after June graduation, her mother had poorly concealed her eagerness for the present visit. But, so far, the visit hadn't been a bit dull—with the boys, and dates, and all. And her Aunt Ruby (her mother's sister) and Uncle Jack Robinson were extremely nice to her—she felt sometimes it was because they had no children of their own.

Now Verna took pains to keep her mother comfortable with long, frank letters about her activities—especially her dates; but somehow she had never mentioned her strange initial fear—fear, not of the boys, or of the big city, although Chicago was at first bewildering, but of herself. She had experienced a brand-new feeling in this very different house, stirrings inside her that were at once confusing and sometimes faintly frightening. But that had been in the beginning. Since then, vague, imperceptible changes had taken place, each defying a neat label; but there was no change in the intensity of her involvement. The fear returned occasionally, but never with its old alarm, and what finally remained was—well, to Verna, it was bliss; still something akin to dread; ecstatically satisfying, yet itself unsatisfied.

The tub was two-thirds full now, and, after turning off the water, she went back into her tidy bedroom. She took her blue dress from the closet and laid it out across the bed. The style of the dress and its shade of blue, an ultramarine, always pleased her, as did the perfect way it fit her, giving her the quiet, worldly air she craved. She turned to look at herself in the dresser mirror, and raised the palms of both hands to her freshly-done hair and fluffed it into a more casual shape. But it was always well-groomed because she cared for it with one of those harsh little passions she directed at certain special things in her life. The velvety brown of her skin, with its peach fuzz, the almond eyes, the curved, ample mouth, all combined to convey the tender, fondled look that drove her handsome Uncle Jack Robinson to refer to her as "quail." He would put his burly arm around her shoulders and squeeze her hard against his heaving ribs, and tease, "You little quail, you!" This had terrified her at first, but now no more—although she was still flustered if her Aunt Ruby happened to be looking. Aunt Ruby would give her high, fluttering, nervous laugh, and say, but not too boldly, "You let that child alone, Jack Robinson!"

Verna heard the telephone ring downstairs, as she picked up the dress off the bed and held it out in front of her. She had decided to wear it that evening because Stanley, her date, had seen it once before and said he liked it; but he was probably jiving, she thought—all these Chicago boys were so full of jive, and so grown up! What would her mother ever say about *them!*—even the real young ones; they were certainly different from the boys in Memphis. But Stanley wasn't too bad—he just thought he was such a man; it really made him funny, if he only knew it. Yet he was a merry, off-beat date— you never knew exactly what was going to happen, but you always had a good time. And he liked her. They were both going away to college in September—or rather, she was supposed to go, if her mother could raise a few more dollars. But Stanley wasn't as nice as Curtis down in Memphis; Curtis was more of a gentleman, certainly; he always helped her off the bus, and made sure she was walking on the inside of the sidewalk. And he'd never tried to force her mouth open when he kissed her—nor had he ever told her how "fine" he bet she was, like Stanley had once.

"*Verna*, baby!" It was Aunt Ruby's jumpy, soprano voice from the living room downstairs.

". . . Yes?" Verna's voice was soft like a child's. She liked her Aunt Ruby, but with a trace of condescension.

"What time's your date, honey? That was your Uncle Jack Robinson on the phone—he wants to take us to the ball game tonight. I told him you had a date, but he said for you to bring your date along."

"Oh . . . Gee." Verna stepped to the head of the stairs. "I don't know . . . Stanley said we were going over to a friend of his to listen to records."

"Well, you know how your uncle is. He wants to run everything and everybody." Ruby emitted the fluttering laugh.

"We can ask Stanley, Aunt Ruby—when he comes. It'll be around eight."

"That may be too late for your Uncle Jack Robinson," Ruby said, in thoughtful apprehension.

Verna was thoughtful too. Her mother had warned her to be nice to her uncle, who had hinted at helping out with her college tuition—he operated two big taverns. "Well . . ."— she hesitated—"maybe we'd better wait, then; and ask him, when he gets home . . . ." She felt exhilarating jitters.

"All right then, honey," Ruby said from the foot of the stairs—she was a light-skinned, flabby-fat woman of thirty-nine who looked easily ten years older from the cruel lines in her already-sagging face; she ate insatiably, feared God and her husband, and kept a clean house. When she was a thin, rather slow-witted quadroon of nineteen, she ran away from home in Memphis to marry Jack Robinson Brown, and ever since had thought herself extremely happy, despite her inevitable stomach-writhings whenever he was around. "It's four-thirty now," she called up to Verna. "He'll be home around six, I guess."

". . . Okay." Verna, on her way back to the bedroom, had already started undressing for her bath. She felt strange— and eager—now. She was naked when she began looking around the room for her robe. Suddenly she paused in front of the mirror. She cautiously viewed herself. Her nut-brown breasts were small and firm, and the nipples were almost black; the fertile curvature of her hips and thighs expressed the ripened child-woman, and she was pleased with herself.

Ruby and Verna were in the kitchen when, about six-fifteen, Jack Robinson let himself in at the front door. He was tall, medium-brown, and weighed a muscular two hundred pounds in his business suit. His rather sharp, severe jaw jutted forward prominently, and was swathed in a smooth beard-shadow; and he clenched a wet cigar butt between his teeth.

"Hey!" he greeted them, tossing his soft straw hat onto the rack before coming into the kitchen. Verna looked wide-eyed at his strong hands. "What're you two up to *now?*" he asked with a raffish grin, his prankster's eyes roving the room.

"We're up to fixing you a nice dinner, honey!" Ruby beamed. "That's what we're up to!"

Verna, wearing a tiny white apron around her waist over the blue dress, stood behind her Aunt Ruby and smiled out shyly at him—but somehow she felt exposed. She couldn't help wondering what he'd been like when he was Stanley's or Curtis's age, for instance. Had he always been so rash, so daredevilish?—he was forty-eight now, she knew. She had never seen any man like him—not even in the movies; and, apprehensively watching him, she shuddered from the primeval hurt in her loins—a dulcet, gossamer hurt, that cringed in the face of half-wished-for cruelties. She was helplessly confused, and longed to run and hide.

"A nice dinner, eh!" hectored Jack Robinson. "Well, that's mighty white of you—as the white folks say." With his long arm reaching high over his head, he pulled open a top door of the cabinet and took down a fifth of Gordon's gin. "And what've you been doing with *yourself* all day, gingerbread?"

he asked without looking at Verna—he was taking down a glass now.

Near panic, she said nothing, until he turned to her. "Oh . . . not much . . . have we?"—she looked at her Aunt Ruby.

"Not much," affirmed Ruby. "We did go to the supermarket, around noon."

Jack Robinson now opened the freezer compartment of the refrigerator and lifted out a small bucket of ice cubes, and then, for a mixer, took out a cold bottle of Squirt from the section below. "Will anybody join me?" he asked—his grin was a leer. He stepped to the kitchen table, half-singing, half-reciting, " 'Whiskey for the head; rum for the feet; and gin for in between!' "

"Jack Robinson! You *stop* that!" cried Ruby, giggling. "That child's not used to talk like that! Her mother'd die! Now you stop it!"

Jack Robinson's shoulders shook a little as he chortled, and poured a half glass of gin over frosted ice, before adding Squirt. As he stirred the drink with his forefinger, he gazed at Verna with the tenderest, most gentle smile.

She felt needles on her face and neck; yet she wanted to laugh; the man could be so funny at times!—but crafty and wicked too, she sensed. She looked at him, and gave a little laugh.

"Look at her!" scolded Ruby, but still giggling. "She's embarrassed!"

"Hummph!" grunted Jack Robinson after drinking off half the glass at one sally. "If she keeps on runnin' around with these little purse-snatchers here in Chicago, she won't be getting embarrassed long—I'll guarantee you that!" He backed up and took a seat on the tall kitchen stool.

"Now, honey! Those're nice boys Verna goes out with—and you know it!"

"Nice my eye! Nice, till they get her cornered! You'll see how nice they are *then!* And that's when you'll have to come out to Cook County jail to see *me!*" Jack Robinson hit himself on the chest twice with the protruding thumb of his clenched first—and his voice was rising now, as the gin hit home.

"Now, *honeeeey!*" Ruby whinnied.

Verna, her mind now clear and alert, wished her Aunt Ruby would hurry up and ask about the ball game. She knew— deep in her clever heart—she wanted to go; the heck with Stanley. Then Jack Robinson, perched on the tall stool, looked across the kitchen at her. "Come over here, sugar," he beckoned with his noisy glass, "and tell Uncle Jack Robinson if any of those boys're tryin' to take advantage of you."

Verna crossed the kitchen and stood submissively at his side—she thought he smelled deliciously of strong tobacco. She reflected for an instant how she might have been different if only she could have grown up in a house with a man in it—she'd had no father since the age of five. "No . . . the boys are all nice," she said. He put his arm around her waist and gazed in her eyes, his grim face shadowed with tenderness. "Little quail," he said, "you know you've always got your Uncle Jack Robinson to look after you, don't you?—y'know that."

"Yes," Verna said, trembling at his touch—she had never in her brief life's experience felt the way she felt now. Wild- fire sensations climbed her spine, and the young flesh on her face and neck went ablaze; she stood numbly rigid, afraid of falling.

Ruby was putting the rolls in the oven now, and, after clos- ing the oven door, turned and beamed at her husband and Verna. "That's right, honey," she said to Verna. "Your uncle means that." She did not see her husband's face cloud up at the intrusion. He released Verna, and she quickly sat down in a kitchen chair. No one spoke. Then he vengefully tossed off the rest of his drink, and set the glass down hard.

"Why don't you go wash up, honey?" Ruby coaxed him. "As soon as the rolls are brown, we'll be ready."

He looked at her coldly. "Don't rush me," he said. "I'm gonna have another drink." He began mixing a second strong gin-and-Squirt. But soon he took it with him upstairs.

Ruby leaned over the table and whispered to Verna, "Don't pay him any mind, honey; he'll be all right afterwhile—something's on his mind . . . something's bothering him."

Verna looked at her aunt, and was inwardly annoyed with her.

When Jack Robinson came down to the kitchen again, the glass in his hand was empty; yet he seemed more composed. He did not look at Verna. "Did the newspaper come yet, Babe?" he asked Ruby.

"Yes, honey—but dinner's ready now," Ruby said.

They sat down to dinner. And Ruby and Verna bowed their heads, as Ruby, in wheedling tones, began saying grace. When she got to: ". . . please bless this food, dear Lord, and sanctify it for its intended purpose . . . ," she opened her eyes wide, and seemed to stare up at the pink kitchen curtains, her high voice rising and falling. When they began to eat, Jack Robinson suddenly seemed cheerful. There was chuck roast and potatoes, and Ruby stealthily waited until the other plates were served before she helped her own, diverting attention from the heaping portions she gave herself.

Soon, with a trace of eagerness, Jack Robinson said, "Let's all go out to that game tonight—and watch the Yankees lynch the White Sox! They do it every time they come here—it'll be the same again tonight!" His laugh was a scoff.

Verna's heart vaulted.

"Honey," Ruby said, this time directing the wheedling tone

at her husband, "I told you on the phone — Verna's got a date. *She* can't come."

"Yeah, *I* know," Jack Robinson scowled. He turned on Verna. "Date with who?"

"With Stanley."

"Where you going?"

"Over to a friend of his—to listen to records."

"Who is this *'friend'?*" Jack Robinson's voice was getting high and hoarse.

"I've never met him—at least, I don't remember him. Stanley says I met him once at a dance, though—when I first came. His name is Julius."

"Where's Julius's *place?*" He spat the words.

"*I* don't know." Verna's voice broke—and soon tears were wetting her long lashes.

"*Honey!*" Ruby pleaded with Jack Robinson, "don't be so rough! Look—you've spoiled her dinner! . . . Stanley's a nice boy—you know that!"

"I don't know any such a *damn thing!*" Jack Robinson exploded. "To *me*, all them little reefer-smokers are alike!"

Verna looked on in awe through the glaze of her tears at his fury. And she felt guilty to find no zeal in her heart for defending Stanley. She said nothing.

The three ate in silence. The electric clock over the refrigerator made a faint whirring sound as the long second hand made its slow trek around the dial. Verna's tears dried readily; she was not hurt. She felt a disheveled relief—as at the violent settling, once and for all, of a burning question. She ate well, and relished her food. Suddenly, Jack Robinson, ignoring her, said to Ruby. "All right then—get your things on. *We'll* go." He finished his meal in a sullen silence.

Stanley arrived shortly before eight. When he rang the doorbell, Jack Robinson, who had been pretending to read the newspaper, got up and stalked off upstairs. Verna, all ready to go, realized he was willing to be late for the ball game rather than leave her to greet Stanley alone. She was nervous, and very glad Stanley was on time; and got him out of the house quickly—before he could sit down. Walking to the bus stop, she was silent, preoccupied.

When the bus finally came, and they had boarded and taken seats, Stanley, with a quizzical little frown, turned to her and said, "What's eating you?"

"Nothing's eating me," she quietly lied.

"All you do is look out the window." He watched her. He was a tall, gangling, brown-skinned boy, and wore an Ivy League summer suit and a pair of big black-rimmed glasses he did not need. He was doing most of the talking.

Verna sat inert; re-living dinner and its revelation; and once more she was afraid—afraid of herself. In her *mind* she had ceased to be chaste already. Aunt Ruby, was right— but for the wrong reason—Verna's mother *would* die, if she knew. A feeling of doom came over her, and she saw all too clearly what she must do—but this thought of leaving Chicago plunged her into despair, and made the past eight weeks seem a nostalgic Shangri-La.

By the time the bus reached Eighty-second Street, where they were to get off, glib Stanley, now thoroughly dejected, had stopped talking; but as they left the bus, Verna, sorry for him, resolved to be more cheerful. It was almost dark as they started walking the two blocks to Julius's. People were out sprinkling their lawns, and the children were whooping and romping on the wet sidewalks.

"Who's going to be there?"—Verna was smiling now, and seemed lighthearted.

"Slick Fambro and Gwen Smith," Stanley said, still glum. "And Julius, of course—and Dotty, his girl. You've heard of Slick—he's the prep basketball star."

"I hope Julius has got some good records." She was making conversation.

"Don't worry about a thing. He's *got* 'em." Stanley was so positive—she was amused.

Julius lived with his mother and father in a small, one-story brick with a trim little lawn. When he opened the door to them, Verna did remember him—as Stanley said. The music was going and everybody was there already, in the attractive living room that seemed large for the house. Both Dotty and Gwen were young like Verna, but they viewed her with anxious interest when Julius introduced her around. Slick stood up when introduced, and then grinned over at Stanley, giving him a low little whistle of congratulations. The music was cool, progressive jazz, coming out of the stereo speakers in the far corner, and Gwen was busily searching through a stack of albums on the floor for the next record. When Julius had finished serving everyone rum and coke, he went and brought his mother—a tiny woman—for Verna to meet.

They were all gay—sometimes hilarious—and even Verna, at times, sipping her drink, was drawn away from the fever of the earlier evening. She danced with all the boys, and smiled when Slick furtively told her how beautiful she was. But as the evening wore on, her mood began to change—to darken. She was thinking of herself again: of how poised she was among these kids; how experienced; how bored. *They* hadn't lived—they just thought they had. She kept a set smile on her face, and felt detached. It did not occur to her now that only two months before, fresh up from Memphis, she would not have felt so secure among these same "kids" now the object of her mild hauteur.

After an hour they were still dancing, and when Julius put a very modern version of "Stella by Starlight" on the turntable, Stanley avidly claimed Verna, and they danced. He was possessive, and held her tightly. "I'm overboard about you," he said. "Real gone. You know that. I just can't get you out of my head . . . you're all I think about—morning, noon, and night." He put his cheek down against her hair and held her even tighter. She tried to keep her breathing in, and say nothing—as her mind shot away. Stanley was offensive to her now, and she longed to wriggle free.

When the record finished playing, everyone sat down. "Now, how about some *listening* music?" Julius said, kneeling on the floor to go through the stack of records.

"Oh, play something by the Soft Sounds Trio, Julius!" Dotty cried, bounding over to him and looking over his shoulder at each record.

Verna sat on the sofa, with Stanley, his drink in his hand, sprawled on the floor at her feet.

When Julius and Dotty finally found the record, and Julius was putting it on, Stanley yelled at him, "Hey, man, d'you need all this light?—you said *listening* music!" Everybody laughed, and Julius reached over and turned off one of the table lamps, transforming the room into a soft gloaming.

When the first pensive notes of the piano came out of the stereo speakers, Gwen squealed. "Oh, it's 'The Party's Over'! I *love* this!" The music played by the smooth combo echoed the break-up of a love affair. It was bittersweet and haunting, and no one spoke. Its mood somehow caught them up in the spell of their own fantasies and dreams of love—yet to be lived—with all the filmy visions of romance with the ideal boy or girl, broken up for a time by some dazzling intruder, but ultimately and rapturously restored in a blaze of passion, tears and remorse. But not Verna. She felt *her* dreams were in the past already. Then the aching deep in her returned, and she felt flawed and contemptible. She reflected bitterly *she* didn't feel moon-struck by the music. She felt cursed. Her mind had returned to early evening in the kitchen, when she had stood beside the tall stool—to the ecstasy, the near swooning, the ravish-wish. She was convinced now she must return to her mother—and at once.

Stanley brought her home in a taxi around midnight. She was moody and would not let him kiss her. As she quietly let herself in the house, she hoped nobody was still up. As usual, the squat little lamp on the kitchen table had been left lighted for her. She went into the kitchen, opened the refrigerator, and stared in absently—she knew she wasn't hungry. But maybe milk would hasten sleep. She took down a glass from the cupboard and poured herself a glass of milk, and sat down at the kitchen table to sip it. Her mind was listless now—she had thought too much for one day. Yet the images of her mother and Cindy came to her clearly, and would not go away. How the weeks did fly! Cindy would be fifteen in October. What would she say when Verna came home so unexpectedly—Cindy could be so nosey! But her mother would *never* understand—and she could never tell her. And college was probably out of the question now—wouldn't her mother be furious! Curtis, though, would be glad she'd come back. But she didn't care about any of these things, really. They were nothing to the sickening feeling in her heart at leaving. There had never been an iron will in her house, since she could remember—and what a difference that made; otherwise maybe she wouldn't be so mesmerized now. And *he* had never had a daughter—maybe he'd be different, too. It was all so everlastingly mixed up—she wanted to cry, but she knew her stony heart wouldn't let her.

She finished the glass of milk and turned out the light. And as she slowly climbed the dimly-lit stairs, she thought of the ball game, and how she had yearned to go—there'd never be another.

She entered her room and switched on the light; and was startled by the white sheet of paper lying in the center of the bed. She picked it up, and recognized her Aunt Ruby's pencilled handwriting:

> Verna, honey,
> Your Uncle Jack Robinson asked me to write you this. He's so sorry the way he acted at dinner. He says he's been upset lately about some things. He never tells me much, so I don't know what things. But he don't want you to feel upset and mad at him, because he said to tell you he loves you. He's a wonderful guy, honey, a wonderful guy, when you get to know him. This note is all his idea — so you see?
> The Yankees won! Just like he said!
> Nighty night,
> Aunt Ruby

Verna slowly sank down on the edge of the bed, clutching the note in her hand, her fingernails digging into the flesh of her palms. The old beautiful, dulcet feeling had returned, creeping and glowing over her like a meadow haze; and it hurt, too—terribly. But she accepted it—with its portent— gladly, eagerly, her decision forgotten. She knew now she would never go home—*never*. Instinctively she went into the bathroom to brush her teeth, and when she returned she fancied herself no longer alone in the room, and started undressing feverishly, heaping all her clothes on a chair, and then flicked out the light and, naked, leapt into bed.

A Chance Meeting

This October afternoon was sunny, but gusty. The wind, flinging smoke from the burning leaves, threshed the tall trees along Berkeley Avenue as black children in bright sweaters and sturdy shoes played along the sidewalk. An elderly, light brown-skinned man walked down the street, the wind flapping his topcoattails against his thin legs. Hanging from his right hand, pendant-like, was a half-full shopping bag and cupped in his left a book, as unnoticed he passed the children.

"*Ford!*" a falsetto voice called out from across the street. "Ford!"

He snapped his head to the left in the caller's direction, eyes wide. Then his facial muscles relaxed. "Hello there, Spivey," he called.

Across the street a big brown-skinned man in his sixties, well enough dressed, waved excitedly as he stood at the curb waiting for two cars to pass. Then he quickly crossed over and, grinning broadly, stuck out his fat hand. "I *thought* that wuz you! I started to go on, but I just knew it wuz you! How in the world you doin', Ford?"

"Pretty good, Spivey." Ford managed a smile as he slipped

the book down inside the shopping bag, changed the bag over, and shook hands. "How're *you* doing?"

"Fine! Fine, so far! I ain't sendin' out to the laundry more'n one shirt at a time, though—and I ain't startin' any continued stories!" Spivey laughed shrilly, showing his short yellow teeth, and then he let go of Ford's hand. "Howya been? I guess it's five'r six years since I saw you last—when L.B.J. was runnin' for President."

"Is that right? Has it been that long, Spivey?"

"Why sure, and before that, a long time. I remember the last time, though, because you said Missus Cate was for Johnson and I wondered how anybody with all her money could ever be for a Democrat!"

They both laughed, Ford softly.

"And y'know how I first recognized you from across the street there?" Spivey said, hitching up the long belt required to encircle his paunch.

"No."

"Why, by that damn book you was carryin'—I could sure tell it was you, all right. It's about music, too. I'll bet you. I'll lay you a bet."

"Well . . . I still read some. I've got more time now." Ford sighed as he carefully set the shopping bag down on the pavement.

"Am I holdin' you up?" Spivey asked quickly.

"No, that's all right. I just got back from downtown and had to stop off at the grocery." Ford thrust both hands into the pockets of his neat grey topcoat and stood up straight.

"*I* was just killin' some time," Spivey said. "M'wife ain't home yet."

"How is your wife, Spivey?"

"Oh, she's fine. Just got a new Olds—and never home. Out in th' street in it all the time. You see me walkin', don't you?"

"Yes, I do," Ford smiled.

"Say . . . how about goin' up here to the corner and havin' one on me? What I wanta do is get a line on you—on what you been doin' with yourself all these years since I left you at the Cates. How long wuz it, Ford, we worked there together?"

"I don't remember offhand—some time, though. I've got my butter and milk in here, Spivey." Ford pointed down at the shopping bag. "I think maybe I'd better go on home." Spivey was silent. In a moment Ford in a flat voice, said, "You can come on along with me if you want to—up to my place. I can probably find a drink or two up there."

"It won't putya to a lot of trouble, will it?" Spivey perked up.

"No," Ford said, resigned, as he reached down for the handles of his shopping bag.

The two men walked down the street together, big Spivey lumbering on the outside and Ford, slight, almost wizened, abreast. Dead leaves swirled about their feet as the wind blew thin, acrid smoke in all directions. Some red and yellow leaves were still on the trees. The driver of a big, red, coal dump-truck was blasting his horn at a black woman in a creeping, dilapidated Chrysler.

The smoke had aroused Ford's frail cough. "What're you doing now, Spivey?" he asked hoarsely.

"M'wife and I got a beauty parlor." Spivey's strident laugh made his small eyes dart. "Six operators—and doin' okay, too."

"Well, good."

"You doin' anything?"

"I'm down at the Library—running a freight elevator," Ford said quietly. "Mrs. Cate got me on down there after Mr. Cate passed. She gave up the big place out in Lake Forest, you know, and came on into the city."

"I saw in the papers about her death."

"Yes." The corners of Ford's mouth set.

"Say, whatever happened to them kids? I guess they're scattered all over by now. That little Peggy was a cute child, wasn't she?—with her blond head—and th' funniest damn questions!"

"Peg and Roger are here. She writes poetry, you know. John's in San Francisco, in a bank. And Sally, she married a Frenchman. She's living over there now."

"Ford, actually how long was you with them people?"

"Thirty-seven years—that is, lacking two months."

"I knew it was a long time, all right. You'd been there a long time when I come."

"I was twenty-eight when I went there."

"And ain't married yet."

Ford smiled wanly. "No . . . that's for you fellows that know all about women."

They had walked two blocks when Ford turned in at a tall iron gate. "Here we are," he said. A cement walk crossed a small lawn to the entrance of the large apartment building and when they had entered the vestibule Ford took out some keys and opened the door into the stairwell. They climbed the carpeted stairs to the third floor where he used two more keys to let them into a single-room apartment, flicking on the ceiling light as they entered.

"Jeee-*sus!*" Spivey cried, stopping abruptly and staring at the walls.

The green walls were a mass of photograph-clippings, snipped from magazines and newspapers and stuck onto the wallpaper with scotch tape.

"Who're all these?" big Spivey screeched, breathing heavily as he struggled out of his topcoat.

Ford was casual—a bit majestic. "Oh, singers . . . and conductors, pianists, violinists—famous musicians that I've heard or seen at one time or another."

"You sure have got a lot of 'em!"

"Yes, they have accumulated, haven't they?" Ford pulled the book out of the shopping bag and laid it on a table and took the bag to the small refrigerator in the back, while Spivey stood in the center of the room, with hands in hip pockets, smug, as he looked around him. One wall had mahogany-stained double doors concealing a folding bed. The room, fully carpeted, contained modest but comfortable furniture, and was tidy enough. But the air was stale.

Ford took off his coat and hat and hung them, with Spivey's, near the door.

"Here's Missus Cate!" Spivey blurted out, snatching up a large studio photograph from the radio-phonograph against the wall. The subject was a handsome woman in her early fifties with soft, light-brown hair and wearing a strand of pearls.

"Yes," Ford said, bent over as he peered into the little refrigerator. "Peg gave me that about a week after Mrs. Cate passed. It was taken a good while ago, though."

"Yeah, but just like her! Just like her for the world! She's gettin' ready right now to say to me 'And Daniel, please don't be all day about it.'" Spivey then picked up the book from the little table and looked at it importantly. "Verdy," he said, rocking back on his heels.

"Verdi," repeated Ford, correcting the pronunciation. "A composer—you know—operas."

"Yeah? Bet *you'd* know, all right." Spivey put the book down and, taking out his glasses, began to look closely at the clippings on the wall. "Some of these names are jaw-breakers, y'know it? Who's this homely sister?"

Ford came to his side and looked. "That's Galli-Curci—a great opera star—Italian. One of the last of the titans, Mrs. Cate used to say."

"Is that so," Spivey finally said, but as if unimpressed.

"Here's old Toscanini—the Maestro himself," Ford pointed out. "He's gone now. This is Rosa Ponselle, here. Bruno Walter. Lotte Lehmann. Melchior, here. Martinelli. And Lily Pons. Here's Stock!—the first symphony conductor I ever heard— Frederick Stock and his wing collar."

"Here's Pinza!" Spivey said suddenly—and proudly. "He was in *South Pacific.* M'wife saw it."

"Yes," Ford smiled, amused, "and he was in a couple of other things, too." He turned away for a moment. "Let's see what I've got back there. There ought to be some bourbon— a little, anyhow." He went to the back and reached up into some shelves over the refrigerator and brought down what had been a fifth of Old Grand Dad. He held the dusty bottle by the neck up to the light as Spivey watched him. It was almost a third full. "There's not too much of it," Ford said.

"Aw, there's some in there all right." Spivey's small eyes glittered.

Ford brought the bottle and a large glass of water and set them on the little table and then brought two glasses containing ice cubes. The two men sat down and each mixed his own drink.

"Ah-h, that hits the spot," Spivey said, taking a long swallow and smacking his lips. "I was real dry."

"Good." Ford held his very pale drink awkwardly.

"Y'got a cozy little place here, Ford."

"It's not much. I've been here since we moved in from Lake Forest. I had three nice little rooms over the garage out there. Chicago's so noisy. It's terrible."

"Say," Spivey said, leaning forward confidentially, "I'm not tryin' to pry into your business, but ever since I read about Missus Cate's death I just wundered whether she ever remembered you in her property or not."

Ford, surprised, uncrossed his legs. "Well . . . yes———,"

he finally said, "yes, she did. She was a very noble and generous woman, you know."

"You'd been awful faithful to 'em, though. I just wundered."

Ford was silent for a moment and then he said, slowly as in a dream, "The thing about it is, I never thought she'd go before me." He bent forward in his chair and put his forearms on his knees, grinding his moist palms together. "Her health was always so good, and mine so poor—and although she was four years older, I always *felt* older."

"Was she sick long?"

"Sick long! She wasn't sick at all. Peg called me up one Saturday morning at eight o'clock and said her mother had passed in her sleep. She called me right along with the family."

"Well, I declare."

"She'd lived a good life, though—she was entitled to go that way, if she had to go. But things like that are not easy to understand sometimes. Peg and I were the only ones there when the morticians came. She was just asleep—or seemed so. After they took her, Peg said we had to have a drink, and we did."

Both were silent for a moment—then finally Spivey said, "She sure liked her music, didn't she? She really ought to followed that."

"We'll never know, of course." Ford's voice was almost a whisper.

"That's how *you* come to like it," Spivey needled.

"Not exactly," retorted Ford. "I liked serious music before. You know, I went to Tuskegee Institute two years—I told you about that—and sang in the choir. Baritone. We didn't sing just spirituals all the time either, but Handel's *Messiah*, Mendelssohn's *Elijah*, and so forth. In fact, the first time I ever saw her in my life was after a symphony concert— down at Orchestra Hall. I was standing on the sidewalk out front, watching all the socialites coming out and getting in their cars. All of a sudden, *she* came out—in a sweeping eve-ning dress and furs, with a group of her friends—and Mr. Cate right at her heels." Ford's voice was softening now. "I'd never seen anybody like that before. So queenly . . . beau-tiful. She was in her early thirties then."

"Aw yes," Spivey conceded, "she was a fine lookin' woman, all right."

"The news photographers were taking pictures right and left," Ford went on, eyes shining, "and next day, all the so-ciety pages carried *her* picture. That's how I found out who she was, because I didn't go to work for them for over a year and a half after that. And that's another story in itself. It took some doing, believe me, because I didn't have a single letter of reference. It wasn't easy." Bemused, Ford smiled as he gazed out the window.

Spivey's little eyes watched him.

"I cut out one of the pictures and saved it," Ford said. "She never knew it, of course—and when she passed I gave it to Peg." He paused. "At first, Peg laughed—she was de-lighted—and then she looked at me and started bawling like a baby. That's when she gave me that picture, there." Ford pointed to the silver-framed portrait on the radio-phonograph.

"Yeah, they all liked you, Ford." Spivey poured himself another drink and handed the bottle to Ford, who set it down. Half his first drink remained.

"But it was a long time before she ever knew I liked mu-sic," Ford said. "The first two or three years after I went there I was one of the chauffeurs, along with the other work they had me doing. But later on, they sort of put me in charge of things, and I had more contact with her then. That's when she found out I liked some of the same music she liked and that I'd heard some of the great ones, too. They had that big library there, you know, in the north wing—and I could take books out. That's how I started the reading. She encouraged it."

Spivey raised his glass and took a drink, his little finger sticking straight up.

"Sometimes I even went in with them to concerts and the opera," Ford said, laughing quietly. "I would sit up front with the chauffeur—with you sometimes."

Spivey's head nodded in assent, as he fidgeted now.

"And when we'd get there, they'd go to their box and I'd go to the gallery. I'd enjoy it as much as they would, too— probably *more* than he would. And coming home, they'd ask me what I thought of the performance. Ah, those were great times," Ford reminisced. "You had real aristocracy then. She was so kind and just—never an immoral thought in her life."

Spivey smothered a yawn as he glanced as his wrist watch. "Well, the day's gettin' on, ain't it?" He looked around the room and out the window.

"There're a couple of drinks there yet," Ford said quickly, pointing to the bottle. "Let's split it. Don't leave any."

"I still got some." Spivey picked up the bottle and handed it to Ford, who carefully poured himself very little.

"You take the rest." Ford passed the bottle.

"Naw, not the rest. I'm feelin' pretty good right now." But Spivey poured a part of the whiskey, making his dark drink darker still, and added water.

Ford hardly sipped his drink at all, as he talked on: "She liked Koussevitzky best—of all the conductors. Believe me, when you left one of *his* concerts, you walked out into the street in a daze. I've got a lot of his recordings—over there— with the Boston Symphony." He pointed to an open-faced phonograph record cabinet against the wall, its shelves tightly packed with old 78 r.p.m. records.

Spivey was silent. Then he said, seriously, "You've lost a little weight, Ford. I kinda thought you'd probably be married by now . . . to some good woman. Y'know, when a man gets to be our age, he oughta have a wife." His high-pitched speech came thickly now, the words slurred.

"I've told you already what I think about that," Ford said abruptly.

"Well, I was only tellin' you what I thought."

"I know, I know. That's okay." Both were silent.

Finally Spivey said, his beady eyes narrowing as he leaned forward in his chair, "Did you ever know she fired me?"

"No . . . I didn't. You told me you were quitting to go back to Texas."

"Never mind what I *told* you. She fired me."

"What for?"

"What does anybody fire you for? To get rid of you! That's why."

Ford looked at Spivey, but said nothing.

"Whatever went with that fella anyhow?" Spivey said. "The lover! Ha! What was his name? Vantin? Was that it? Vantin . . . Emil Vantin."

"*Emile* Vantin, you mean—the pianist. Oh, he's dead—a long time now. He was great—very great."

"Didn't she take lessons from him?"

"A few. Not many, though. He wasn't in Chicago that much. Sometimes he'd stay with us when he played here. Maybe he'd give her a lesson or two then."

"It was more'n any one or two, Ford."

"Well, maybe—but not many."

Spivey's eyes narrowed again. "That fella was a wrong guy, Ford. I'm tellin' you. He was a wrong guy—if I ever saw one."

"Why so?"

"Aw, he was such an overbearin' bastard—one of them foreigners that probably thought a servant oughta be whipped ever' once in a while. I used to drive Missus Cate and him around town quite a bit, y' know—to concerts, the Art Institute, luncheons all over. She only had the two children then, I think. Well anyhow, she sure'n hell used to get on my nerves— bein' so damn proud to be seen with that man."

"Well, he was world famous."

"Okay, so what? He *thought* he was God! The thing that got me was that she couldn't see through him—she couldn't even tell what he was up to. Bein' a man, *I* could tell. I think he caught on, too—that I had his number—b'cause he couldn't stand me. I could see him in the car rear-view mirror some-times. They'd be facin' each other—and lookin' into each other's eyes—and holdin' hands too, probably. I couldn't see that."

A soft pallor had come to Ford's face. "You've sure got some imagination, Spivey," he said, with a frozen half-smile.

Spivey drank the rest of his drink in a gulp and set the glass down noisily. "Yeah. I probably got a little more'n *you* got, Ford," he said, not smiling.

Ford got up and turned on a large floor lamp near Spivey's chair and walked across the room to the door and flicked off the bright ceiling light. The room was different. The green of the wallpaper was less stark and the varnished wood surfaces no longer shone. The room was smaller—more confined. Ford looked tired as he sat down again.

"Vantin was the artistic type—romantic, maybe," he said. "And she admired artistic people—tremendously. I think more than anything in the world she'd loved to have been a serious musician and, of course, when he played for her, especially Brahms, she was greatly moved. But by the *music*, Spivey!— by the music."

"Aw, for Chrissake, Ford! I saw him huggin' her one night. Down there by the lily pond. *God bein' my judge*, I did! Why d'ya think I got fired?"

Ford did not move at all—and said nothing. His eyes took

on a tubercular brightness as his jaw gave way, parting his dry lips slightly.

Spivey stood up unsteadily. "I'm goin' now, Ford," he babbled. "I gotta go."

Ford still did not move, except that he looked at Spivey who walked over to his coat and slowly wrestled it on and then took down his hat. Ford finally got up, his face ashen and immobile, and stood silently with both arms at his side.

"Glad I run into you," driveled Spivey. "Take care of yourself, hear? You're a rare one, for sure—always up on the mountain top. Take care of yourself, hear, Ford?"

"Yes. Okay," Ford said huskily, as he followed Spivey to the door.

The big man opened the door and felt his way out into the dim hallway. As he reeled down the stairs, he called back, "Be seein' you, Ford—good to run into you. Just a chance meetin'!"

Ford stood in the door and vacantly watched his heavy descent. At length, he pushed the door quietly shut, groped back to his chair and, dazed, stood there gazing out on the fading autumn afternoon. He stood there for a long, long time, as if incapable of moving, until the sun, now a molten scarlet wafer, was level with the window sill. It was only with the onset of twilight, pink-hued and somber, that he approached the little table, gathered up the whiskey bottle and glasses, and walked back slowly toward the sink.

The Rescue

Tuesday morning. Essie was still in her pajamas. An old bathrobe thrown about her shoulders, she sat slumped in a rickety kitchen chair, drinking a glass of Alka-Seltzer. She slowly emptied the fizzing glass and set it down, breathing heavily, and feebly wiped her mouth with the back of her hand. Her hair, newly-straightened, stood up in short, pliant streaks over her head, and gave her puffy-eyed brown face the appearance of floating under an ocean of clear water.

She'd never learn, she was telling herself. When you got so high you forgot to take a couple of Alka-Seltzers before you went to bed, you just suffered next morning, that's all—just suffered. Lonzo—he could drink a barrel of whiskey, and get up next morning like nothing'd ever happened. She'd never seen anybody like him! But he drank only plain water with his liquor; none of that sugar—cokes and ginger ale—that always murdered *her*. No—she'd never learn.

Limping back through the shabby little apartment to the bedroom, she stood guiltily before the mirror. She could see—and not for the first time—that there were far too many creasy lines in her face for her thirty years. But then she always tried to steer her mind away from such things—it was no good to go letting your memory loose all the time, to roam back over what *could* have been; it only made you miserable; and pretty soon you were drunk again. She shrugged off the robe, and was about to get back in bed—when the telephone rang.

Moving a step to the bedstand, she picked it up. "Hello."

"Hi—It's me," the female voice in the phone said.

". . . Yeah?" Essie yawned and sat down on the bed.

"You sound sleepy. It's eleven o'clock."

"I was up," said Essie.

"You don't sound like it . . . Say, I gotta get my cleaning out today. Can you let me have twenty dollars—'til Monday?"

". . . Yeah . . . I guess-s so. Why can't you wait?"

"I gotta couple of dresses in I'll need before then."

"Need for what?"

"Oh, I'll tell you!—Can I come on by?"

". . . Okay," Essie sighed, placing the phone back thoughtfully.

She sat there on the bed awhile. Finally she lifted her legs around up onto the bed and lay back wearily, her eyes up on the mottled ceiling. Whenever she thought about her sister, she wanted to be quiet, undisturbed. Still the answers never came. What was Bernice up to *now?* Where did all her money go anyhow? Twenty now, ten last week. She made ninety dollars a week—what'n the hell did she do with it! And she was getting wilder by the minute—just one man after another. She needed a damn good talking to! But she knew Bernice wouldn't appreciate that—not from *her* anyway. "Who're *you*," she was likely to snap, "to be lecturing me?—*you*, living right out in the open with a man!" Essie half-moaned and rolled over fitfully on her side, facing the wall—the motion brought back the queasy sinking in her stomach and her temples pounded.

She thought of how her mother would twist in her grave if she could see Bernice now. And it looked like she *never* wanted to get married. She, herself, *had* been married, twice—before she let Lonzo talk her into moving in with him. She was broke and out of a job at the time—Mama had always said she was lazy. Now Lonzo acted like he owned her; had beaten her up twice. And he drank like a fish. He could be so mean and evil, too, when he was drinking, and she had to be damn careful what she said to him then. She realized she was getting fed up . . . but he *was* a meal ticket; going it alone meant hard work, slaving in some laundry six days a week like Bernice did—or like Bernice *used* to do. Bernice was a cute little chick, though, and Dispetto, her boss, had her out front now, on the counter, waiting on the customers. *Some* stuff! But Essie knew there was more to that story.

She lay there staring at the wall, finally realizing she couldn't go back to sleep. Soon she got up and lit a cigarette, and then went back into the kitchen to make coffee.

Barely thirty minutes later the doorbell rang. She went into the living room, pressed the buzzer, and opened the door, holding it ajar, as Bernice, a slender, brown-skinned girl, came running up the stairs, pointing back down behind her.

"My God!"—she was out of breath—"Don't your janitor ever sweep that vestibule, or the stairway?"

"That old man's drunk most'a the time," Essie smiled wearily, closing the door behind her sister. "Don't be too hard on him."

Bernice, wearing a bright yellow spring coat, cocked her head to one side and twinkled at Essie. "Looks kinda like *you* tied one on, yourself, last night."

"You're mighty goddam sassy for somebody runnin' up here for money, I'll tell you that!" Essie sank into a chair, as Bernice laughed and waved her off belittlingly.

"Y'got a can of beer back there?" she asked, nodding toward the kitchen.

"Now it's beer!" cried Essie. "Have *you* got the gimmies! Go on—get you a can." She grinned at Bernice indulgently.

Bernice went into the kitchen, and soon came back with an opened can of cold beer and flopped down in a chair.

"Where you going that you gotta have your cleaning so quick?" asked Essie.

"Detroit."

"Detroit!"

"Yeah. What's so awful about *that?*"

"What'n the world's in Detroit?"

"Rosetta's going up there to see her boy friend—she's gonna quit the laundry pretty soon, and get a job up there."

"Lord God! Whatta 'bout *your* job? You're fixin' to get fired, that's what you're fixin' to do!"

Bernice was smug. "No, I won't get fired."

"Oh, no! I forgot! Not *you!* Dispetto—he wouldn't fire *you!*"

Bernice looked injured—then sullen.

"If you ain't got th' money to get your cleaning out, how'n world're you goin' to Detroit?"

"In a car."

"Rosetta ain't got no car."

"Roy's going up."

"Oh-h-h, *now* it's comin' out! 'Roy's goin' up,'" mimicked Essie. "Well, what's Roy's wife gonna be doin' while you'n him're layin' up in some cheap hotel in Detroit!"

"Well, how d'you like *that!*" Bernice set the can of beer down. "Look who's talking!"

"You listen to *me*, Miss Know-It-All!" Essie shrilled, scooting forward in her chair. "*You* better slow down! You're ridin' for a fall!—sure's your name's what it is. What'n the world would Mama say, if she could see the way you're carryin' on! Just tell me that! What would she say? Why, she'd be fit to be tied, and you know it! She wouldn't pay *me* no mind—she put *me* down long time ago. But *you*—her 'little girl'—why, it'd break her heart!"

Bernice's eyes were blazing. She craned forward on the edge of her chair. "Why *is* it! Why is it you're always jumping on *me!*—and getting some of the damnedest ideas! What've *I* done? Sure I go out with fellows! Don'tcha think I'm entitled to some fun once in awhile!—I work everyday, don't I? Whatta you *want* me to do?—sit up in that damned room all the time, I guess!"

"Y'oughta be thinkin' about marryin' some nice boy, that's what y'*oughta* be thinkin' about."

"*Any* fool woman can get married! *You* tried it—twice already! I see you didn't stay in it long. No, you like other arrangements better! Well, I got news for you! It'll be a helluva long time before *I* ever get into it!—a helluva long time!"

Essie was quiet now—grave. "Bernice, you're not foolin' me—not one bit. I'm onto you. But you always try to cover up. It won't do you no good, though. I'm your sister, and I don't like to see you goin' to the dogs like you are. Mama'd simply be wild if she knew I hadn't kept closer track of you. She'd blame it all on me. But it ain't all my fault. Part of it's your own bull-headedness—nobody can tell you a thing. You know *every*thing." Essie's face crinkled in distress. "Why don't you move out'a that flat—and start rooming with some nice church family? The way you're livin' now, you don't have nobody to look after you—and that's what you need. I don't care *what* you say, you oughta be married—never mind about *me*, we're not talking about *my* life; you never heard me braggin', did you? You oughta be married to some decent fella, and have some kids—there ain't nothin' wrong with that; and it ain't a bit too soon—you're twenty-two. What future is there in the way you're livin' I ask you? I *ask* you! The men're just makin' a chump out'a you, that's all—even that goddam Dispetto (I could shoot that bald-headed bastard). You think you're so fancy—why, he wouldn't take you into a drug store for a hamburger. Oh sure, he'll sleep with you, and pay you a pretty good salary—and even buy you a trinket once in awhile. But what's he think of you? Huh? Just what's he think of you?"

Bernice had jumped up. "I'm not gonna sit here and listen to any more of this! I'm damn sick and tired of your insults!" She started for the door.

"Bernice! I *know* what's best for you. You're talkin' to somebody that's been through the mill. I *know!* I wish *I* could start all over again—there'd be some changes, believe me. That's the reason I keep after you all the time! Now don't go runnin' off all mad, like some spoiled child." Essie had gotten up and was following Bernice to the door. "Wait! *I'll* get you the money. Wait a minute. *I'll* get it."

Bernice had hesitated and now shook her head sadly. "No, I can get along without it. I just get so tired listening to you preach all the time. *I* know you think it's for my own good. But I'm living my life the way *I* want to—and that's the way it's gonna be." Her right hand behind her back was groping for the door knob. "I'll call you when I get back from Detroit."

"Wait—*I'll* get the twenty bucks. *I'd* rather be the one to give it to you than to have Dispetto, or Roy—or somebody else—."

Bernice caught her breath. "You see there!" she yelled. "You see what I mean? In *your* mind I can *do* no right!—Never! . . . I don't want your damn money! I don't want it!" She rushed outside into the hallway and slammed the door wildly.

Essie stood helpless in the middle of the floor. Finally she moped back to her chair and sat down again, and pressed both her palms to her temples to hold in the dull throbbing. Her mother's angry, hovering image clouded her mind. Yes, Bernice was just like Mama, awful temper and all. The brooding, guilty feeling she always got after quarreling with Bernice returned: Bernice might have been different if she had only set her a better example. Mama had seen and feared it all, in her final weeks. She didn't start railing at Essie until she realized death was very near; she had hoped for a reprieve, and was bitter. The hospital scene was branded on Essie's brain: Mama shrieked at her that she was too trifling and low-down to ever look after Bernice. All of Essie's tearful promises were hurled back in her teeth.

She understood now her mother had never really loved her since the time, at seventeen, she got pregnant. Outraged, Mama had rounded up the scared boy and forced the marriage, only to have Essie miscarry in the sixth month. And she remembered after that nobody seemed to care a hang what happened to her. The marriage didn't last a year. She was merely overlooked at home—not seen. It was Bernice who got focused devotion.

Now she suddenly realized she was feeling sorry for herself. She got up and hobbled back into the bedroom and lay down again, staring at the smudged wallpaper. But in spite of everything, she thought, she, herself, was mainly to blame for her life. She'd had chance after chance to pick herself up, to make a clean break. She hadn't taken a steady job in nearly three years! So she wondered now whether it was too late—for both her and Bernice—to turn the tables and start again. She wasn't sure. She wasn't sure she even had the guts to try it. Bernice had gotten so hard-headed—the little fool! If she could only see what was up the road for her, she wouldn't be so damned cocky! Something or somebody had to jerk her around into her senses—and soon!

That evening Essie stood at the stove in her sooty little kitchen, cooking dinner. Lonzo was already overdue. She moved about stolidly—Bernice still preyed on her thoughts;

she had tried phoning her that afternoon, but Bernice had slammed down the phone. She could be so cruel—no wonder Lonzo never tired taunting her about Bernice; they hated each other and barely spoke; Essie knew she could never discuss her with *him*—he could turn into a maniac about nothing in a matter of seconds if you got him stirred up. Yet she could understand his bitterness toward Bernice, for he knew how she mocked Essie for living with a man who didn't even carry life insurance, and who could up and leave her tomorrow or whenever he pleased. Hadn't he walked out on the last woman he was living with? Bernice had scoffed.

Essie stepped to the sink and emptied a little saucepan of hot water. Momentarily she expected to hear Lonzo's key in the front door. Of late, this had set off a thumping panic inside her. Still she refused to admit her dark fear of him—and his knife. Bernice didn't know about his crazed jealousy. Essie knew there was no chance he would leave—*she* was the one who wanted to leave. She thought of it so often now, and the wilder Bernice got, the more gravely she thought of it. But whenever she looked at Lonzo, she understood the risks.

Shortly after six o'clock she heard him coming in at the front door. Little waves of fright went over the dry skin of her whole body. Soon he walked into the kitchen—a squat, chunky, black man, about forty; wearing heavy, lime-dusted, working shoes and a soiled khaki windbreaker. The long welt of a knife scar came off his cheekbone and ran down alongside his jaw almost to the point of his chin.

"How'ya feel, Baby?" he grinned, his large black and white eyeballs bulging as he slapped at her girdle. "You sure raised *yo*'self a boatload o' hell las' night, didn't you!"

Essie smiled ruefully. "Yeah? Well, *you're* sure an iron man."

"No ah ain't. Ah'm whupped." He dropped into a kitchen

chair. "Ah'm goin' to bed to*night*. He watched Essie as she mournfully lifted a big skillet off the stove.

"Whut time did you git up?" he asked.

"Oh . . . *I* don't know. It wasn't early."

"You sho look beat. Y'better lay off that stuff awhile." Soon he got up and went into the bathroom to wash.

She realized now how desperately she wanted to be rid of him. A quivering revulsion welled inside her. But she knew she'd have to get out of Chicago—and fast. It all depended on Bernice. Would she go too?—or else there'd be no point. She vowed to give her no peace. She'd talk some sense in her hard head or else, by God! Now she coolly made plans: she must work on Bernice gradually; be nice to her; use more patience; stop scolding her so much—it only made her worse. And if everything went okay, they could go to St. Louis, or to Cleveland, maybe—or *any* place away from Chicago. They'd find work all right—could even have their own apartment. Her excitement soared with her thoughts.

When Lonzo returned to the kitchen, she was standing over the stove. He walked over, grappled her around the waist, and rubbed his stubble-rough chin against her cheek. "But ah ain't too whupped for a little friggin'," he grinned, his eyes popping. "An' ah know *you* ain't either—'cause you been sleepin' all day."

"Let's eat," she said, grinning back. "Have *you* got big ideas!" She was conscious of her own cunning, and felt the need now to sweet-talk him.

Then, as he was sitting down at the table, he said offhandedly, "Ah been thinkin' lately—maybe we oughta go on and git married."

Essie's knees weakened. She leaned against the stove for support. Finally, turning her face away to hide the shock, she clutched up a pan and carried it to the sink.

"Did'ja hear me?" he growled, watching her.

Her voice had withered to a whisper. ". . . Yes, I heard you." Then she tried a cool laugh. "What's got into you?"

"Nothin's got into me. Ah been thinkin' 'bout it a good while."

"Why d'you want to *marry* me?"

"Ain't *that* a helluva question!—Christ!"

"I think you're kiddin'," she sparred, smiling as she sat down at the table.

Lonzo was roiled. *"Kiddin'!* Whut th' hell're you talkin' 'bout!"* He laid down his knife and fork and glowered at her. *"Ah don't kid!"*

She still smiled but said nothing, and nervously heaped her plate with spaghetti.

"We kin git the license my first day off," he said, calmer now—he was eating noisily, and raised a full can of beer to his mouth and nearly emptied it.

Essie chewed her food and kept her eyes in her plate—but her heart was hammering.

When they had finished eating, he would not let her do the dishes—before he pulled her into the bedroom.

An hour later, Lonzo lay on his back in bed, his short arms and legs spread-eagled, snoring in rattling grunts. Essie sat spent and trembling in the living room, staring vacantly at the lighted TV screen. Only the noisier, more frantic lines of the actors pierced her thoughts. Married to that pig! God!— had he lost his mind! and had *she!* What in God Almighty's name could have made her take up with him! Bernice was right, she had sunk pretty low; he could never have gotten within a mile of *her*—Bernice would have starved first. Essie's brain was gyrating: she must find Bernice!—and before she left for Detroit. It was time to *do* something! She'd try phoning again . . . then she realized—she couldn't talk from the bedroom.

But she got up and tiptoed into the bedroom—with its throaty noises—felt her way to the head of the bed, and pulled the chain on the little bedstand lamp. Weak, yellow light flooded the tousled bed; one short black leg lay exposed, and Lonzo's liverish lips were parted in a silly leer. She knelt quietly at the telephone, dialed Bernice's number, and waited—her heart thudding at her ribs. Promptly the other phone rang . . . once . . . twice . . . and then she heard Bernice's eager voice say "Hello." Gently she placed the phone back in its cradle.

But now she dare not circle the bed for her coat in the closet! She pulled the light out and went softly out of the room; and soon, without a coat, left the apartment by the front door. Going down the stairs to the street and into the chill May evening, she felt a mouth-drying fright—but a sense of crisis, too. She wouldn't take any goddam foolishness off Bernice tonight—they'd have it out, once and for all. Then she remembered: she must take it easy—go slow; but that was about the hardest thing in the world to do—the last thing she remembered, and the first thing she forgot! She *would* get Bernice out of Chicago, though! She kept telling herself now she mustn't be afraid—of Lonzo *or* Bernice; when you were afraid, you couldn't think straight. She wasn't broke, that was one good thing—she knew exactly what she had in her postal savings account: two hundred and fifty-seven dollars and some cents. But Bernice wouldn't have much except her clothes.

Shivering, she walked over to 43rd and King Drive, and stood waiting for a southbound jitney. One finally came along carrying two passengers already—men—and she bravely sat between them. The driver's window was down too far, and she was chilled through. It was just dark, and threatening rain; the air was heavy, and to the south and east dark purple thunderheads were scudding in from Lake Michigan as orange flashes of lightning lit up the sky—the loud rock 'n roll music coming out of the driver's radio was frequently jammed by the violent bursts of static.

Apparently the two men passengers were strangers—they weren't talking.

"How far you goin', Miss?" the driver asked.

Oh! Had she forgotten to tell him? "I want 58th!" she said. She had been combing her brain for pretexts in case Lonzo woke up and found her gone. But surely he wouldn't!—he'd had only three hours sleep the night before and had downed almost a fifth of whiskey . . . . But would *Bernice* still be home when she got there? *That* was the question!

The inky-black old man at her left was smoking a huge cigar. He turned to her—smiling. "Kin you stand this?" he asked, holding up the cigar.

"I think so," she laughed. She suddenly felt close to him.

"Are you used to 'em—does your husband smoke 'em?" He gave a wizened, toothless grin.

". . . No . . . just cigarettes," she stammered. Husband!— My God! If he only knew what he was saying! Her woes all seemed to rush back at her at once.

As the jitney rattled on out King Drive, the rain started. Big, splashy drops pelted the windshield, as the wipers labored. She felt the old man watching her now. Pretty soon he said, "Where's your coat?—you're gonna git wet."

"I don't think I'll need it," she lied. "I'll be all right—I'll run. It ain't far."

"Fifty-ninth's my stop. I'll git off at 58th—you kin throw my coat over you."

She put her hand on his arm, protesting. But they had already reached 58th; both now paid the driver and climbed out. The old man insisted on taking off his topcoat and tossing it over her head, as he squinted in the rain. "Which way?" he asked.

They scurried four apartment buildings up 58th Street, and

darted into Bernice's entrance. "Here we are," she said, lifting the coat off her head and returning it to him. "Thanks," her voice faltered, ". . . You're sure nice," she tried to say. The old man's thin face puckered in another grin—and then he was gone.

She stood for a moment in the vestibule, trying to compose herself. Finally she rang the bell. Then suddenly she wondered if Bernice had "company" tonight—if she did she knew she'd never answer the bell. Waiting, the seconds seemed minutes. At last the faint buzz came. She dove for the door knob and, weary with relief, entered the drab stairwell.

Bernice was already leaning over the second-floor banister, calling down sharply, "Who *is* it?"

"It's me." Essie had started the slow climb.

"Essie?"

"Yeah."

Bernice turned stony.

When Essie reached the second floor and entered, Bernice retreated dourly before her into the clean, but battered, little kitchenette. The ironing board was up—she had been ironing a pink blouse. Her cleaning, in three white paper bags, was hanging primly in the corner—so she got it out after all, thought Essie.

Bernice, brown and slender in a tightly-belted bathrobe, and wearing felt bedroom slippers, frowned at her sister. "You was lucky to catch me," she said. "I was getting ready to take a bath and go out—I gotta date."

Essie was calm as she sat down. "Go ahead and *take* your bath—*I* ain't stoppin' you."

"I leave tomorrow, you know."

"My, ain't *you* busy?"

Bernice, vexation on her young face, resumed her ironing

Essie began unsurely. ". . . I wanted to talk to you. . .

So I thought I'd just come on over here and take a chance on catchin' you. I'm thinkin' about leaving town."

Bernice set the iron upon its end, and stared. "What?"

"I'm thinkin' about going to Cleveland, maybe—and gettin' a job."

"Yeah? What about Lonzo?—is he going?"

"No." Essie was very composed.

"Are you crazy? He'll *kill* you!"

"He won't know it—'til I'm gone. He can't find me then. If I stay with him much longer, he's gonna end up killin' me anyhow," Essie shrugged.

"Well!"—Bernice breathed nervously.

"And I want you to go with me," Essie said quite casually.

Bernice dropped both arms to her side, gaping. Then she smiled bitterly. "Are you losin' your weak mind?"

"*You* know I ain't! You know *damn* well I ain't!" Essie's voice shrilled out before she thought. But now she talked softly again. "It's the thing to do—for both of us, Bernice, baby; to get a new start—the *right* start, this time. *We* won't have any trouble gettin' jobs, and we can even have our own little apartment. Wouldn't Mama like *that!*—you know she would."

Then Bernice thundered down her slippered foot on the floor, rocking the ironing board. "What'n the *hell's* eatin' you!" she screamed. "A job's a helluva thing for *you* to be talking about! I got a ninety-dollar-a-week job here, where I don't have to be sweating all day over some damn mangle, and *you* come tellin' me, 'Come on, let's leave all that, so we can go to Cleveland—or some other goddam place—and get us a *good* job!' And join the church too, eh?—I guess! Yes, you are!—you're losin' your weak mind! Besides, whoever said *you* liked to work? You'd have a job about a month! No!—I ain't *studyin'* you! You go, if you want to. *I* ain't goin' nowhere! *Nowhere!*"

Essie had strained forward in her chair. Now she fell back

limply—silent. Bernice stood over the ironing board, panting.
There were long moments of silence before she spoke again.
"You just don't understand, Essie! Chicago's the *only* place
for me—can't you see that? Why don't *you* go. *You* go on
and go."

Essie's lip quivered. "An' leave you?"

Bernice pulled the iron cord from the wall socket, and said
nothing.

Slowly Essie rose to go.

Then Bernice said anxiously, "I'll be back sometime late
Sunday night. I'll call you Monday. You take it easy, hear?
. . . Say, where's your *coat?*"

Essie said nothing.

"Where's your *coat*, Essie! You'll catch your death of cold!
Here, wait!" Bernice hurried to the little closet and took out
her winter coat, and held it while Essie got into it. Then Essie
walked out the door.

Finally, on King Drive, she flagged a cab. Climbing in, she
said to the driver, "Pete's Tavern—43rd and Prairie."

Later that night, about 1:30, Essie came home—eyes glazed
and mouth hanging open as she lurched up the stairs. Finally,
despite the weaving, she got her key into the lock and let herself in. She slowly wrestled off Bernice's coat and left it heaped
in the middle of the floor. Then she staggered into the bedroom,
groping for the light switch, and flicked on the blinding-bright
ceiling light. Lonzo still lay deathlike, exactly as she had left
him—only he was snoring softly now; a thin string of clear
saliva had wandered down over his cheekbone scar and back
under his earlobe onto the pillow.

Essie swayed over the bed for a moment. Then she took her
right foot back—slowly, deliberately—and crashed it against
the foot of the bed. The warped floor boards quivered and the

iron bed rang. Lonzo vaulted straight up—his bulging eyes bloodshot and wild.

Then Essie screamed at him. "*Yes!* You *black bastard*, you! *I'll* marry you!"

Lonzo blinked and choked. "Woman, whut th' goddam hell's wrong with you!"

"*Yes! You rotten, no-good, black son of a bitch*, you! *I'll* marry you!"

Then she fell kicking and sobbing across the bed.

The Lookout

Wild torrents of snow darkened the view ahead as, its windshield wipers laboring, the Buick crept down the street into the blizzard. The young woman inside leaned forward over the steering wheel trying to see out through the foggy glass. Alone, she wore a blue winter coat, white gloves on her brown hands, and was bareheaded. She glanced at her watch; it was one-forty-five. "They'll start getting there around two," she told herself. It was Saturday afternoon. She hoped she'd be lucky enough to get just the right parking spot—one from which she would see without being seen. The swirling snow would help. She turned left to circle the block in order to park across the street from Laura's big house on Woodlawn Avenue.

It was a sense of compulsion that had sent Mildred out of the house into the bad weather, leaving her husband and two boys to think up some Saturday diversion for themselves. She hadn't said where she was going, which, in itself, was a little unusual. But Wes was so agreeable, so easy-going . . . . Sometimes she wished to God he weren't! The boys would have questions, though . . . .

Coming now from the opposite direction, Mildred eased her car into the well-chosen space, lifting a resolute chin to find

the curb almost hidden in the drifting snow. After turning off
the motor, she felt in her purse for a cigarette. She was a handsome woman of thirty-eight, with smooth coppery skin, and
soft hair blandished by a chic haircut. Her serious turn of
mind and self-possession blended in rather naturally with her
recent moodiness and, with her cool good looks, created a
curiously sensual amalgam. Mashing the red-hot dash lighter
against the cigarette-end, she blew a jet of pearl-grey smoke
against the windshield and then settled back to wait.

Woodlawn was a wide residential street. Traffic was especially light today, with the bad weather. As she sat smoking,
Mildred realized how tense and uneasy she was. It was a risky
foolish thing she was doing—one of those catty women going
into Laura Font's bridge-luncheon could see and recognize
her. That would be bad, she knew, for recently she had made
a quietly desperate effort at indifference; she had been careful not to show any awareness that she had not kept pace with
her former friends. To be caught here now would be the fatal
admission. She could hardly withstand the urge to reach for
the ignition key and start the motor. But she wouldn't—she
couldn't.

It had been only by sheer coincidence in a telephone talk
that she learned of Laura's party in the first place. And now,
having spent the whole morning mustering the courage to
come, she must hazard staying at least long enough to see
who went in and what they were wearing—at least until she'd
seen Janice, the guest of honor, arrive. She wasn't parked directly in front of Laura's anyway, but down the street a bit.
No one would see her through the sifting veil of snow. But if
they did! If they did, they'd wonder, of course, why she didn't
come in. And after a while, when she didn't, they'd know she
wasn't invited. Still, she must take the chance.

She had heard of Laura's huge fireplace, and she knew
she'd have it blazing today for all those vain, lucky women.

Yes, vain—because of the financial strain they constantly kept their husbands under to outdo each other in the trappings of success. And lucky too—for the husbands, despite all, had somehow borne up physically. It *was* luck—she knew now you could never tell beforehand whether a man "had it" or not.

When Wes came out of the university, everyone said he was going places, and they said the same later on, when they were married. For the first five years he *had* grown; he was ambitious for big things. Then something happened—the plateau; he stopped maturing. And now, after fifteen years he had what *he* considered a good job with the insurance company he'd started out with. He was content to go to the football games in the fall, and for the rest of the year to have in a few cronies periodically for poker in front of his tidy bar. Lately, to her secret disgust, he had been watching the late TV movies. He had long ago left the supervision of the two boys completely to her and sometimes she found she had three boys on her hands instead of two.

Mildred sat and waited and watched the snow. The houses in the area were large and well back from the street; to Mildred, they were remote and ghostly in the white swirl. A small delivery truck with large letters on its side reading "Bristol Pastries" pulled up from the other direction and stopped in front of Laura's. The young driver climbed out with a package held carefully in both hands and carried it around to a rear door. Yes, the cake, thought Mildred. She lit another cigarette and drew the smoke in hungrily.

Laura's success had surprised everybody. She had taken little Herbie, who it was true was very bright in school, and she had somehow urged him to the top. Now Herbie—with his kinky red hair and blue eyes—was an outstanding physician; he had his own clinic and staff of doctors. And Laura, herself, had everything to go with her station in life—a stately stone house (owned formerly by a wealthy Jewish family), a Mercedes-Benz car for herself, and two house servants. For a girl whose father had been a postman, she had done well indeed. In school Laura hadn't been nearly as good-looking as she, Mildred, and at the University of Illinois, she didn't go out with the popular fellows that Mildred knew. She was humble, and Mildred proud—proud of Wes, who was slender and handsome then, and who reveled in the smoldering traces of jealousy Mildred always tried to hide. Looking back, it was all so incredibly fantastic!

Soon a Ford station wagon came down the other side of the street toward her. It slowed and pulled to the curb in front of Laura's. Mildred put the window down a little, and saw a mousy-looking young woman in a scanty broadtail jacket get out. She gasped. Hilda Simpson!—married to a pharmacist. Even Wes made more money than Ted Simpson! But Hilda's father had been a classics professor at Fisk University. That made the difference—*her* father was a caterer. Mildred smiled to herself. Hilda *would* be the first one there—so glad to be invited. And imagine anyone wearing a broadtail jacket in this weather instead of a warm cloth coat. You couldn't impress *that* crowd with broadtail.

The snow was coming down more slowly now, in big, spinning flakes. Mildred started the motor for a few seconds to let the windshield wipers clear the glass. Soon a Lincoln Continental drew up slowly from behind and parked just ahead of her. She tensed. Two women got out from different sides of the car, closed the doors and, talking, started across the street toward Laura's big iron gate. Mildred gently exhaled a cloud of smoke. Both were light-skinned, and the one who had driven the car was beautiful. Mildred didn't know her, but recognized the other one as Mae Todd, the old-maid high school principal. She watched the two women mount Laura's stone steps. Suddenly it came to her. The beautiful one must be Evelyn Todd, Dr. Herman Todd's new wife, and Mae's new sister-in-law. Mildred smiled again, knowing that old Mrs. Todd, the doctor's jealous first wife, must surely be turning over about now—out there in Burr-Oak Cemetery. So that was the beauty from Boston, so *soignée* in her casual-style Matara Alaskan seal, and plum-colored suede pumps worn bravely in the snow. Mildred sat and watched them enter through the big arched door.

The impulse to leave gripped her, but she tried to ignore it. She leaned forward and glanced at her face in the rear-view mirror, and then sat back, absently pulling at a ravel in her glove. She knew if she left now she'd miss seeing Janice arrive—lucky Janice, home from New York just to be feted by the elite. Was this the same girl who grew up with Mildred, stayed whole week ends at her house, and so often double-dated with her? Janice had roomed with her all during their junior and seniors years at Illinois. She knew Janice had been in Chicago since Tuesday—last year when she came home she'd at least phoned. How callous could you get? But *her* husband was a successful publisher, and husbands were the key to everything.

No one arrived now for ten minutes. Then two new Cadillacs followed by a Plymouth came down the other side of the street toward her, all moving slowly in the accumulated snow. The Cadillacs plowed over to the curb near Laura's car, and the Plymouth went on. There was the slow indecisive parking by women, a clambering out of silk and mink, and a slamming of heavy car doors. Mildred, jittery, sat back from the car window and watched. It was Sadie Tate and her gang—a cruel, vicious coterie of social brigands. All boasted northern university degrees and light skins. There were no black or dark brown women among these vocal members of the NAACP, Mildred knew—these implacable foes of discrimination. She watched Sadie lead them slowly up the wide stone steps— Sadie, over the years, had consumed so many *hors d'oeuvres* and martinis that she was now barrel-shaped. A sense of awe held Mildred—this was a life she could never know. It was too late. She lit another cigarette and tried to relax by tilting her head far back and blowing the smoke up against the ceiling.

Then the cars all seemed to come at once. Mildred was frightened, for it had almost stopped snowing. The guests were pulling up from both directions now and hunting parking space. Soon a big beige Imperial eased up from behind and was opposite her car window before she knew it. She fell back terrified. The car stopped. There were three women in the front seat, and a man wearing a chauffeur's cap sitting in the back. He got out and opened the right front door for the women. Mildred recognized the first one out—Nan Hawthorne, well-off, and a snob of snobs. Then she saw only the long legs of the next woman sliding out, but she knew that it was Janice. She was laughing as she got an assist from the chauffeur and then, waiting for Betty Bond, the driver, to be helped out, she stooped over and brushed a fluff of snow from her ankle. All three were soon talking and laughing again as they stood waiting for the chauffeur to pull off and let them cross the street. Suddenly Janice glanced around toward Mildred's car. Fear congealed her. But Janice hadn't seen—she was too busily amused at something Nan Hawthorne was saying. The three then crossed the street abreast, tall Janice in the middle.

Janice was wearing a soft, rippling, full-length mink. Mildred watched her proud carriage. She'd never known Janice to look patrician before. Her legs were still too skinny, but she was dressed so tastefully that her thin body lent elegance to the finished impression she made. And she looked terribly happy, Mildred thought—for there'd be other parties, you could see. Where tonight, for instance? To Sadie's? Mildred had heard that the men servants at Sadie's wore mauve jackets. Maybe Nan Hawthorne, who abhorred large cocktail parties, would have in a favored few. Or Betty Bond might be giving something—a dinner, perhaps. Each occasion would be smart and lavish and cultivated.

Just then Audrey Johnson, mannish as ever, drove up in an Oldsmobile station wagon, looking for a place to park. Audrey was one of the very few in that group who was still nice to Mildred, but she had always had her doubts about Audrey.

Two boys trudged by in the snow, one dragging a sled. They were about the age of Mildred's boys. She spent a good deal of her time nowadays thinking about her sons and what they'd make of themselves. She hoped they'd turn out to be real men, with a passionate pride in accomplishment—still, not at a sacrifice in tenderness to their wives. And then, as always lately, her thoughts turned inward. She could testify that the woman should never be stronger than the man. Only calamity ensued. She knew that her incessant yearning for the life she'd seen today was futile.

She'd tried hard to manage herself accordingly—no fairminded person would deny that. Yet, here she sat, in this snowy lookout—like a member of the FBI. It was insane. If only she hadn't found out about Janice being in town! It had set her back and jarred her resolve. They had been so close once. She used to tell Janice what she ought and ought not do. She wondered if she ever thought about it now. Perhaps Janice laughed now at the thought. She had a perfect right to, certainly; but she'd no doubt forgotten it all. Probably no impression remained—not even of Mildred. It was just as well . . . .

She mashed out her cigarette and started the motor. There was only one thing she was sure of now: she didn't want to go home. And she wouldn't—at least for a while. Then, in plain view, she pulled away from the curb, no longer caring who saw her, and drove off. But there was no place to go—yes, perhaps to Mama's, but no place else. Poor, uncomprehending

Mama—who thought "Millie" was "doing simply grand."
Wesley was so wonderful to her. "They've got *everything*—an
automatic dishwasher and a *stereo*. Goodness! I would've
thought I was a queen! But Millie now thinks nothing of it."

On Fifty-fifth Street Mildred pulled over in front of a liquor
store. She'd take along a fifth of 100-proof bourbon, and she
and Mama could make some good strong Manhattans. She
went in and bought the whiskey, and it was only as she drove
away that she remembered the drinks would start Mama talking, blubbering probably about Charlie, Mildred's aimless
brother. She hadn't considered that. On such occasions Mama
could get pretty loathsome. But it would be better than going
home. And she, herself, could have a half dozen Manhattans—
even more, if they were required—until she would yearn for
nothing. Mama didn't give a damn . . . .

She was operating the car instinctively now, stopping for
red lights by seeming automation. It had stopped snowing
completely, and she regretted this. She had always loved the
snow; it made the world look so unreal and insubstantial.
Dreams had a better chance of coming true in a world of un-
reality. Sometimes she went out walking alone in the falling
snow, feeling the strange urge to be caught up in it somehow
and made dizzy, completely out of her head, by its crazy, swirling madness. But sooner or later the snowing always stopped—
as it had today—and she had nothing to do but to return to
earth with a cold and bitter heart.

Girl Friend

Lester stood alone at his window looking out on a weary plum sun setting across the patches of snow on the housetops. His plain apartment, where he had confined himself all day, seemed to him a hushed prison cell. He was tense, jumpy—waiting for the telephone to ring. Would Annette *never* call!—the afternoon was almost gone!

A widower for one month now, he was confused, at cross-purposes with himself. He didn't know where his life was heading. But he made excuses: A man who'd been married for thirty-four years and is then suddenly cut adrift, could be expected to make a few false starts, to require a little time to orient himself. Lottie had been a serious, bustling wife—his conscience seemed now to cast up all the good things about her—but she had harbored a tautly-disguised passion to administer his life for him. To rule. He remembered her as a born supervisor, who soon brought him, and later their two daughters, Reba and Lillian, under her artful, but firm control. They were a black family and this mother-leader arrangement had seemed to them all perfectly right. Even the twenty-nine years he worked for "the Government," as a Chicago postal clerk, were taken by them mostly for granted—simply because Lottie had handled his money so well. *She* was the paragon, the family star. He could still hear her assured but strained laugh as she would say to them: "My, my, what'n the world will you all do when I'm gone!" He and the girls would laugh too, and one of them might say: "You ain't going nowhere, Mama!"

Yet she *was* gone. And he didn't feel grief so much as bewilderment. But already his daughters, with husbands, children, and homes of their own now, were steeped in their mother's methods. They were devising new—and less subtle—means of steering his life for him. "We gotta look after Papa," they quickly agreed, "and see that he eats right, and gets his rest. And that nobody comes messing around with him." He well knew what this last sentiment meant—no women. Yet he was only fifty-six, and well-preserved, he thought—although getting very bald. But he held the passbook to the savings account, representing money accumulated by Lottie from his pay checks over those long, tedious years, and he sensed his daughters' sharp, hawk-eyed concern. Christ! he thought. . . . what if they knew about Annette! They would die—simply die, that's all . . . of conniption fits, or a stroke at least! And Annette married! He could not help smiling.

But why, oh *why*, didn't Annette hurry up and call—like she'd promised! Time dragged so—the telephone seemed dead! But the *doorbell* was ringing! He froze—then turned around in stony displeasure . . . but made no move toward the buzzer. Annette would never come by without calling first. Then came a long, alarming ring. He took his sullen time going to the door, pressed the buzzer, and pulled the door open. Someone was starting up the stairs already.

"Papa!"

A scowling silence hit him. Lillian.

"Papa!"

"Yeah—that you, Lil?" he finally said. He had tried his best to sound pleasant.

She soon reached the second floor and walked in boldly—a tall, dark brown-skinned girl, nearly thirty, and very heavy-bosomed. "I wasn't sure I'd catch you," she said, out of breath.

"You almost didn't," he lied. "I was getting ready to go out." But he smiled at her.

She studied him. "I was over at the meat market picking up my roast, and thought I'd ring your bell. Can I give you a lift somewhere, Papa?"

"No, my car's right down there on the street."

She was wearing a heavy grey winter coat and fur-trimmed boots, and began looking around for a chair. "Have you got a minute . . . to let me catch my breath?"

He paused—furious inside. ". . . Okay, Lil," he finally said, his blood in angry riot now—"I'll go put on a necktie, eh?" He sensed her distrust and his resentment soared. He knew she was hell-bent on detecting where he was going without actually asking him. He went into the bedroom and, standing before the dresser mirror, jerked a necktie off the rack. One hell of a time for her to come! They were such damned snoopers!—both of them. He didn't know which one was worse: Reba, with her hard, cold ways—or now nosy, nervous Lillian! He tied his necktie, frowning unhappily. Then he picked up a stiff-bristled hairbrush and fiercely stroked the stubborn horseshoe of hair around his head.

"Have you heard from Reba today, Papa?" Lillian called from the living room.

"No, not yet."

"She said she was goin' to call you."—Lillian lay back in the chair, her coat unbuttoned, her uneasy eyes roving the room; she knew every square foot of its dusty plainness, with the dated furniture and ornaments on which she felt her mother had squandered unnecessary patience and care. There was the false fireplace, with its narrow, wooden mantelpiece, and clock not lately wound; the gaunt television standing in the corner, its tall V-aerial perched atop it like feelers on a giant insect; the old lamp shades, now grey and lackluster under their thin skin of dust; and the unwrapped magazines her mother subscribed to, accumulated on the table like a pile of little logs.

Lillian sat there remembering her mother with a fanatical, almost maudlin, devotion. She wondered now in her exasperation why her mother hadn't taken some of the money she'd so faithfully saved up for the family all those years and gone downtown and bought herself the nice, new furniture she was always talking about, or at least got some new, pretty clothes. No, she was always worrying about the family! Lillian chafed. Her mother was the only really adequate person she had ever known and she constantly found herself comparing her with others—to their detriment. This included her father. She had somehow never thought him quite worthy of the marriage actually—despite his years of silent, faithful effort to support them all. She couldn't understand why she felt this way; he hadn't been a harsh father—her mother was by far the sterner of the two—but Lillian had sometimes sensed in him traces of indifference toward his family, of boredom even.

The telephone rang! Its clanging seemed to Lester to rattle the very window panes! He panicked . . . and sprang into the living room for it. But Lillian was already there—her hand in the instant just reaching the phone—a sad, innocent look on her face. In the act of picking it up, she said to him: "Reba, probably." His angular body quivered with pent-up anxiety and fury. But before he could speak, Lillian was saying "Hello."

There was a pause. She repeated harshly—"*Hello!*" Another pause. Then she stiffened—and said slowly, acidly: "*Yes* . . . he *is* . . . you just hold *on.*" Training her small, convicting eyes on her father, she surrendered the phone.

He took it limply, lifted it to his ear, and held it there, help-lessly—as Lillian, her dark nostrils flaring, sank into her chair again.

Then he heard Annette's voice in the phone. "Lester! . . . is that you, Lester?"

"Yes." His voice was reedy.

"Listen, I know you can't talk! I know why. I'll talk—you listen. I can come out tonight for a little while if you want me to. . . . Do you want to meet me about eight-thirty in Walgreen's drug store at 47th and Michigan? Can you do that? . . . about eight-thirty?"

"Yes," he breathed gratefully. He returned the phone to its cradle. "I'll get my coat now," he said to Lillian, and tried to be casual.

She stared wildly in her lap and said nothing.

He went to the hall-tree and began putting on his overshoes; then his hat and overcoat. "Ready?" he said brightly, squaring his shoulders.

Suddenly Lillian was scrambling in her purse for a hand-kerchief; and jabbed it up under her nose, her heavy bosom shuddering and heaving under the winter coat. *"One month!"* she gasped. "One lousy month!" Then she choked up, and tears flooded her face, soaking the handkerchief.

He stood and looked on in silence. Finally he turned his back on her and walked dejectedly to the window.

"I'm gonna tell Reba!" she spluttered and moaned. "You see if I don't! You see! . . . *Poor* Mama, *poor* Mama!"

He was frightened now—and sad. It was a horrible thing, he thought, to make enemies out of your own flesh-and-blood daughters! What had got into him! . . . Why had he done it! He could have waited a decent time, at least. It was shoddy. But he knew he had *had* to do it; and had lost control in this brand new—blissful—experience; yet he felt sordid.

Lillian, the corners of her mouth bent down grotesquely

like an African sculpture, got up now and stumbled toward
the door. The tears had streaked her brown cosmetic, and one
of her stockings was slack and twisted on her skinny leg. He
looked at her—as if for the first revelatory time. He had not
realized before that she was ugly. Then at once he felt despicable—wasn't she his own daughter?

He knew now there was no further use in pretending he
was going out—the game was up. As Lillian stood at the door,
waiting for some placating gesture from him, he began taking
off his coat instead, and then peeled off his overshoes. At this
she began sobbing again. And finally, violently jerking open
the door, she rushed out, and down the stairs.

By eight-thirty that night a wet snow was falling. Lester,
still shaken, stood in Walgreen's drug store near the front door,
gazing out at the sluggish flakes settling onto the sidewalk. The
cashier, a mountainous black girl, chatted gleefully with the
customers filing in and out past her cigarette counter, and
the porter at the entrance repeatedly swung his mop across
the slushy floor. Lester yawned from nervousness, then sighed
and stood up straight. Annette wouldn't be late if she could
help it, he knew. It was something!—the way she always managed to be on time, regardless of all hindrances, and despite
her whining husband, who was almost always home now with
his arthritis. Curiously, it was the fact of this affliction that
had first thrown Lester and Annette in contact. It seemed to
Lester now a long time ago—yet it was actually only a year.
He recalled it in wonder.

It had been, of all things, *fraternal* business!—Lester smiled
guiltily to himself. As a member of his lodge's Sick Commit-
tee, he had gone to call on Brother Andrew Sikes, then bed-
ridden with his arthritis. And sloe-eyed Annette had met him
at the door—that was how it all began. He remembered how
he smiled so gravely, to hide his shock at her fleshy, almost

carnal beauty—he had always had a solemn, wayward eye for the ample female limb; it was a trait his wife Lottie sensed but could never quite pin down. Sometimes he felt now, though, she had passed along warnings to her daughters.

He recalled how Annette took him into her husband's bedroom, and left them almost immediately. He did not see her again until, leaving, he returned to the living room. "Thanks, Mr. Billups . . . for coming," she said, and smiled, as she stood close to him at the door—"Andrew's taking it kind of hard. It's awfully painful, you know. Then he gets cross sometimes. So it'll help him, I think, to know the fellows hadn't forgotten him." Still he had caught an annoyance in her voice, an impatience, as she spoke of her husband.

But it was his own giddy excitement at the time that stood out now like a white light in his memory—as they had said good-bye, she shook his hand sincerely, caressingly. Wild sensations climbed his vertebrae. He could never get her out of his mind after that. He would often lie awake in the dead of night, beside Lottie, thinking of her—of her quick smile, her lovely lightish-brown skin, her tantalizing figure, her occasional easy languor. And the fact that she was the age of his daughters only whetted his suppressed passionate craving for her, his mooning love; it was ridiculous, even comic, he knew.

He saw her only once after that before Lottie died. It was in a large supermarket—one Saturday afternoon. Shopping alone, he had clumsily pulled down a tall stack of toilet tissue, sending the rolls scurrying along the floor in all directions. Just as he floundered about, trying to pick them up, Annette pushed her cart around the corner—confronting him squarely. Both were startled—and embarrassed. Then suddenly they laughed.

"Let me help you," she said, and stooped down to retrieve a pink roll for him.

"Thank you . . . thanks!" he stammered. "I'm not so good at this—as you can see."

But they exchanged only a few more words—about nothing. Then she wheeled her cart on. His heart sank, watching her go. And he thought her slightly thinner—but still voluptuous and wonderful. Afterwards for days he was plagued with what he might have said to her—impressive, witty, perhaps daring things—had he not been so muddled and confused. And again, during the long, still nights, while Lottie slept, he would lie awake, thinking about Annette.

Now she was entering the drug store!

She must have seen him first, for she was smiling. He took a quick step toward her, then self-consciously held back, smiling also.

"Hi!" she said. He always thought her teeth so pretty when she smiled. "Have you been waiting long?"

"Oh, no!" he said.

She shook her head. "I couldn't get started any sooner. *You* know." She was wearing a blue belted coat, a little blue felt cloche-type hat, and boots.

He touched her elbow and guided her back to the door. "Let's walk over to the Brass Rail," he said.

"Oh, swell."

Both looked at each other and each saw the strain in the other's face.

They went out into the wet snow and headed east on 47th Street. She ran her arm through his impulsively, smiling and leaning against him as they walked; and making him tense and uneasy as he thought of Lillian!—or of being recognized by someone on the street. Yet the bursting shower of elation inside him made him heady and reckless.

They crossed through the heavy traffic on Indiana Avenue. Cars, some sounding their horns, crept by under the snow-hazy street lights. On the sidewalks the denizens of the ghetto sauntered or hurried about their Saturday night business. But he felt conspicuous—yet so proud of Annette.

"I got *you* off the hook today," she teased him with a nervous little laugh.

"That's what *you* think." He grinned at her. "How did you figure out what was up?"

"You wouldn't have any *other* woman in your apartment except your daughter, would you?—You'd better not!" she laughed.

"Oh, no!" he said, frightened.

Lester considered the Brass Rail very classy for a saloon; it catered to all the leading Southside sportsmen and big shots. He and Annette entered the dimly-lit place somewhat unsurely and wandered back through the blue haze, past the bar, to a rear booth. The juke box was playing soft jazz, as the waitresses moved back and forth among the well-heeled patrons. Someone at the bar was saying: "Yeah, but the White Sox'll have better pitching this year, you watch!" Lester, a baseball fan himself, privately agreed, as he hung up Annette's coat.

Soon a squat, brown-skinned waitress, immaculate in white, came over, stood at their booth, and casually looked off in another direction.

"What would you like?" Lester whispered to Annette.

". . . Same as usual, I guess."

"Two bourbons and ginger ale, please," he said to the waitress, who, as she left, seemed to smile at the order.

Annette was wearing dark costume jewelry at her throat; it contrasted with her clear skin. She took a pack of cigarettes from her purse, and he reached across the table for matches. When he had lit her cigarette, she sat back, smiled, and asked: "Did you think I wasn't going to call?"

"I wasn't sure there for a while."

"You wouldn't kid me, would you?—You knew I would."

"Well . . . I thought so, but after Lillian came by, I was

hoping you wouldn't—not right then anyway. Wouldn't she time it just right!" He smiled and shook his bald head.

Soon the waitress brought the drinks and left.

"What did happen when I called?" Annette asked him, then tasted her drink.

He gave her the full account.

She was intent on his every word, and when he had finished, she shook her head slowly, with finality. "Your daughters would hate me."

He was silent, and peered down into his drink.

"Yes, they would hate me," she repeated, in a monotone.

He fidgeted; then knitted his brow. "I just contacted you too soon, that's all," he said. "I should've waited awhile. Two or three months, maybe—even six."

"What difference would it've made to them?—with me married. I'm glad you didn't wait now."

He made no reply . . . as his mind soared back over the past three hectic weeks; and he felt the guilt of those weeks, for when they began, Lottie had been in the ground only eight days! He recalled it all too well—the afternoon he saw Annette's husband from a distance. Andrew Sikes was hobbling painfully down the street on a cane. Lester jammed on the brakes of his car, jumped out, and ran into a hamburger stand, where he searched out the telephone number and dialed Annette. Afterwards he concluded it was the wickedest, craziest thing a man ever did and got away with. She of course was dumbfounded by his call. She had heard of Lottie's death, and was about to offer him her sympathy, when he cut her short and begged her to meet him—it was something urgent, he had insisted; something personal, involving just the two of them! Still puzzled, but curious, almost alarmed, she finally agreed to see him. They met downtown the next afternoon, in a little sandwich shoppe on Adams Street, and he recalled how hoarse and shaky his voice got as he laid bare to her his feelings about her: how she had fired his thoughts for a whole year now, how mixed up he was, how guilty he felt.

Annette, her eyes big, had just sat there, astounded; then, after awhile, fascinated; but only after she had tried discouragement, resistance, pleading, coldness, scoffing. Nothing fazed him. After that day they began seeing each other often—two or three times a week. There were rash car rides along Lake Michigan, and rendezvous in downtown movies, or in Southside bars. Once she went to his apartment.

"But I still say I called you too soon!" Lester insisted again now, frowning; he sipped his highball. "I should've waited awhile. I had always wondered, though, after that day in the supermarket, if I'd ever see you again . . . or *how* I'd ever see you. When I spotted Andrew out walking that afternoon, I just lost my head, that's all. Otherwise, it might have been a whole lot longer—if ever."

Annette smiled wryly, ironically—"And he hadn't been out of the house in weeks; he's only been out once *since* then. How's that for fate, or something?" Her pretty nose crinkled in what he thought a rather raucous laugh, but he sensed her desperation. He lit another cigarette for her. Then she started humming along with the music coming out of the juke box. "It's getting to be hell for me to stay in the house any more," she said—"You've made me like the lights." She went on humming—he watched her, hypnotized. "And that's not good," she finally said, with a sensuous smile.

"Is that what I mean to you—lights?" he said.

"Yes . . . but more." She looked away thoughtfully, rolling the highball glass between her palms.

He grinned at her. "I'm not so sure. I'm the guy that gets you out once in awhile, that's all."

"That's *all!* My God, that's a lot—you don't know."

"Ah, but don't I? My daughters, remember?"

"Yes . . . ," she said drearily, ". . . your daughters—

and my husband." They sat now without talking. Then she saw him watching her and she bent her head over her drink.

Soon he said, quite evenly: "Would you marry me?"

"Why would you ask that! How could I?"

"But would you, if you could?"

"You know I would," she said in exasperation.

"Well, I'm glad. I'm a lot older than you are, you know."

"You're only six years older than Andrew—and he's been sick almost four years. Age hasn't got everything to do with it." Then she smiled ruefully. "And *you* know you're sort of handsome, all right."

"*Ho!*" he laughed. "Am I? With *my* bald head? But only 'sort of,' eh? I could take offense at that."

But she was serious now. "It's been tough around the house, real tough—low funds and big doctor bills. We couldn't make it at all if it wasn't for a small health insurance he had, and help from his two brothers, and also now his nephew—God! He doesn't want me to go back to my job, you know, like I should, really. He's so grumpy—stays in the dumps. . . . Oh, but you didn't come here to listen to all this," she sighed, then smiled again, primly patting her dark processed hair.

He put down his glass in agitation. "I'll help you! . . . I'll help you any way I can," he said—"*Any* way."

"Well, thanks!" she laughed. "Quite a gold digger, me, eh?" Then she finished her drink and said grimly: "But money won't cure what's wrong with me."

"What's wrong with you?" he grinned again. "*I* haven't seen much."

"I don't know whether I know, myself, or not. Maybe it's that I'm just existing. Not living—just existing. Oh, that's so damn corny! . . . but I *am* only existing! It's true!"

"Ask me," he said wearily—"I know all about it. It's a helluva feeling, all right." Soon he waved for the squat waitress and ordered two more drinks.

"That'll be my last," Annette said, glancing at her watch. "Liquor's not much help."

He became impetuous. "I'd marry you so quick it'd make your head swim!"

"Yes," she laughed, "and your daughters would shoot us both."

He scooted forward on the seat. "Then, will you be my girl friend? Will you? I'll take care of you. I *will!* I'm not broke!"

"Your girl friend! I'm your girl friend *now*—or I thought I was!" She laughed sadly.

"You think it's funny. *I* don't."

"No, Lester, honey,"—she patted his fist across the table— "it's not funny. But we gotta act like it is."

He shook his head again. "I don't get you! . . . I don't get you at all!"

Soon the waitress brought the second pair of drinks and as she went away Lester began talking faster and louder, for the juke box was playing a little louder now. "Don't you understand?" he cried. "I can't marry you!—you gotta husband already! But I can take care of you! . . . *he's* not! Did you ever hear of love? I *love* you!"

"*Shhhhh!*"—she glanced toward the bar, putting a hand on his forearm—". . . they'll hear you."

"What do I care."

She sat deep in gloom. ". . . So does Andrew love me. Can't you see that's what makes it so crappy—he loves me." She gulped half her drink.

"Chrrr-ist!" Lester sputtered. "—It's too God-damned complicated for me."

"Taking your money wouldn't bring me freedom—and I need money. But I need freedom more."

He took a drink and sulked. "I've spoiled everything now— you don't like me."

"Oh, Lester! How can you say that!—when I've turned my

husband into a raving maniac by running out in the street to meet *you*." Then she leaned forward and whispered bitterly: "And I've been in your bed!" Both were shocked into silence.

". . . What's up the road for us?" he asked finally.

"Oh, in time, you'll get tired waiting around on street corners for me to get out to meet you in some drug store, or movie, or tavern—there're too many women around not caged in like I am. You'll see."

"Are you happy when you're with me?"

"Yes," she said submissively.

"I've never felt about a woman the way I feel about you."

She tried to laugh "That's just it!—you haven't felt, period. We're twins like that—we haven't felt, we haven't lived!"

"But I'm living now—because I *do* feel. I didn't for thirty-four whole years, though. And I had to wait till I was fifty-six to find out—how about that?—and with only a few short years left."

"Oh, I don't know," she shrugged. "I may be all wrong about it . . . all wrong." She slowly drained her glass and set it down.

Suddenly trembling, he seized both her hands. "Will you go home with me again tonight?" he whispered.

For an instant an odd terror gripped her heart—before she said wearily: ". . . Oh, why not."

Rapport

The two babies squealed their delight, waddling back and forth across the grass, as their sapling mother sat hunched on the bench, her legs crossed, reading *True Confessions*. Jackson Park that summer afternoon was an urban woods. The elms stretched their branches out over the gravel paths, the orange-cup lily beds, and the horseshoe pit; and just the breath of a breeze came skimming in from the golf course and the distant softball diamond.

Old Alf Sewell, who looked part black, greater part Indian, sat on another bench nearby, beaming as he watched the children. He was gaunt now, with iron-grey hair, and his leathery, hawkish face verged on a scowl each time he smiled. Only in his gnarled hands did there seem to remain a trace of his former strength.

The tiniest boy, about two years old, stumbled over to him, holding out a red rubber ball. The old man grimaced and smiled at the same time, pursing his lips to hold his dentures snug. "Oh! You wanta give me your ball, do you?" He took the ball in his cupped hands. "Well, you're mighty generous, I must say. *Mighty* generous." The child watched him. But soon his brother, a little towhead about two years older, edged up and put out his hand for the ball. "Oh, you're here to take it back already?" and Alf drew back in mock surprise.

"That's ours," the older child said, looking around toward his mother, who after a moment managed to lift her head from the magazine.

"Ronnie," she said in a lazy nasal voice, "bring Frank over here. Come on, now, and stop bothering the man——."

"Oh, they're not bothering me," interrupted Alf in disbelief, surrendering the ball to Ronnie. "They're two cute ones."

The mother, chewing gum, gave a grudging little smile and went back to her love story, as the children started galloping around her bench again. Alf sat and watched them with a sober stare. Though never a father himself, all his long life children had fascinated him; but now, a widower, he could only surmise what it might have been like—just as in his many empty hours his mind would range back over the victories and frustrations, the highs and lows, of his life, and the bleak prospects. For he had reaped more leisure than he either needed or wanted, and now too many of his afternoons were idled away in the park as he unwittingly sought to fill his vacant days watching the doings of strangers. After awhile he ventured to speak to the mother again:

"You're mighty lucky . . . to have the nice children," he smiled. "—Got any more?"

She finally looked up from the magazine. "Just the two," she said, and stroked her frazzled, yellow hair—her fingernails were bitten to the quick.

"You're still young yet, though," Alf counselled.

She glanced at him and appeared to nod agreement, as she turned the page.

He felt himself getting edgy. And soon he got up and brushed off the seat of his trousers and started up toward The Hut, at the number one golf tee. He'd get an Eskimo pie and watch some golf shots. His thick shoes clumped along the narrow, cemented walk as his eyes bored straight ahead. There was an unconceded bewilderment inside his head that he hadn't felt since he first came to Chicago as a stripling from Oklahoma. Yet back then he had soon rid himself of this vague, cut-adrift feeling—but now, he wasn't so sure. Before, there had been the lure of the future; and youth—a physical, bull-like splendor, sorrel skin, black hair like a horse's mane, a beaked nose, with a trace of the African genes showing in his full lips. And though it was true that this last mark stamped him—inescapably—in his harsh world, he had then known too little of life to be daunted.

When he reached The Hut, he bought an Eskimo pie and took a seat in the last row of benches behind the number one golf tee. A foursome of two women and two men was about to tee off. Both men wore gay Bermuda shorts. The goofs! thought Alf, nibbling the ice cream bar. The women hit short, lobbing drives into the wide, green fairway, but the first man, after addressing his ball interminably, hooked a wild shot into the second fairway. The other whiffed his shot completely, as Alf laughed and crossed his leg.

After a while he noticed a white-haired old man, older than himself, sitting stooped over in the left section of benches . . . . Could that be Ben Feldman? . . . He got up and walked around to the old man's left before speaking. It was Ben all right!

"Counsel, how are you?" Alf beamed, standing over the old criminal lawyer. "Remember me?"

Feldman, white stubble on his pinched, pink face, squinted up through thick glasses. "Of course," he said in a quavering voice. "Sergeant Sewell." He gave a quiet little laugh and gripped Alf's hand.

"That's what you used to call me," Alf laughed, sitting down beside him. " 'Sergeant'—but I never was."

"I know, I know—but I called *all* you cops 'Sergeant'." He

was chortling as he moved over on the bench to make room. "I got a damnsight more cooperation out of you guys that way . . . now didn't I? How've you been?"

"Pretty good, I guess. My prostate ain't what it used to be," Alf laughed—"I don't sleep so good sometimes. But I get along."

"You'll get over all that—ha, with a little surgery! I had the same complaint when I was your age—before I retired." Feldman twinkled.

Alf observed his heavy cane, heard his shaking voice, and was unconvinced. But he said, "You know what it's like, then . . . . Say, I didn't know you lived on the Southside."

"Right over there." Feldman pointed proudly. "—on 69th Street, with my youngest daughter and husband—and kids."

Alf felt a darting streak of malice and changed the subject: "Did you see Judge Burke's picture in the *Trib* the other day— blowing out all those candles on his birthday cake?"

"No, but he's still around, I know. So's his wife. . . . Are you close here to the park?"

"Not far—at the Webster Hotel, on 63rd."

"Oh . . . hotel."

"I lost my wife—almost two years ago."

Feldman sadly shook his head. "That can be rough—real rough. It's almost ten years now since I lost mine. I know what you're up against."

"I tried batching it," Alf said, "but I didn't like it. I finally got rid of the furniture."

"Well, well . . . ," old Feldman sighed, squinting at his wristwatch. With his right hand clutching his cane and the other the bench in front of him, he slowly hoisted himself. "I'd better get going," he panted. "The grandchildren get back from camp today—and they'll make a helluva fuss if I'm not on hand to greet each and every one of them. One *hell*uva fuss."

The two men soon shook hands again and said goodbye, and Feldman hobbled off in a slow, crouching gait.

Alf sat for awhile; apathetic now toward what went on around him: the concentration of the golfers; the whispered chatter of the spectators behind the tee; the tall, gawky young woman pushing her bicycle past alongside a short, Italian-looking man; the noisy vigor of the softball game three hundred yards off to his right; the big, droning super-jet high overhead like a lazy platinum catfish, its silvery tail flashing in the watery sunlight.

Finally he got up and sauntered off in the direction of the softball game. But before very far, a little boy, with a blond cowlick and a dirty face, came toward him carrying three scuffed-up golf balls in his hand.

"Wanta buy some golf balls, Mister?"

"How much?" Alf smiled, feigning interest.

"Fifty cents—all three."

"My! That's pretty high, ain't it?" Alf joked.

"No, sir. This one here's a Spalding Dot." The boy picked out a scarred ball.

"Where'd you get 'em?"

"Over on the eleventh hole—the water hole."

"Why don't you keep 'em? You'll be playing yourself before long," Alf laughed.

The boy began to look away, bored by the long negotiations.

"How old are you?" Alf asked. "—You're old enough to play *now*."

The boy did not hear; he had sighted two women as they approached pulling golf carts and, without looking back, he hurried over to them—as Alf groped in his pocket for fifty cents.

"Wanta buy some golf balls, lady?" the boy called out.

The women apparently were not interested, for he continued

walking past them on toward the softball diamond, leaving Alf standing with his hand in his pocket.

Alf watched the boy. Then he slowly turned and started back toward The Hut, which was near the street and the bus stop. He was not hurrying; for somehow he was suddenly tired—too tired to walk to the hotel. Evening had begun to settle on the park, and the freshly-mowed grass gave off a cool, sweet-clover fragrance; and there had now appeared thin, horizontal streaks of tinted clouds that crossed the dying sun like tight ropes of dripping moss. In his prosaic way, he was moved by the redolence and the sunset, hating, really, to leave the park he had learned to love even with its uncaring strangers. The park was always better, for instance, than the monotonous hotel where he had to live because of what inflation did to a pensioner's check. It was better, too, than Mrs. Turner's painted-over dining room at the hotel, and her sporadic courtesy. It was better than a lot of things he had come to know lately. He kept walking toward the bus stop.

After a short ride, the bus put him off at the Webster. When he entered the lobby he found himself surrounded by a mob of barnstorming baseball players, still in their steaming uniforms. He threaded his way through them to the new automatic elevator, where three of the players and a woman were waiting to go up.

"You boys win today?" the woman asked.

"We always win," answered the burly black, with mock seriousness.

"Haw!" his skinny teammate horse-laughed to the woman. "He means, when *he* don't play!"

Alf laughed out loud, and the big player looked at him hard. "Wuz it *that* funny, *Dad?*" he growled in jest.

"It sure was, *I* thought," said Alf brightly.

The elevator doors parted and the five stepped in, the third ball player cuddling a brown paper bag in his arms. From deep inside the bag came faint sounds of clinking glass.

"Did you git any ice?" the big player asked him.

"Naw, Sims is gonna bring it—if he don't get scared of runnin' into the boss."

The three players got off at Alf's floor, the fourth. His room was to the left at the end of the hall and they were going in the same direction, so he joined them.

"Want a drink, Dad?" the bag carrier asked him with a prankish grin.

Alf, who did not drink, hesitated; his heart quickened as he smiled at the player and fumbled for an answer. Nice of him, he thought. Then he saw the other two players glowering at the inviter as if he had dropped the precious bag on a concrete sidewalk. Alf froze and his smile faded. "No thanks—not this evening," he said with politeness, and walked on ahead.

The players reached their room first—Alf heard their key in the lock. Then, as he reached his own door, he heard the burly player explode at the bag carrier, "God dammit!—you losin' your weak mind? He coulda come in here and drunk up *all* th' whiskey—and nobody coulda said a fuckin' word!"

Alf unlocked his door and quickly stepped in. Shaken, he thought of the old days when he'd have had plenty to say—and do—to a bully like that. But now he put his hat on the bookcase and sank in a chair.

The room, a television set in the corner, was old-fashioned and cluttered, but not small, and held the pungent smells of wash cloths and half-eaten, now dried apples. From her picture atop the high chest of drawers, Carrie, his wife, brown and lantern-jawed, smiled somehow not down on him but across the room. He stared at her, but their gazes would not meet. He remembered that blue print dress; it was a favorite of hers, and on one occasion she had given the dry cleaners a bad time about it. He brought up first one tired knee to his chin and then the other in order to loosen his shoe laces and let the shoes lie where they fell; and then he slid down in the chair with his legs straight out and stiff and his arms dangling over the sides of the chair—still watching Carrie.

He well knew her mood when she half-smiled like that. She was pleased, self-satisfied—as whenever she beat him at checkers or five-up, or came up with the proof for her side in an argument, as she had the time she insisted that Lincoln had said if saving the Union required that he not free a single slave, he would save the Union. Sometimes her behavior bordered on arrogance. But she had her reasons, he remembered with contrition; he had been a provoking husband at one tenuous stage of their marriage—his wild stage. They had split up for a week on two occasions, and there was that time at the breakfast table when she hurled the half-grapefruit at his head. He realized now, though, all this might have been different if they had had children. But the doctor had said it wasn't "in the cards" for them.

He remembered coming home one afternoon to find her sitting alone in the kitchen sipping some sweet red wine she bought occasionally and kept in the buffet; he abhorred the syrupy stuff and was cool to her as he walked through to the bedroom; but she followed him, glass in hand. "I was thinking today,"—she was slightly unsteady— ". . . we could adopt a little boy maybe." His coolness vanished and he thrust his arm around her. "Sure we can," he said tenderly. "Let's see about it right away. That's a wonderful idea." But somehow she looked at him as if she doubted him, and next day when he broached the matter of how one went about adopting a child, she showed only a casual interest. Once in awhile the subject would pop up in their conversation—until both were past forty—but nothing ever came of it. They had each other then. Things weren't so bad after all. And their later years together, especially the seven after his retirement from the police force, were their finest. They were inseparable. She seemed to relish the time she spent in the kitchen on his pet dishes. And he would stop at Tony's, the curbstone florist, and get her little bunches of white or bronze or lavender pompons, which she always kept before her in a glass of water on the kitchen shelf. Or sometimes he would bring her a small azalea plant which, for some unknown reason, she always put on the window sill in the bathroom. Now he sat and watched her picture; these remembered days seemed so long ago.

In a little while he pushed himself up from the chair, and went in to run a tub of water. He'd feel better, maybe, after a bath—and some dinner.

Mrs. Turner's Dining Room was on the lobby level of the hotel. The muggy un-air-conditioned place was well over half full of her faithful black patrons as Alf entered just as he had on what seemed to him countless evenings before. The room had been redecorated only a month earlier in a fresh peach, and the new chairs were chrome steel. The cash register was located in the corner nearest the entrance and shuddered under the vibrations of a giant, whirring electric fan behind it, aimed out at the diners from atop a tall steel shaft.

As always, Mrs. Turner was perched on her high, cushioned chair behind the cash register. She was a dark brown-skinned woman addicted to scarlet lipstick and when she smiled she exposed pink gums above her gold-capped incisors. She would have taken deep offense at the suggestion she might be fifty. Somehow she always made Alf jumpy; he could never be sure whether, after greeting him, she was to remain friendly and attentive throughout the meal or go fawning after somebody else. This generally depended on who was present. Occasionally one or two of the black physicians or lawyers from the corner office building would drop in for coffee or a sandwich, invariably bringing Mrs. Turner fluttering down from her perch, her big rump and spindle legs abustling. "The bitch," Alf would sputter inside. But her food was clean and tasty— and today she seemed okay.

"Hello, there," she grinned. "Did you get in last evening, Mr. Sewell?"

"I had leg of lamb." Alf was a little smug.

"Oh, sure you did—right over there." She pointed to one of the small tables on her left. "Why, yes."

"That's right." Alf was gallant now as he sidled through the larger tables in the center to get over to a small one again. He pulled out the chair and sat down.

Soon an athletic-looking fellow wearing a seersucker sport shirt walked toward the cash register to pay his check. There was sex in Mrs. Turner's smile as she preened forward in her high chair awaiting him. He handed her the check and reached in his hip pocket for his wallet.

"Did you enjoy your dinner, sir?" she inquired with a wet, lip-curling smile.

"Yes, I did, thank you." He looked like one of the more genteel ball players, and placed down a ten dollar bill on the glass cigar counter.

She took her eyes off him long enough to lift her chin and examine the check through her bi-focals. "Two twenty-one," she simpered, slamming the check down dangerously on the sharp spindle. "Gotta penny, sir?"

"Sure," the fellow said, going into his pocket.

Alf smoldered as he watched her and waited for a waitress. Yet when the waitress finally came he had not looked at the menu. He quickly picked it up as she stood over him with her pencil on her order pad; but he could not decide.

"What's good tonight, Pearl?" He was sheepish.

"Oh, I don't know," she sighed and smiled. "The short ribs *look* good. You like cream-of-tomato soup, Mr. Sewell—that's on there."

"Okay, Pearlie—you're the expert. Soup and short ribs it'll be, then—and iced tea."

Alf was in the middle of his meal when Cootie Silverette came in with his wife and another woman. Cootie was an old-fashioned band leader, a hot sax player, who lived at the Webster and was wearing a beautiful beige suit, with his hair still "processed" and gleaming. They took the table at Alf's right, and Cootie's wife, who looked almost white, appeared to have had a few drinks. She was talking loud and giggling, but Cootie and the other woman were dignified. He seemed bored as he picked up the menu and studied it. "Well . . . whut's th' deal today?" he soliloquized, ignoring the women.

"I wanta steak, baby," his wife said.

"Okay, Alberta," Cootie said. The other woman waited for the one menu.

Then, looking toward the entrance, Alberta uttered a groan. "God, would you look at that?" she said. Alf turned and stared with the others. A hulking, unkempt woman had entered, pulling behind her a little black girl about six years old. The child was dirty and her hair was woolly and matted. "Emmy Scales," Alberta said, shaking her head. "They sure must be hard up for somewhere to place foster kids nowadays."

Mrs. Turner pretended not to see Emmy, who had to fend for herself; still pulling the child, she lumbered toward the back through tables and diners, looking from side to side with chalky eyes popping from a massive ebony face. Finally she sighted the small table at Alf's left elbow and made straight for it. Noncommittal, Alf continued eating.

As soon as the child climbed onto her chair, she began picking her nose.

"Stop that, Earline!" Emmy exploded in a loud whisper. "I'm gonna whup hell outa you, if you don't!"

The child gave her a look of contempt and started bumping up and down on the chair. Then she jerked her topsy head right and left and rolled the whites of her eyes and stretched her mouth open wide, showing opossum teeth. Alf watched her out of the tail of his eye and decided her skin was the blackest of any human being in his memory.

The waitress was glum as she approached Emmy's table.

"We just wanta sandwich," Emmy said.

"What kind?"

"What kind you got?"

"They're all on the menu there."

Emmy was displeased. "I don't want no menu. Gim'me two hamburgers—and two Pepsi Colas."

The waitress did not bother to write it down, and walked off.

The child now had both hands on top of the white table cloth as if playing a piano, dirt caked under her fingernails. Soon she jostled a spoon off the table.

"Keep on," Emmy warned in hushed breath. She pushed back to look for the spoon. "I'm gonna take care *o'you* when when we git home."

The child turned and looked at Alf, as if expecting him to retrieve the spoon. He pushed his chair back, slowly leaned over, and picked it up. He offered it to her and she took it with her bright eyes fastened on him.

"Your name is Earline, is it?" he said, smiling.

"Yis." Her answer was barely audible as, still holding the spoon, she studied him.

"I don't believe I've seen *you* around here before," he said.

"No," Emmy butted in, "—and you ain't likely to again soon."

Alf ignored the remark, as the bewildered child looked first at Emmy and then at him.

"Little girls like you don't eat in big restaurants much, do they?" Alf asked. "—Do you like to?"

Earline started to answer, but she looked at Emmy again and fell silent.

Soon their waitress brought the hamburgers and the Pepsi Colas. Earline sat up at once and, looking once more at Emmy, reached for the sandwich. She wolfed her food, as Alf looked on. She poured Pepsi Cola into a glass, seized the glass in both hands and gulped like a stevedore, the dark beverage dripping off the corners of her puckish mouth. As she drank, she watched Alf with big sad eyes.

He had intended nothing else from the kitchen, but now, as Pearl, the waitress, returned, he ordered more iced tea.

When Emmy had finished her sandwich she leaned over to Alf and whispered, "Mista, have you got a cigarette?"

"I don't smoke," Alf said coldly. He smiled at Earline again. "The circus was in town last week. Did you ever go to the circus . . . and see all the animals?"

Earline shook her head, rubbing her greasy fingers against her dress for a napkin.

"You mean you never saw the lions, and the tigers, and the big elephants! . . . You never saw the clowns all painted up and making funny faces at the children?"

Earline shook her head, this time emphatically, and smiled for the first time.

"Well, you will someday," Alf said. "You'll have fun— you'll be a big girl, and you'll have fun."

Earline now gave him a radiant smile, and then looked at Emmy—who was pouting.

"You remember that, Earline," Alf said.

Pearl brought his iced tea at about the same time Emmy's waitress brought her check. Emmy had received quick service, he observed. She pulled a giant black purse up onto her lap and prepared to get up from the table.

"All right, let's go," she said to Earline, pushing her bulk back from the table.

Earline did not move, but looked at Alf.

"I said, let's go!" Emmy blurted.

Earline's face lengthened and tears began to shine in her eyes as she looked ruefully at Emmy.

". . . Well, goodbye, Earline," Alf smiled. He had not touched the iced tea.

Emmy stood up. "All right, Earline! Did you hear me? *Git up* from there!"

Earline started crying, softly at first; but soon began wailing. Big crystal tears rolled off her blueback face onto her dress. "I don't wanta go! I don't want to!" she cried. "I wanta stay here! I wanta stay here with him!" She was pointing at Alf and howling.

Emmy had seized her by the arm now and was dragging her from the chair. "Just wait'll I git you home!" she breathed through grinding teeth. "Just wait!"

Now Mrs. Turner was coming over. "What's the matter here?" she said. "Goodness!"

Emmy ignored her in jerking the screaming, kicking child toward the cash register. She paid the check in an uproar— and soon they were gone.

Alf took one sip of his iced tea, and pushed the glass away. He sat for a while. Finally he beckoned to Pearl for his check and, leaving a small tip, got up and walked to the cash register. Afterwards, he couldn't remember whether Mrs. Turner had been friendly or brusque when he paid her. He couldn't remember hearing anything she may have said. He didn't care. As he walked to the elevator, an alien feeling suffused him, blurring his vision. And stepping from the elevator and down the hall to his room, he seemed weightless, and the faintest smile softened the rigors of his face as he entered his room and quietly closed the door. "That little doll," he whispered, ". . . that little black doll."

Mary's Convert

Forty-third Street, near the "el," the street of rib joints and taverns, was more cluttered and overrun than usual. It was the heat. It lay on the sidewalk like an electric blanket and scores of restless people were in motion. Driven from their baking kitchenettes, they looked uprooted and a little dazed, as some stood at the curb and moped, or turned in at a corner door for beer.

Jerome stood wiry tall and casual at the newsstand, inspecting the headlines and the cover girls; he looked young even for a teen-ager, and wore skin-tight, hep cat pants.

"Whutaaya want, boy? —a comic book?" the dirty man selling newspapers said.

Jerome made no reply, but watched as an old Cadillac with a roasting radiator crept by, and two clowning loafers shouted obscenities across the street at each other. Then he resumed with the headlines.

"These here papers are for *sale*," the newsman insisted, joking. "This ain't no library."

Jerome paused and gave him an unruffled look. Finally he said, "Okay, gim'me a comic book."

The newsman's black horny hand reached up for a book.

Jerome's shirt was open at the throat but despite the heat, the long sleeves were buttoned at the wrists. He extracted a tightly-folded dollar bill from his pants watch pocket.

"Ten," the newsman said, taking the dollar bill and handing over the comic book. He gave back ninety cents change, and Jerome checked the two quarters and four dimes in his palm before sticking them in his watch pocket. Then he hesitated, his young, brown face expressionless, and viewed the newsman. "Seen the Red Lion 'round here this afternoon?" he asked.

The grimy newsman stiffened. He stood staring at Jerome. "Whut'd you say?" he scowled.

"Seen the Red Lion 'round?" Jerome repeated.

"You git outa my face," the newsman whispered. "—you little bastard, you. You ain't sixteen!"

"What's it to you?" Jerome's face was all flat nose, so spreading flat that there were only slits for nostrils. He watched the newsman with a level gaze. "You know Tommy," he said, ". . . you take care o' him all right."

"I ain't even talkin' to you." The newsman turned his sweaty back. "Go on, *beat it!*"

Jerome studied him. "Okay . . . ole *Red Lion*," he said. Then he sauntered off, leaving the newsman glowering.

Along 43rd Street, the few people still left in the hot, mangy, brick and stone kitchenette buildings were hanging out of their windows in hope of a breath of air. They were mostly frowzy women, of all shapes and colors, who would often yell down at their children or passing friends on the sidewalk where the pigeons were liberal with droppings and floss. Jerome was in no hurry as he walked. The hell with the Lion . . . who was he trying to kid; not him. He'd wait and see Tommy that evening; no problem. Tommy'd go to the Lion for him; Tommy was great people; swell, big-hearted—had given him his first fix. That was last spring, almost five months now. It seemed longer. They'd had many a one together since then. But Tommy always said any guy with sense could kick the habit, whenever he wanted to—and that a guy with sense always knew when he'd better *start* kicking too. Tommy was smart; never got puff-headed about anything—more like a brother, a big brother. And religious too—real religious; belonged to the Church of God in Christ.

Jerome opened the comic book as he walked and, casually turning the pages, scanned the cartoons. He hadn't meant to buy it—had let the Red Lion rush him, and still hadn't done any business with him; only got chased away. He approached the corner of 43rd and Calumet. Then he saw her. She was a young, brown-skinned woman—and wore flowing white robes. She was passing out leaflets and darted from one passer-by to the next, gesticulating, exhorting, thrusting her literature at them. Her head was draped to the shoulders in the same heavy, white fabric of her robes and despite the 95-degree heat no part of her body was visible except occasionally her feet, in high-heeled shoes, and her hands and face. But what Jerome could see of her face attracted him. There were gaudy rhinestone rings on her fingers and when she turned to face him he could see huge golden earrings dangling back up under her white head covering.

She jumped at him, shooting out a leaflet. "Young man, have you talked with Jesus today?" She blocked his path.

He said nothing and tried to step around her.

"Young man! Have you talked with Him?—just once today?" She pushed the leaflet at his chest.

Jerome was cowed. "No'm," he said.

"Then read this! Read it." She shook the leaflet at him.

Slow anger gathered in his face. "I don't want it, lady." He side-stepped toward the curb.

Suddenly she snatched the comic book from his hand and, breathing in his face, dropped it to the sidewalk.

His first impulse was to swing at her. But he stood motionless. Then someone behind him gripped his arm. As he spun around, a squinty-eyed black man, his face deeply pitted, grinned and pointed at the woman. "Don't pay her no mind," he sniggered. "That's Sanctified Mary." He turned to her. "Whut's th' matter, Mary? You off the stuff again? Kicked it, eh?—fuh a week or two—an' took up Jesus." He laughed.

Mary was sullen, silent.

"She's savin' souls *now*," the man said to Jerome, "but jus' ask her t'pull up that Kluxer sheet an' show you her arm. Go on—ask her."

Jerome looked at him, and then at Mary, but said nothing.

Suddenly the man leapt forward and seized her by the wrist, and yanked her to him.

She went raving wild. "You son of a bitch, you!" she screamed, fighting and clawing him. "Take your filthy hands offa me, Jug Smith!" Her leaflets scattered to the sidewalk.

The man struggled and tugged her around in front of Jerome and with his free hand slid her robe sleeve up her arm to the shoulder. "Look!" he breathed. "Look here! Whut's Jesus gotta say 'bout *that?*" Near the elbow on the inside of her arm were a dozen purple-dotted needle scars. "Y'see?" Jug panted. "She's a mainliner. Y'*see?* Now you git t'hell outa here," he grinned at her, "an' leave this kid alone." He turned her loose.

She was incoherent. "*I'll kill you!*" she finally shrieked, lunging at him. Still grinning, he grabbed both her arms and held her off.

Someone yelled from across the street. "You-all better cut out all that 'who struck John' over there, Jug! See that squad car?—up in fronta the drug store."

Jug looked up toward the drug store and laughed. But he turned Mary loose again and trotted across the street.

She was ready to cry. Jerome stood by, helpless. Soon he stooped down and picked up a few of the scattered leaflets, glancing at one. There was much fine print, but the caption in bold type read: KEEP LOOKING UP—JESUS NEVER FAILS. He offered her the leaflets, which she finally took grudgingly, still whispering curses to herself at Jug Smith.

"Don't worry 'bout that guy," Jerome said. "He ain't nothing but a hoodlum."

She still fought tears. "He made me forget m'self—and say all those bad words!" she whimpered, "and I been tryin' so hard . . . to do what Jesus wants. *So* hard."

Jerome began inching away. The heat from the pavement was coming through the soles of his shoes and his shirt was sticky.

Mary came alive. "Young man!"—she shoved a wrinkled leaflet at him—"put this in your pocket an' read it when you get home! An' keep on reading it. HE never fails."

Jerome took the leaflet and stuffed it in his shirt pocket, and then continued down the street, leaving his comic book lying on the sidewalk.

About an hour later he was home, climbing the creaking stairs of the apartment building where he lived with his uncle and aunt. He was bored. He'd kill some time till Tommy got off from work at 5:30 . . . but he couldn't get Sanctified Mary off his mind; imagine *her* a hop-head; some nut; a real screw-ball; not a bad looking chick, though; if she just didn't wear all that mad get-up—robes! Jug Smith had identified them with the Klan. Kluxer sheets he called them; she wasn't a day over twenty-three or four; how could she put on all that hot crap in August and go out in the boiling sun and pass out leaflets about Jesus? He didn't get it; it didn't make *any* kind of sense; he'd tell Tommy. Tommy was religious.

He took out his key and let himself in. The blinds were all the way down, and he stumbled against a chair as he groped for the light switch. No one was home and the place was suffocating, with the windows shut tight and the sun outside on the west wall. But he knew not to open a window—his Aunt Bertha would raise hell for him "acting like a fool and letting in all that street heat." He went into the kitchen, opened the refrigerator and took out a cold bottle of milk. He uncapped the bottle, upped it and swilled almost half before he slumped in a kitchen chair, still holding the bottle, and sat staring at the sooty vacant wall, thinking of old fine Mary wearing her sharp high heels under the robes! and all that fake jewelry on both hands! that didn't look very religious to *him;* maybe she'd just forget to take the rings off whenever she'd switch over from sinning; and she could sin a while too, he bet—once you got her in a groovey mood; and a mainliner!—she was all mixed up; needed help; Tommy should see her; *she* hadn't kicked it; it *wasn't* all that easy, probably; she sure looked sexy, though—even in the funky robes.

He got up and put the milk back in the refrigerator. He stretched and yawned. His face rippled like rubber around his pancake-flat nose—and his boredom deepened. Then he remembered the leaflet in his shirt pocket and took it out to examine it. Soon he was sprawled in the chair again, reading:

KEEP LOOKING UP—JESUS NEVER FAILS

Elder Griffin, the great preacher and spiritual leader, asks: Have you talked with Jesus today? If you have not, or without success, then come to the Temple at 4178 Calumet, and pray with me. Only a small silver offering is asked. Open 8 AM to 10 PM, daily and Sundays.

The Elder says: Come to me if you are troubled and almost beat down to the ground. Are you sick, unhappy, disgusted with life? Does bad luck seem to follow you wherever you go? Then come to the Temple. I am here to help you see the mysteries of God's work—His mercy, and your salvation. I can do these things only through His will. *I* am nothing—Jesus is all. But to receive His Comfort and blessings, you must get right with God.

May I ask you the most important question in your whole life? It is this: Are you prepared to meet God? Your joy or your sorrow for all eternity depends upon this one question. If you are not, then you must make a start now. You must prepare! The Word of God tells us that because we are sinners we are condemned to die. "For the wages of sin is death." Romans 6:23. "Sin bringeth forth death." James 1:15. What does it mean to be a sinner condemned to die? It means separation from God, the Father, for all eternity. As you read this, won't you hear the voice of Jesus as He beckons you to come? "Ho, everyone that thirsteth, come ye to the waters." Isa. 55:1. "Incline your ear and come unto Me. Hear, and your soul shall live." Isa. 55:3.

Jerome read to the end and sat deep in thought. Finally he gave the leaflet a methodical fold and put it back in his shirt pocket. Soon he got up and wandered into the living room. That stuff sounded like Aunt Bertha; she was nutty on religion too, but she was older. It was okay for older people to be so religious if they wanted to, but Mary . . . what could she see in an old bastard like Griffin? . . . *Elder* Griffin! . . . Ah, but maybe he wasn't so old; maybe he was a young stud; hip to the tip—with a line for all the chicks; he'd love to see the Elder once; a real weird deal, this was; he'd talk to Tommy about it. Finally he strolled out the front door of the apartment and down into the hot street again. Maybe if he went back down on 43rd, he'd run into Mary again.

When he reached 43rd and Calumet, Mary was nowhere to be seen. He stood in the doorway of a sweltering fish shack and listened to the juke box pouring out the blues—"Just a dre-e-e-e-am ah had on mah mind! . . . ." Finally he went in and sat at the counter and bought a grape pop. Maybe Mary was up on King Drive with her handbills by now, he thought, swigging the pop; or else she'd gone on home—to get out of those steamy robes; and take a bath; she'd probably had enough of Jesus and Elder Griffin for one day—in all that heat; she was just climbing in the tub now, maybe—buck naked. He wondered if she knew the Red Lion—when she had been sinning, that is; all the mainliners at one time or another knew the

Lion; couldn't she get mad easy!—flipped her lid on the street
there when Jug got after her . . . and made her backslide;
Aunt Bertha always said there was nothing in the world worse
than a backslider—because they never had any religion in
the first place; but she didn't know Mary; that was okay too;
she'd hate Mary; Aunt Bertha was always talking about how
she didn't want anything to do with any "low-down people"—
whiskey-heads, and bad women, and all that; and hop-heads!
Lord!—she'd skin him alive if she knew about him and Tommy
and all the fixes they'd had together; maybe he ought to put
Tommy down—and kick the habit; he could kick it if he
wanted to; maybe Tommy couldn't though, no matter what he
said; Mary hadn't. He sat at the counter with the sweating
bottle of pop in his hand, wishing he knew Mary better, wishing he knew where to find her; she probably wouldn't have
any time for somebody sixteen years old, though. But before
very long he finished the pop, got up, and sauntered out of the
fish shack into the street again.

It was quarter to five when he stood in the vestibule of a
run-down apartment building on 48th Street bending forward
to scan the stacks of penciled names over the mail boxes. He
had just come from the Temple, a large bare room with a few
folding chairs over a pool hall, where a woman, also in white
robes, had given him Mary's ("Sister Mary Bivens's") address. Looking now at the names over one of the mail boxes,
he saw that Mary lived, apparently with many relatives, on the
third floor. There was no doorbell to ring, so he went up. When
he reached the third floor, right side, he knocked. Inside he
could hear noisy children. Soon the door was opened by a little
black girl, with a tooth out in front. She appraised him.
"Miss Mary home?" he asked. He was shy.
The child viewed him with misgiving, and called back into

the apartment. "Mama! A man wants to see Aunt Mary!" Now three more children came galloping to the door.

Finally a woman wearing worn-out bedroom slippers appeared. She was sweating. "My sister's 'sleep," she said. "Whatayou want?"

"Oh, I just wanted to see her." Jerome was offhand. "I was talkin' with her today—down on 43rd Street—and just thought I'd drop by. I can see her some other time."

"Are you from Elder Griffin's?" Her curtness softened some.

"I just came over from the Temple—yes'm." Jerome was quick.

"Are you one of Mary's converts?"

". . . Yes'm . . . ."

The woman studied him. ". . . Okay," she finally said, "come on in. I'll see if she'll come out." She stepped aside to let him in. "She's awful tired," she said, shuffling from the room.

Jerome stood in the middle of the bare floor. The children had lost interest in him now and were romping again. A pair of large oval portraits under glass hung on the wall over the sofa. They were apparently of grandparents, and were enlarged and touched-up in a blurry pastel-tint; the old man had a grey kinky beard, and wore a shirt fastened at the neck with a brass collar button but no collar or tie; the woman looked like a New Orleans creole, with her hair severely parted in the middle and her dress padded and built-up at the shoulders. But nothing in the room reminded him of Mary. Wouldn't she be surprised to see *him!*—she'd remember him all right. But she might be mad at him for seeing her disgraced right there on the street in front of him.

Mary's sister came back in the room. "Come on—in here," she summoned. He followed her into Mary's humid bedroom. Mary sat barefooted on the side of the bed in a dressing gown. She did look tired. On a chair in front of her was a tiny, whirring electric fan. As they entered, she quickly pulled the sheet around her and let it drape down to hide her feet. She still wore the rhinestone rings on her fingers.

"Well . . . ." She gave him a weary smile.

"Hello, Miss Mary." His voice was weak and bashful.

"Uh-huh, I knew it." She spoke with conviction. "You been thinking about what I told you—I can see it. You been talkin' to Jesus, like I told you." She smiled. "Ain't that right?"

"Yes'm." Jerome grinned and looked at the floor.

"Let me talk to him, Dillie." She was abrupt with her sister who stood in the doorway. Dillie left the room with a long face.

"What's your name, son?" Mary said.

"Jerome."

"Jerome what?"

"Jerome Williams."

"Uh-huh, and why'd you come here, Jerome?"

He hesitated—stumped. Then he thought of the leaflet. He fumbled in his shirt pocket, pulled it out, and stood holding it, saying nothing.

"My sister said you just come over from the Temple," Mary said. Then she saw the leaflet—"What's that you got there?"

"It's what you was passing out today," Jerome said.

"Well, bless your heart! Ain't that nice. Do you understand what Elder Griffin was gettin' at?" She pulled up the bed sheet to swing her legs around onto the bed, as Jerome coolly glimpsed her bare knees before she could cover them. His quiet breath came faster. "That's why you came," she said, "you don't understand it all, do you?" She pointed at the leaflet in his hand. "Sit down there," she nodded toward a straight-back chair at the side of the dresser.

Reluctantly he backed away from the bed and sat down. The window was up and the sharp cries of playing children reached up from the sidewalks below.

"Jerome . . . y'know what?"

"No'm."

"I want you to go out tomorrow—with me—and pass out literature."

He looked at her. ". . . okay," he finally said.

"You been getting the message all right . . . or you wouldn't be here. I told you—Jesus never fails."

Jerome shifted his feet.

"Now, what is there about it you don't seem to understand?" Unconsciously she wiggled her toes under the peak of the sheet.

He was too distracted to answer.

"Here, gim'me that," she said, and stretched from the bed toward him, took the leaflet, and then lay back again. She began to read: "What does it mean to be a sinner, condemned to die? It means separation from God, the Father, for all eternity." She stopped and looked at him. "Jerome, that's terrible . . . but it's true. D'you see the Elder's message there?"

Jerome hesitated. "I think so."

She took another passage. "The Word of God tells us that because we are sinners we are condemned to die. For the wages of sin is death. Romans 6:23. Sin bringeth forth death. James 1:15." She raised herself up now and stared out the window into space. ". . . Ah, we all understand *that*," she mused aloud.

Her dressing gown had fallen away from one shoulder, revealing an untidy brassiere strap. He sensed she hadn't bathed yet. But her face looked clean, and free of make-up. He recognized the break in the line of one eyebrow as scar tissue, put there by men's fists. She held the leaflet in her lap, still gazing off in space. Suddenly he noticed that the left sleeve of her dressing gown had worked up, exposing her forearm, and again he saw the needle scars.

She quickly caught him staring. "What's th' matter with you, Jerome? What you looking at?"

His eyes swept up to her face.

"You were lookin' at my *arms!*" she suddenly cried, thrusting both arms out straight. The dark purple dots glared. Jerome, flustered, shook his head no. "Yes, you were too!" Her eyes blazed. "Is that what you come here for?—outa curiosity—to make fun of me?" She hurled back the bed sheet and sprang out of bed, the dressing gown parting and showing her thighs.

"Aw, no, Miss Mary!" He cringed in his chair as she stood over him. "I didn't come here for that, Miss Mary!"

"You damned little liar, you!" She began shaking him. "An' coming in her with my literature stuck in your pocket! Now, what'd you come here for? *Tell* me!" She gave him a savage shaking.

Jerome trying to fend off her hands could smell the sweaty perfume on her body and underwear. "I come here to see *you,* Miss Mary."

She stepped back from him. "Don't lie to me, boy! Don't you lie, now!—Did Jug Smith tell you t'come here!—to pester me some more, to make it harder for me?—because I won't have nothing to do with dogs like him no more! *Did he?*"

"No'm! I *told* you!" Jerome pleaded.

She seemed not to hear him. "Nobody don't know, or care, about what I'm goin' through! Nobody!"

"You're wrong about me, Miss Mary."

"No, I ain't, either!" She stood over him again and glared.

Then slowly he began unbuttoning the left sleeve of his shirt. He turned the inside of his arm up and pushed the sleeve above the elbow. There sat a welter of purple-dotted needle scars.

". . . Oh!" Mary gasped, and turned her back. She would not look at him and sank on the bed. "You poor boy, you!

You poor boy!" Soon she was crying.

Jerome sat and watched her.

"I'm so sorry!" she moaned, crying in the bed sheet she held to her eyes. "I'm *so* sorry!"

Jerome was confident now. Tommy should see him, he thought. He got up boldly and went to the bed and sat down beside her. The shouts of the children in the street below overcame the faint whirr of the little electric fan, as it fluttered the bed sheet against her leg. He put his arm around her waist. "I didn't mean to make you cry, Miss Mary."

"You came here for help," she looked at him through tear-wet lashes, "and I acted awful . . . cussed you out . . . . Oh, forgive me, baby—you're only a baby."

He held her tighter now. Soon he pressed his lips hard against the side of her face. They sat silently. She seemed to relax.

She looked at him again. ". . . You're only a baby," she repeated, softly like a mother, and stroked his forehead, and then his flat nose, with her sensitive fingers. He could smell the musky-sweetish perfume and was racked with impatience. Suddenly he seized her and, moaning softly, crushed her mouth open with his lips.

Then she viewed him sadly. ". . . And you've started your bad ways so young," she said. "You shouldn't be like me— weak. I'm weak—*so* weak."

He felt the tornado inside him. But he kept his arm around her waist and waited.

Finally she gazed in his vacant face. "Go close the door, Jerome," she said, ". . . and throw the lock."

He sprang at the door, eased it shut, and threw the lock. Hanging on the nail was her long white robe.

Black for Dinner

It was ten o'clock on Wednesday morning, and Anita sat alone at the table in her polished copper kitchen, sipping coffee. She was a pert little brown-skinned woman, short and very plump, almost dumpy, and wore sparkling rimless glasses. All her life she had been a vacillator. Despite almost thirty years as a well-off housewife, she abhorred making decisions and was never quite sure of them when made, but would stew and fret and finally end up asking her husband, Dave, what she should do. But Dave Hill, a wise, tolerant man, never seemed to mind.

For instance, two days hence—on Friday—she was to have in ten people for sit-down dinner; and the responsibilities involved were looming larger by the hour. She had invited Kate Horton, the undoubted social queen of the posh Hyde Park-Kenwood black community; and was then surprised, a little awed even, when Kate accepted. It meant effort, she now realized; for everything had to be just so; and Alice Smiley, another guest, and Kate's close friend, was just as fastidious as Kate. Neither had been to Anita's in over two years—not since the downstairs of her big house had been re-done, complete with sumptuous draperies and a new sofa. So she knew

everything—furnishings, food, wines—would undergo, albeit
with gracious smiles, a searching examination. Yet she felt
inert, immobile—unable to plan beyond the menu. Bemused,
she lit a cigarette, and stared off into space.

The rib roast had been ordered—there would be Yorkshire
pudding to go with it, and Burgundy. And Mrs. Adams had
been engaged to do everything—this was no job for Thelma,
the regular cook. Thelma could help with the serving. Also,
the linen, china and silver must be put out and made ready—
tomorrow would be time enough for polishing the silver. She
knew she didn't have the silver Kate Horton had, but what
she did have was just as fine—twelve place settings: the knife,
fork, spoon, salad fork, dessert spoon, and butter spreader.
Kate of course had everything—plain and pierced serving
spoons, gravy ladles, jelly servers, lemon forks, nut spoons,
olive forks, cheese knives, cake servers, relish spoons, and varied other silver instruments Anita could not presently call to
mind. And she remembered Kate's china was just as elaborate.

She wished *so* Dave were there. She needed him to lean
against, to consult. He had been in New York on business now
for two days, and would return that afternoon. But really he
couldn't help her, she knew. Planning dinners and such were
the remotest things from his world. His life was real estate.
But she could at least think out loud to him if he were there—
he always listened. She sat for awhile, then absently mashed
out her cigarette, and went up the hall toward the living room.

She was proudest of the front part of her house—especially
since the refurbishing. The parlor was large, with great ex-
panses of red oriental rugs stretching back under dark, bur-
nished furniture. A Chinese cabinet, pale blue, and beautifully
filigreed, stood near the front of the hallway and contained
displays of her mother's Meissen figures—red-coated porce-
lain soldiers, brown and green shepherds, curtsying ladies of
the court, and a flesh-pink, indolent Cupid. On the one un-

broken wall of the parlor hung two large oils—a peasant girl, and an Italian landscape—and rouge damask draperies swept back from the windows.

She touched a finger down on an end table for dust, but knew Thelma dusted every day; then she bent over to knead the down-filled cushions on the new sofa, and puttered briefly with the draperies. But what she longed to do was go upstairs, and take out her new dress again—her new black silk dress. Once already that morning she had taken it from her bedroom closet to inspect it with a mute delight. The very day Kate Horton and Alice Smiley said they could come, she had gone out to Saks and bought it; and it was the only dress she could ever remember liking from the very first moment the saleslady brought it out, her own plumpness notwithstanding—lately she preferred darker colors that played down her pudgy shape. She felt the dress did this, and was chic and elegant besides—*decolletage*, with a softly-full skirt, cut on a bias. Kate and Alice would approve, she was certain, for they—and the others too, for that matter—recognized fine clothes at a glance. Dave didn't know about the dress as yet, she reflected; it was delivered only yesterday; and it *was* expensive. He would only shrug, though, and smile.

She also remembered now she must have him check his liquor supply. She had already ordered the Burgundy, and a case of very good champagne—she had felt she needed his special permission for the champagne; but you could not serve *these* people a shoddy champagne. As he left for New York, Dave had smiled and agreed—he could be so casual when he was amused at her. He seemed tired these days, though; yet he never complained. Ah, and he must be warned against making any unfunny cracks about Alice's French poodles, for instance—or about Doug Horton's big boat. Anita smiled; and then started up the carpeted stairs—to see her dress again.

That afternoon, about four o'clock, Dave came home, letting himself in at the front door. For a man in his mid-fifties, he looked youngish; brown, thick-set, of medium height, he wore a neat gabardine topcoat over his grey suit. But merely carrying his luggage in from the taxi seemed to have exhausted him, for he was breathing hard.

Thelma, the husky young cook, smiled as she hurried up the hall to greet him. "Hi, Mister Dave!"

"Hi, child." He looked around wearily. "Where's everybody?"

"Mrs. Hill's upstairs. Here, let me have your bag. You look beat." Thelma took the bag and started up the stairs, as Dave removed his topcoat and hat and hung them in the stairs closet. Soon he too started upstairs.

When he turned at the landing and looked up, Anita was standing at the top with a big smile for him. "Hi, honey!" she said.

"Hi, Peachie."

"How *was* little old New York?—And the flight?"

"Okay." He kissed her. "The flight was a little bumpy, in spots—coming back."

"Oh, I'd have been scared to death!"

He was impassive as they entered her bedroom.

"What've you been doing with yourself?" He held his smile on her.

"Now, what do you think!" she laughed.

"How *is* the party shaping up?"

She turned to sit down again at her dressing table. ". . . Okay—I guess." She was tentative. Then, as he stood behind her, she watched him in the mirror. "You're tired," she said.

"Oh, traveling always tires you out some." He walked across the hall to his own room now, and began opening his luggage. Soon he returned and handed her a small wrapped gift; and then went back to his room.

"Oh, my! Thank you! Say, this isn't a peace offering, is it?" she laughed to him across the hall. "Have you been a good boy?" She stretched over for the big pair of scissors on her writing desk, cut the thin gold twine from the package, and took out a small strand of cultured pearls. "Oh, pearls!" she cried.

"Cultured pearls," he said.

"Oh, they're lovely just the same! Lovely!" She held the necklace to her throat before the mirror. "I can wear these with my new black dress!"

Across the hall he was silent.

Thelma appeared at his bedroom door now, with two bourbons and water on a silver tray. "My friend," Dave smiled to her, "you've been reading my mind, you have. If you'll just tote that across the hall there, I'll be right with you."

When he returned to Anita, he was glum, preoccupied. He lifted his drink off the tray and sank into her big chair. "Why don't you wear a gay dress?" he said, ". . . green, or white, or something—red, even. We'll have the champagne—and shoot 'em up a little." He grinned at her. "You've got the champagne crowd coming, haven't you?"

"Oh, now, honey!—I've got a *new* dress. It's quiet—real elegant. I couldn't promise how I'd look in some loud color, with *my* derriere."

"Your what?"

Anita laughed and adjusted her sparkling glasses. "Oh, forget it, please—we'll talk about it." They were silent, as she grew pensive—then irritable. "You promised we were going down to the Virgin Islands after Christmas," she said. "But you haven't mentioned it lately at all. Why? You need a vacation—I know that. I'm going to take the bull by the horns, Mister, and make the arrangements myself."

He inspected his drink and said nothing. "Aw, hell, Peachie," he finally said, "let's talk about that later, too.

You'd better be thinking now about feeding all those swells you've got coming in here." He grinned at her again as he stood up to leave the room, holding his drink high as if to give a toast. "Whatta you say, kiddo?—let's shoot 'em up Friday night. And wear something *gay*, will you?"

Friday evening arrived cold and rainy in early darkness. From outer Lake Michigan a wet November wind drove the slanting rain inland, dousing streets, parked cars, and the huge, swirling trees around Anita's big house, which from basement to attic was a schooner of blazing lights wallowing in the gale; and, inside, a wild fire leapt up the blackened cave of the fireplace, casting great, weird, frolicking shadows up against the paintings on the far wall.

Mrs. Adams, the cateress, and her staff had arrived and were in full charge. There were two white-coated bar boys— one to mix, and one to serve; a sensual-looking brown-skinned waitress, whom Thelma would assist; and Mrs. Adams, her- self—fat, but very efficient. Mrs. Adams at the moment was in the kitchen collecting the oven drippings from the standing rib roast for making the Yorkshire pudding. She checked the clock; it was only six, and things were well along already. The guests weren't due until seven—which, Mrs. Adams knew, meant seven-thirty—so she hummed while she worked.

Dave had left his office at three o'clock and come home early to take a rest before evening. He fixed a drink and took it with him upstairs to his bedroom. He was somehow eager, keyed up, over the dinner. It was Anita's party, and he was doting, proud—the best people were coming. It was a good chore for her; might do something for her anemic self-confi- dence. He sat down, loosened his tie, and sipped his drink. He was convinced it was the *people* that made a party. You could have the finest house, foods, wines and all that, and then waste them on a bunch of boors—like casting pearls. But it wasn't that way tonight.

He undressed, put on a robe, and lay across the bed for awhile. Later he took a slow tub bath, and rubbed himself vigorously. He stepped on the bathroom scales—175; weight about okay; down to where Cartwright said it had *better* be. Cartwright loved to warn you; he was an indelicate bastard for a heart man—most doctors were not. A man ought to be left alone to take what's coming to him in his own way, if he's got to take it. Cartwright had deprived him of cigarettes, and to what purpose? But so far, Anita had been kept in the dark about the whole matter—that was the important thing. He gave himself a lazy, methodical shave, and by six-thirty he was all dressed—in a trim grey suit and striped maroon tie; and then went downstairs to watch the preparations.

Upstairs, Anita's bedroom door was closed. She had wanted a nap, but her excitement was like caffeine. Bathed and warm, in mules and a silk robe, she lolled on her chaise longue, listening to the cold rain outside pelt the window panes. It seemed to her she had supervised a thousand details, and still she combed her brain for some disastrous oversight. And the dress. It had trapped her thoughts for two whole days now, holding her in a tumult of indecision; and Dave could not help in this. In fact, he had caused it all. She felt wronged—the dress was brand new, and she liked it *so;* had wanted to look her tasteful best, to wear something simple, expensive, secure. Red!— He was out of his mind. Nothing could be so frustrating as a man who didn't understand that what a woman wore sometimes depended on how she felt. But he had asked specially, which was unusual for him. Telling her what to wear!—he'd never done it before. It was sweet of him though, maybe; you never really knew, he was such a riddle sometimes. Yet so gentle always—a strange, tender man. The whole twenty-nine years of their marriage had been like this—wonderful years. She had just trusted him, and things always came out okay.

It was the same way before they were married—when they were college students at Howard, in Washington. He was poor and required two jobs on the side; but his grades were always good, far better than hers, despite all the free time she had to study—her father, a Richmond physician, underwrote her education completely. She knew she had not been a good student; hadn't been able to study, couldn't concentrate, and would sit for hours gazing out the University library window daydreaming. Sometimes Dave would help her with her math, but on examinations she felt abandoned. And when he graduated a year and a half ahead of her, she despaired of ever finishing—and could only pray that he would ask her to marry him. That was all she wanted from life—she shut out thought of her future without it. Married to him, she would be rid of all her plaguing anxieties. Wherever they lived, whatever their life, richer or poorer, she would be set—always.

Her father too had liked Dave, from the beginning—but was often obliged to reassure her mother. "The boy is solid," he would say, "Solid." Anita knew how right he was, and still held the tenderest memories of him for helping her land Dave. Above everything her father ever did for her, this was the greatest by far; and when she finally graduated and married, he often visited them in Chicago. To her extravagant delight the two men became cronies. By then, Dave, already with a job in a Southside real estate firm, was scheming to save the money to establish his own business. It was some eight years later, when his business was finally going well, that she had been able to make a thirty thousand dollar contribution to it—at her father's death—and thus satisfy a burning urge to do something really outstanding for their marriage. For this urge had become acute the year before that, when their one child, Timmie, four years old, had died of polio, plunging young

Dave into months of a desperate, silent grief that wrenched her heart.

But soon after, things began going better for them—and Dave made money. They traveled now, and some of her finest memories were linked to trips to California, Canada, the Caribbean, and once to South America. This was before they went to Europe, where now they had been three times. Dave loved Italy; and adored Florence—which they had just revisited the past spring. She had never known his moods so bright, his talk so free, as when they tramped the streets of Florence, or he badgered her about her walking shoes, and claimed her feet were flat. He loved to stand in the cloister of *Santa Croce*—of the year 1294 A.D.—and merely touch the crumbling bricks and mortar with his finger tips. And sometimes, with a drink in their hotel room before dinner, he would grow expansive, philosophical, a little wistful; she especially remembered one early evening, after their return from a trek up to the heights of the little church of *San Miniato*.

"The finest view of Florence is from *San Miniato*," he said, sprawled in a big chair in his robe. "You get the oddest feeling up there—looking down across the river onto the cathedral, and that big old dome of Brunelleschi's, and the bell tower. It's a tremendous sight. These church builders were artists—and were probably self-important as hell; they knew when they were putting up these stone piles their names would live for centuries. I guess everybody wishes for something like that, in one way or another—to be remembered; but only a few make it. Most of us are so damned mediocre and insignificant we're forgotten as soon as we're gone." He reflected— ". . . Maybe it's not the going so much, as the forgetting."

Anita recalled how she felt, listening to him; it was a feeling of awe, of gratitude to be married to him. That's what she loved so about their trips—he talked more; and although sometimes pensive, he seemed freer. She felt it was the change

of scene, of routine, and dreamed now only of their next trip—
to the Virgin Islands.

Ah, but the dress again—what of the dress? She lay on the
chaise longue as her mind probed and strained and her eyes
roved the ceiling. Maybe he'd understand—if she took the
time to explain. A "dressy" dress just wouldn't do; besides,
she'd bought the dress especially for tonight. Perhaps he didn't
really care that much—for months he'd heard her mourn her
figure. Yet he knew this when he asked her to wear something
"gay"—and still had asked her. She began to weaken now,
feeling she should do his bidding, with no questions—he
asked so few things of her. Then she thought of Kate and Alice;
she wanted *so* to show them she too knew the meaning of good
taste. Did it really mean so much to him—*that* much? . . .
She could ask him. Yet if she asked him, and he persisted,
she couldn't refuse. But if she took a chance and didn't ask
him, she might be surprised to find he'd forgotten all about
it. She sat up and stared at the wall awhile. Finally she got
up, went to the closet, and resolutely took out the black dress.

At seven o'clock sharp the household was ready. The bar
boys idled in the pantry, with their highball and cocktail
glasses in neat rows and the liquor bottles capped with shining
little spouts—as Thelma and the hippy waitress, both in white
uniforms, broke the pantry tedium with their hushed, eye-
flashing frivolity. Up front, the blaze in the fireplace spread
a roseate warmth over the whole parlor and dining area ad-
joining, and the paintings on the wall, the gilt mirrors brack-
eting the fireplace, the furniture, the rich draperies and oriental
rugs, all fused to create the gracious, elegant atmosphere of
the house.

Anita was still upstairs. But Dave was in the kitchen now,
in folksy talk with Mrs. Adams. He opened the refrigerator,
pulled out a horizontal bottle of champagne, and patiently

worked the cork out under a covering napkin; then poured them both chilled sparkling glassfuls before, laughing and touching glasses, they drank to the evening's success. Then he paused in thought, and said his wife was probably tired and might like a glass. "Of course," Mrs. Adams said, and went into the pantry for another champagne glass.

When she returned, he was sitting at the kitchen table, limp and perspiring, an ashy-brown color in his face.

"What's the matter, Mr. Hill!"

". . . I guess I had a little sinking spell," he said, with heavy breathing.

"What do you think's the matter?" She stood over him.

"I'll be okay in a minute." He looked shaken. "You needn't say anything to my wife—it's nothing. I'll just sit here for a little bit and—." He stared at the door. There stood smiling Anita—wearing her pearls, and her chic black dress.

She saw the champagne. "Oh! You two have jumped the gun!" she laughed.

He only stared at her.

"We sure have!" nervously laughed Mrs. Adams.

Then Anita looked at Dave—and she knew she had guessed wrong. He had not forgotten. Her briefly buoyant spirits sank. But why his shocked expression? She felt it was all her fault. A rising frustration, and anger at herself, welled up inside her. Yet *he* was acting stubborn too, and a little unfair, she thought—about a dress. Still, she experienced a wretched contrition, and longed to run upstairs and change. But it was too late now; there was not time. A dull, preoccupying anguish settled on her for the evening.

Thelma entered the kitchen now, carrying a tray of glasses.

"Thelma, honey," Anita sighed, "when the guests arrive, will you answer the door, and handle the wraps?"

"Sure," Thelma smiled.

Dave sat at the table stony and detached. Soon he got up and went upstairs.

It was twenty-five minutes after seven when the door chimes at last sounded. Thelma jumped. Then recovering, she smoothed her uniform and hurried into the foyer to the front door—followed by Anita. The door opened on Hortense and "Sully" Weaver, smiling and stamping their wet shoes on the mat outside. Hortense, a highly-styled, light brown-skinned woman, stepped in and grasped both of Anita's hands in her own. "Anita, hon!" she purred. "How *are* you, darling?" Sully, dark-brown with gleaming white teeth, a probate lawyer, entered and bent forward chivalrously to kiss Anita on the cheek. "Hi, sugar!" he said. Dave appeared in the foyer now, his face drawn but smiling, and joined in the welcome. After Thelma took the wraps, the guests were ushered into the parlor.

"Oh, the fire, Sully!" Hortense cried, approaching the fireplace and rubbing her hands together. "It's wonderful!—and on a night like this!" They all sat down, and a bar boy entered with a tray of canapes and, as he passed them around, took orders for drinks.

Anita cut in. "Maybe Mrs. Weaver would like champagne," she said to the boy.

"Oh, I would!" cried Hortense. "May I?"

Sully had the same. "You can't go wrong with that," he laughed, "—until the next morning, that is."

"Make it three," Dave laughed to the bar boy.

As the boy left, the chimes sounded again. Anita stood up before she thought; but then gave Thelma time to reach the door, before following. It was Vashti and Walter Cooper. Vashti was a Wellesley graduate and a very proper person. Tall and olive-skinned, she resembled an East Indian—she had in fact traveled widely in the Orient. "Oh, Anita, how well you look," she said, smiling as she entered. Walter, a savings-and-loan association president, was shorter than his wife, and stood back smiling whimsically through black horn-rimmed glasses. "Nice weather," he laughed to Dave at the first pause in the women's talk,"—*lovely* weather." After their wraps were handed over to Thelma, the new guests were escorted into the parlor with the others, where eager friendly greetings went all around. Vashti sat with Hortense on the French love seat and agreed to champagne, but Walter said if they didn't mind he'd stick to Scotch. Hortense immediately remarked about the silver Chinese bracelet Vashti wore, launching Vashti on a rather tedious, but charming, explanation of the dragon figures the silversmith had so intricately worked. The three husbands huddled with drinks in hand, as Dave, in a feat of geniality, appeared to feel well again.

The young Bishops—Kitty and Roger—were the next to arrive. They came in laughing hilariously about what they referred to as the new escalation clause in their baby sitter's contract. Roger was an English instructor at the University of Chicago, and Kitty, of an excellent Atlanta family, had studied at the Sorbonne. They had three fine children and not the means to entertain on any elaborate scale, but nonetheless moved easily among the Southside's most cultivated people. Kitty was brown and beautiful, a girl with laughing eyes, who, despite her children, had retained her lithe, angular figure. She enjoyed the innocent conversation and flattery of older men—and all wives watched her. Roger, tall and athletic-looking, looked more like a basketball coach than a university instructor—his field was modern literature, and his avocation chess. The pair sparked any party they attended and, notwithstanding Kitty's dangerous beauty, they were on the favored list of every hostess.

Ten minutes later, over the mild noise of talk, the door chimes sounded again. Anita, though seized with jitters, did not move this time, and arose only when she saw Thelma enter the foyer. The remainder of the guests had arrived—the Hortons and the Smileys had come together. Kate and Alice swept in—both were bare-headed and swaddled in mink—followed by burly Douglas Horton and "Fritz" Smiley. Dave, too, was at the door now.

"Oh, Anita," Kate said, "how splendid to see you." She embraced Anita and then held her off at arms' length to look at her. "How are you?"

"Oh, I'm fine, Kate!—just fine!" Anita cried happily.

Then Alice Smiley, whom Anita thought looked thinner than ever, embraced her. "How are you, sweetie?" she said.

"Wonderful, Alice! We're *so* glad you could come!"

As he got out of his overcoat, Doug Horton seemed slightly drunk. He was a light tawny brown; square, beefy, and greying at the temples; and when he smiled exhibited large prominent teeth. He came from one of the most distinguished black families in the country, had inherited wealth, and made money in his own right, as a community banker and publisher. But now at fifty-five, he spent more time in travel, and in sumptuous living, than at work. He was known to like women, and whenever he put his cunning eyes on Kitty Bishop, an animal turbulence was triggered inside him that persisted for days. He smelled of liquor now as he smiled and quickly shook Dave's hand. Then he made a stiff, smiling bow to Anita, and passed on into the parlor.

Fritz Smiley was a surgeon—and contributed to the medical journals. Like his wife, Alice, he was very light-skinned and thin, almost cadaverous; and though he gave Alice all the money she wanted, he was cold and steel-nerved, rarely showing her affection. But he was cordial to Dave now, as they shook hands.

"How're things?" He studied Dave with a friendly, guarded look.

"Okay," Dave said, "and you?—how do you keep your weight like that?"

"I don't get time to eat," Fritz twinkled. They moved into the parlor.

After Thelma walked away with her arms piled high with wraps, Kate, Alice, and Anita stood talking briefly in the foyer. "Your house is so attractive," Alice, looking about her, said to Anita. "Your draperies are beautiful."

Kate stood preoccupied and, glancing toward the parlor, seemed intent on keeping an eye on her husband. She was totally patrician—a beautifully-proportioned woman of fifty, with erect carriage and soft brown skin; although recently, delicate crow's-feet had appeared at the corners of her eyes. Her features were chiseled and severe, almost satanic—relieved only by a pleasant mouth, and eyes that could dance when amused. She was born and grew up in Chicago, was a graduate of the University of Chicago, and spoke careful, immaculate English. An enthusiast of the serious theatre, she occasionally gave play-reading parties that were brilliant and sought-after. With wealth, culture, and a fading beauty, she was the community's supreme hostess and social figure.

Anita soon noticed Kate's absorption, and deftly guided them toward the parlor. Kate looked at her now. "I like your dress, Anita," she smiled.

"Oh, thank you!" At last Anita felt the elation of reward.

The company was at last complete—as the bar boys, in their white jackets, scurried back and forth with drinks. Doug Horton, seated alone, brusquely declined champagne, requesting a dry, "very dry," martini. He then scrutinized a plate of canapes on the coffee table and, after serious study, selected a caviar. He put the morsel to his mouth, skinned off the paste with his top teeth, and dropped the denuded bit of toast in an ash tray. When the martini came, he speared out the anchovy olive and chewed it reflectively; then, lifting the small crystal beaker, coolly drained it off and set it on the coffee table. He looked across the room now at young Kitty Bishop—she was talking rapidly to Dave and to Hortense Weaver—and sighed.

Kitty was telling about her children. ". . . and Gregory caught the poor little kid!—I say 'little', but he was as big as Gregory—and at that point *I* stepped in." Hortense threw her head back and laughed. Dave, now sitting with them, smiled and listened. He thought Kitty more beautiful than he had ever seen her. And the way she talked with her hands!—so self-assured and high-spirited. He felt he'd missed out on women—that is, really alluring women. His nose had been to the grindstone—all the way. He'd played it safe, with Anita. No complications. It was a bit late now, wasn't it, to be over-whelmed, a little sad even, about a beautiful, vibrant girl? She was actually the age to be his daughter. He gave himself a wry smile—yes, a trifle late, old man; but Roger Bishop was plain lucky.

Across the room, Anita took her first glass of champagne from the moving tray. She looked at Dave repeatedly, glad to see his mood improved—even if he persisted in ignoring her. Finally she went over and sat down beside lone Doug Horton.

"I know you hated to put your boat up for the winter," she said brightly.

". . . Oh, sort of,"—Doug was friendly enough—"but the crew got bored, along there toward the last. So it was just as well."

"Oh, Doug, you don't have a drink!" Anita said.

He grinned. "I just finished that martini there." He pointed his big manicured hand at the empty glass.

"Well, you must have another." She looked around for the bar boy.

Doug chuckled. "Katie's watching," he said. "She claims too many drinks before dinner deaden the taste buds."

Anita's laugh was high and forced. Her gloom had not

lifted. She was watching Dave—to catch his eye and smile. But he would not look at her. Soon she was miserable. She couldn't understand him! How silly he could be—and about a dress! 'Silly' wasn't the word for it—it was cruel. He had talked to everyone but her. Her hurt and anger mounted— only to be dissolved in moments by her love.

At eight-thirty Thelma entered and whispered to Anita—it was time to move the guests into the dining room. Anita stood up now, smiling, and announced dinner.

The large dining area, adjacent, featured a glittering crystal chandelier suspended directly over the center of the table. A long mahogany sideboard, highly polished and topped with pink marble, extended along one wall, and the window wall next to it was hung with heavy silk draperies of Prussian blue. Hidden wall speakers leading from Dave's stereo equipment in the rear poured soft tunes from the Broadway musicals into the room. And the entire staff, including Mrs. Adams, had stationed themselves to greet the guests—now led in by Anita, who pointed out the various place cards for seating. Dave sat at the head of the table, with Kate Horton at his right, while Anita, down at the other end, had Doug Horton on her right. Doug had entered the dining room carrying his fourth empty martini glass, and passed it curtly to a bar boy before pulling out Kitty Bishop's chair, next to his. He seated her with a Mephistophelian dead pan, but Kitty seemed very pleased.

As all were seated they found their curry consomme and hot crackers before them. Dave, presiding, though often smiling, seemed tense and formal. He had drunk champagne freely, but it had done him little good. Kate, at his right elbow, pretending exhilaration, hid her pique at Kitty Bishop's placement and bent toward Dave to praise the soup. Then smiling mischievously, she turned to Roger Bishop, on her right, to tell him she knew a twelve-year-old boy at Parkway settlement house (Kate was active in many charities) who, she suspected, could give him a very interesting session at the chessboard. Roger, sipping his soup, laughed and said he didn't doubt it for a second, as chess was largely, as most things in life, a matter of endowment. Alice Smiley, at Dave's left, laughed, and admonished Roger for conceding so readily.

Down at the other end of the long table Anita strove for brilliance, gaiety. With Doug Horton on her right and Fritz Smiley, who used his wit as he used his scalpel, on her left, she felt the need for alertness. But she soon recognized Doug's attention was for Kitty.

"Was this seating by lottery?" Doug, grinning, leaned to young Kitty to ask "—or by design? I never won *any*thing by chance."

"The hostess decides on seating," Kitty laughed, "—as if you didn't know!"

"Well then, Anita's a friend of *mine*," he whispered—as Kate's quick eye came down the table.

Anita had turned to Fritz Smiley to enquire about the Virgin Islands, and said she knew he and Alice had been there twice—or was it three times? Fritz said it was twice, and that he liked it very much, but was afraid Alice hadn't particularly, as he had spent a lot of time on the golf course. "Oh, you men!" cried Anita. "But Dave and I are going—right after the Holidays."

"Is that right?" Fritz said, and then sipped his soup in silence. She'd go only if she was damned lucky, he thought—if what Cartwright had told him at the hospital was correct: that a man with Dave's clogged aorta was a walking miracle. And Cartwright was a hell of a cardiologist. Almost any day or night now, he had said—touch and go. Anita wouldn't exactly have to worry about her next meal, though, Fritz thought— Dave was in good shape, that way.

Hortense Weaver had had her share of champagne and was

now in shrill voice as she talked across the table at Vashti
Cooper, who never drank much and was amused at Hortense.
Vashti leaned against Sully, Hortense's husband, at her left,
and whispered something about Hortense's eyes. Sully laughed
and assured her *he* could drive home. Hortense heard and was
petulant. "Yes, for once!" she cried, "—just once! D'you think
you can, Sully dear—just this once?"

Now came the main course: roast beef, with individual
Yorkshire puddings, French string beans, acorn squash, and
endive salad. The Burgundy was poured into glinting crystal
goblets.

Doug Horton, to his surprise, was enjoying himself more
than anyone. He fingered his second goblet of Burgundy and
turned from Kitty long enough to smile at Anita. "Anita, my
dear," he said dreamily, "you've really slain the fatted calf
tonight. The beef—it's superb, superb. *Every*thing's superb."
Then he turned again to Kitty, who was laughing at him.

Anita was happy momentarily. But then a shadow would
cross her heart. She could not understand her feeling, and
was too busy to wonder at it, to probe it. She only knew it
was there. Then impulsively, with a wistful smile, she stared
straight down the table at Dave. But if he saw her he gave
no sign.

The hubbub of talk and laughter had increased. Once even
Dave had let out a sort of whoop, at one of Roger Bishop's
clever remarks. At the other end of the table Fritz Smiley sat
and watched his friend, Doug, across from him. How in crea-
tion, he wondered, could he swill all that alcohol? those lethal
martinis—and the food! Fritz gazed now at Kitty. She *was*
beautiful—no doubt about it; very. But old Doug would never
get her—she was too slick . . . much too slick for *Doug*.
She was something special. He suspected *her* case required
cold calculation—not liquor. Briefly Fritz imagined himself
her vanquisher and experienced a vague egoistic gusto.

The main course required more than an hour. Finally the table was cleared for dessert: pears, with Bel Paese cheese, coffee, and yellow chartreuse.

Dave had begun to look tired. He smiled mechanically as he spooned his desert. Engaging Kate Horton and Alice Smiley in conversation for over two hours was no joke, and he was glad to see the dinner's end approach. Down his whole left arm, through the fingers, a dull ache distracted him from the talk around him. But his darkest secret was the cowing fear.

By one A.M. the house was empty of guests and servants, the ground floor dark. Wearily, Dave had gone upstairs to his room, taken another bath, this time a shower, and donned fresh pajamas. The wind had risen still higher during the night and slammed about the upper stories of the house. He opened a little cabinet, poured a tiny brandy and, holding the glass, sat down on the bed. When he looked up, Anita, now in her robe, stood in the door with a flippant smile.

"How'd you like the party?" she said.

"Fine—good party." He was grave.

Still she smiled. "Do you realize, Mister, you didn't speak to me *once*, the whole evening?—and acted like you couldn't bear the sight of me?"

He took a sip of the brandy and set the glass down. "No, I wasn't aware," he coolly lied.

Then she came over and sat down on the bed beside him. "What's the matter, honey?" she said. "Have I done something wrong? Tell me, if I have. *Tell* me. But don't keep acting like this."

He sat in silence. Finally he looked at her. "You haven't done anything wrong," he said coldly. Then he stood.

Suddenly she jumped up and ran from the room. And returned immediately—clutching the black dress in her left hand, and the big pair of scissors in her right.

He stood horrified.

She began cutting savagely, and cut the dress from the neck straight down through the bottom hem. Then she cut it in two along the waist. Laughing and crying now, she dropped the fabric to the floor, pitched the scissors onto the bed, and threw her arms around his neck.

"I'll never wear black again, honey!" she cried. "I promise! I promise! *Never!* No matter where we go, or what we do, I'll never wear it! Do you believe that? Do you believe me?"

He held her in his arms with terror in his heart. "Of course, I believe you," he soothed, "of course . . . of course . . . ."

Moot

It was late in the afternoon when the old man started across the street with his mangy old dog at his side. There was a dull yellow light in the sky and the air was sulfurous as the storm impended. They had left the park-playground just in time and the old man flapped along like a phantom goose trying vainly to hurry. The old dog, a little over knee high to him, was at the moment businesslike. Thunder rumbled and a few big drops spattered the dust along the curb as they made it safely to the other side. They went on down the street toward their flat. Lightning streaked and for a moment the old dog squatted in wide-eyed fear, looking up at his master. But they went on.

The flat was a ghetto hovel where they had lived together for almost twelve years. No one but the two of them, Matthew and Mark. Old Matthew in better days had been a Pullman porter, but now he had to manage on his social security and a miserly little pension. The mongrel old dog Mark was most of the time austere yet agreeable. They made a quaint pair. Old Matthew after climbing the stairs now let them both in. Then in the living room he dropped into the musty armchair and let his arms plop over the sides. Old Mark went to his filthy pallet in the corner, sniffed it, circled twice, and dropped down also. There was silence now except for old man Matthew's wheezing.

Then the rain came. Old Matthew roused himself and laughed. "We beat it!" he cackled to old Mark, whose nose was extended on the floor, eyes on his master. The old dog was still businesslike, and interested. Then he yawned, licked his chops, and began to pant, his tongue hanging out six inches. Old Matthew went to the kitchen now and brought back an opened can of dog food, made mostly of cheap cereal, and put a few chunks in the old dog's dish. Mark ate the food quickly and licked his chops again. The rain came in hard now against the windows, and the thunder rolled. "We made it," old Matthew sighed, half to himself. "Dog, we made it." Again he went back to the kitchen and this time poured himself a drink, the cheapest whiskey made, and drank it off. He flinched and shivered but poured himself still another, then took it with him back to the living room and dropped into the chair again as the old dog, his nose once more extended on the floor, observed him with now half-closed eyes. "Yeah, go on and sleep now, you old bastard you," old Matthew said testily. "You've had food. I ain't. I gotta go cook mine—what there is back there. You're whole lot better off'n I am." He took a drink. Old dog Mark frowned, as if to say: "Yeah, but you can drink liquor and I can't. I wish I could—to dull my miserable existence as you do yours."

Old Matthew began to clear his throat loudly now as he did when getting a little tipsy, his only pleasure in the waning days. (He wished for their close, really.) He finally got up and went to the window. The sky was still a dull dangerous yellow and an occasional veined fork of lightning pulsed, then vanished, as the thunder came in. Old Matthew peered out. "Yeah, we beat it," he breathed. He had picked South Carolina cotton when he was eight and even from those days he remembered the power of lightning in the open fields. The sense of danger had become instinctive with him. He was eight and little Lettie was eight. She could pick more cotton than he could. They were sweethearts that early. From his third-floor window now he could see across to the parched and arid park-playground that was now receiving much moisture. Where was Lettie's soul? he wondered. He bitterly concluded it had to be in hell. There was such a long roll of thunder now that the window panes gave a low death rattle and old Mark came up quickly off his vile pallet and went and stood beside his ebony old master. "You got your belly full. What you scared about?" old Matthew said to him, sensing the old dog's nearness though not looking to see. Another filigreed vein of lightning made old Mark squat again. Finally he whined. "Lord Jesus, dog," old Matthew said. "You ain't seen no trouble. Hummmph, scared of lightning." But old Mark still whined as if frightened and sad, or worried, or as if experiencing a foreboding for both himself and his failing master. Wondering who would go first. The two of them were so interdependent. Without Matthew, Mark would starve or, worse, perish in that horrid concentration camp of a dog pound. Without Mark, Matthew would expire of sotted boredom and loneliness.

It need not have been this way, old Matthew knew, as he took a drink. Lettie had not lived up to her bargain. It was the bargain of matrimony. Young sweethearts for ten years, then married for twenty-three, they should have been fortune's shining children. But she had not honored her commitments. Soon after they moved to Alabama as young marrieds, when he got the wonderful job on the Gulf, Mobile & Ohio R. R., she couldn't stand the good life, the milk and honey. Almost every time he had to be gone for two or three straight nights, she would succumb. It was bad. It was a disgrace. She had failed him. Even their little boy, Harlan, their only child, knew what was going on. For he saw the men. And finally *the* man—DuBois Jackson, dice genius. In the end it was DuBois that knifed her, and they buried her under a small granite stone that Matthew, despite his disgust, had paid for. After that he was an empty shell. Even Harlan's death many years later in an Italian mine field in World War II left him callous, uncaring.

There was more adder-tongued lightning now across the sky and old Mark lifted his grizzled snout and howled in certain expectancy of the bolt of thunder that promptly struck. The room shuddered. He whined piteously now and soon set up a frightful howl again. "Lord God, just listen at you," old Matthew said. "You don't know it's too late to git scared, do you? It's way too late. Ain't nothin' goin' to happen to you now except you goin' to die—soon." He drained off his drink and put the glass down on the window sill. The creeping cars were the only sensation of movement he received from the wet street below. The formerly dull yellow sky was darkening now and old Mark pressed hard against his trouser leg, still whining. "Lord Jesus, dog, I never knowed you to carry on so like this. What's got into you? You scared of dying, ain't you? Yeah, that's it, all right. You're scared. That ain't gonna help, though. It's comin' for both of us. I'm ready, myself. You don't hear me whinin', do you? Indeed you don't. It's somethin' you gotta face. We've had a pretty good life together. But it can't go on forever. So stop that damn whinin'. *I* know it ain't the thunder and lightnin' you're tremblin' about. Don't kid *me*." But old Mark still whined and trembled. Finally old Matthew went over and sat down again, snorting.

In a little while they heard the noisy children playing outside in the hallway. At once old Mark looked up gladly, expectantly, at his master. It was the only division between them. Old Mark loved children. Old Matthew detested them. Mark went slowly, feebly, over to the door now, then turned, wagging his stiff old tail twice, and looked back at his master. "Git away from that door, dog," old Matthew said. "I ain't gonna open it." Soon old Mark came away and dropped down on his pallet again. "Ain't no use lookin' so mad," old Matthew said. "Them children don't want to be bothered with you. I opened the door once, remember, and they all run down the stairs screamin', 'Don't touch him!—don't touch that old filthy dog!' You remember it, all right. Now you want me to open the door so you can git the same thing. Ain't you got no pride?—you wanta keep on gittin' insulted, huh?" Old Mark only stretched his nose out on the floor and gazed at his master. "Dog, I can't figure you out," old Matthew said. The old dog only looked at him and soon began panting again.

It was raining steadily now, but gently. The thunder and lightning had stopped. Old Matthew got up and went and peered out the window again. The scrubby park-playground across the way looked better being rained on. The puny trees were dripping water and the old benches were even shiny. Old Matthew finally turned and started back to the kitchen to prepare his dinner. He had a piece of liver he would fry. "Come on, old dog," he said. "I've watched you eat, now you come watch me. Come on." He left. But old Mark did not move. His nose still on the floor, he gazed straight ahead, pouting. But when he was sure he was alone, he got up and crept over to the door again. Outside it the children were still playing and he lay down and lugubriously stretched his nose out on the floor only a foot from the door. Once or twice he tried to wag his stiff old tail again. The children were romping noisily both in the hall and up and down the stairs. But the old dog knew this was not a common situation, for they only played inside when it was raining. Now he began to whine again. And finally he stood up, put his right side, his ribs, against the door panel, and beat his tail against the door in a kind of SOS. He whined again. But nothing happened. Anyway the children were making so much noise they could not have heard.

"Hey, you!" old Matthew called from the kitchen. "Come back here. Come on, now. I'll give you some more grub. Come on, old dog. Don't be so contrary." Old Mark finally went back to the kitchen. Old Matthew was boiling a potato. The old man reached up on the shelf and got the half-pint whiskey bottle, poured the inch of cheap bourbon that remained into his glass, and tossed the bottle in the trash can. He made a half-pint last him three days. The old dog stood disconsolately in the kitchen door and looked at him. The whiskey had old Matthew feeling pretty good now and he grew expansive. "It'll soon be curtains for you and me, old dog," he said. "Lay down over there and listen to me while I fix my dinner." Old Mark came in but sat down only tentatively on his haunches. "Yeah, we've had it," old Matthew said. "We're both 'bout the same age, seventy-two and fourteen, and have had it. I ain't sorry to git it behind me, neither. No, there ain't much time left. I'm goin' to Heaven, though, dog. Where you goin'? Huh? Ever think of that? You ain't goin' no place. This is the end of the road for you. Right? Want some more grub now?" He stepped around the old dog and went and got the can of cereal dog food and shook a little of it out onto a saucer and put it down on the floor before old Mark. But he refused it. "Might as well eat, dog, and quit worryin'," old Matthew said. "Worryin' ain't gonna make it no better." Finally old Mark lay down with his paws out in front of him and looked on as his master dropped the piece of liver into a hot skillet. Now the noise of the children in the hallway and on the stairs seemed to reach a crescendo and old Mark began to whine again.

"What is there about them children out there you like so, dog?" old Matthew said. "I tell you they don't feel the same way 'bout you. The way you look, you scare 'em to death. Just look at your hide all comin' out in patches. And you can't half see. Your teeth're almost gone too. Ain't you a sight? And still wantin' to run around with a bunch of children. You're way past your prime but don't know it. Dog, you're nuts." Old Matthew now poured some hot water into the battered coffee pot. The children still played and yelled and old Mark still whined a little, softly. "Shut up, dog," old Matthew said. "After I eat, we'll go up and look at Huntley and Brinkley."

Later, by the time the two returned to the living room, the children had left the hallway and stairs and gone in to their dinners. It was quiet now. Old Matthew went to the television and turned on the news. Then he sat down in his musty armchair again while old Mark went to his reeky pallet. Everything was routine. After the news was over old Matthew watched "High Chaparral," after that "The Name of the Game," and after that "The Saint." Finally at ten he stood up, stretched his creaking bones, and gave a fetid yawn. He looked over at the pallet. Old Mark lay stretched on his side with his eyes closed. "Come on, dog," Matthew said. "It's time for us to turn in. Your dog bed in the bedroom's better anyhow. Come on and I'll give you some water, you sleepy old fart you." Old Mark did not move. Matthew finally went over and nudged him with his toe. There was no response. Old Mark was dead. Matthew now suspected as much and, heart pounding, knelt down to make sure. The dog's breathing had stopped and his body was limply inert. "Why, you old bastard you," Matthew said nervously, still on his knees looking hard into the old dog's reposeful face. Now in desperation he shook him but there was no reaction. "He's dead, all right!" he whispered, and stood up and stared unbelievingly at the wall. At last he went back and in deep thought and perplexity undressed and went to bed.

Next morning after he'd had his coffee he got out his old Val-Pak and put Mark's carcass in it. Then he left with it and caught a bus way out to the end of the line at the city dump. It was a Saturday and there was no one there to keep him from breaking the law. He took old Mark out of the Val-Pak and deposited him in a big soggy pasteboard carton abandoned between two piles of rusty tin cans. Then he covered him up with wet ashes. He did not tarry long but walked as hurriedly as his old legs permitted the considerable distance back to the bus stop. It was a bright early October day, although it had rained most of the night, and from the bus window he observed the nice tidy lower middle-class houses near the outskirts of the city along the way. White children were playing ball or speeding up and down the side walk on tricycles. And a teen-age youth was on a shiny new ladder washing his mother's windows. Everything was sunshine, blue sky, freshness, newness, health, life. He looked on soberly, then in wonder, awe.

When he returned to his flat he took old Mark's two filthy pallets and went out back and stuffed them in the garbage can. There he also got rid of what remained of the cereal dog food, Mark's old collar, and his feeding dish. There was not a trace of the old dog anywhere in the flat now, not even his acrid smell. Old Matthew wanted a drink but there was no whiskey left, and he could not afford another half-pint until his social security check came next Monday or Tuesday. So he rinsed out the skillet in which he had fried the liver the evening before and made ready to prepare himself some bacon and eggs. Soon he stood at the stove turning the sizzling bacon. "You're next, old dog," he said suddenly. "After I eat, then you eat." He half turned around to the spot where old Mark had often watched him as he cooked and for an instant was stunned to find him not there. "Lord Jesus!" he breathed, staring at the place. "Where are you, old dog? Ah, you're gone, ain't you, you old bastard you. Soon now you'll be rotting. The flies and maggots'll be at you. What an end, old dog. Good God, what an end." Later he sat eating the bacon and eggs, the stale bread, and drinking the tepid coffee. "Gone," he whispered. "The old bastard's gone."

On Tuesday his meager little check came and he went out and bought groceries and another half-pint. Before thinking, he had almost bought three cans of cereal dog food. As he walked home in the early afternoon the weather, though still clear and bright, was unusually crisp for early October. Most of the children were in school at this hour and for the time being the neighborhood was quiet. He went up to his flat and put the groceries away and then poured himself a drink of whiskey. When later he went up in the living room and dropped into the musty armchair again he felt unfamiliar in the surroundings. The room seemed strange and he hardly recognized what he saw. In addition to the armchair and television there was a greasy old sofa, a straight chair, and a piece of carpet on the floor. There was also a little table by his chair that held a lamp. But he did not try to read much now because of his failing eyesight. He got his news from the television. He had not taken much notice of these items before. It was only now that old Mark was gone that he seemed to see them for the first time and they were alien to him. Before, they had been mere inanimate objects unworthy of his notice. Old Mark had held center stage. He turned and gaped at the sofa although it was a relic of his marriage. Ah, Lettie. That bad, bad woman. He pulled open the drawer of the little table beside him and took out an envelope of faded snapshots. One was of lantern-jawed Lettie holding little Harlan, then four. It seemed a century ago. Harlan turned out to be a rather odd, gawky, detached young man. He had not wanted to go to war. His reason was plain now. Yet he'd liked it overseas when not up in the lines with his rifle company. He had especially liked the signorinas. Old Matthew took out a snapshot

Harlan had sent him from Italy showing him with a signorina he called his "girlfriend." She was a very pale, very hungry-looking peasant girl. Next he found another snap of Lettie at a church picnic. She was laughing and showing her buck teeth. "That horny bitch!" he breathed, and threw the pictures back in the drawer. "I didn't have a chance at nothin'. I can see it now. Right, old dog?" He looked around and at once caught himself. Old Mark was gone, he again realized. Rotting, rifled with maggots, out at the city dump. He thought of the futility of all life and, horror-stricken, went gibbering from the room.

By the time school let out later in the afternoon and the noisy children returned, he felt better and made ready to prepare himself a chicken pie for dinner. "I eat well! Better than you do, old dog!" he said loudly in the kitchen. "Come on back here with me and I'll let you taste somethin' good just soon as it comes outa the oven. Man food, not dog food. Come on, you old bastard you!" he bawled. But all the time he was saying these things he knew old Mark was rotting out at the city dump. He said them, however, to indulge himself. "Lay down there, dog, and listen to me," he said. "Do you remember when, and how, I got you? Huh? You ungrateful old bastard, you've forgot already. Ah, I stole you. Remember? It was only two months after I quit the railroad and was so lonesome by myself. Lettie's sister had grabbed Harlan. Yeah, I stole you just like she did Harlan. Stole you out of a cracker's car, right in front of his little children, when him and his wife was in the store. You remember, all right. You didn't wanta come, either, you bastard you. Started whinin' and carryin' on just like you do now. When it was the luckiest day of your life. Look what all I've done for you, what I've put up with all these years—walked you, fed you, cleaned up your shit, took care of you far better'n I did Harlan when I had him. Didn't I? You damn right I did. So, you ungrateful bastard you, whatta you do? Why, you go off'n leave me. And peacefully in your sleep too. What a crummy trick. . . . ah!" The old man sat down at the kitchen table and wept angrily. "You bastard! . . . *you brute!*"

During the next few weeks the neighbors seldom saw the old man. They were accustomed to seeing him and old Mark out walking, or more often sitting, in the park-playground across the way. But now the only time they glimpsed him was when he went out for a little food and an occasional half-pint. They especially thought it strange that they no longer saw the old dog, but otherwise they paid no attention and did not care. They had never liked the old man anyway. He was too strange and, they thought, very mean. He was also frightfully dirty. Even the children shunned him as much as they had the old dog. But there was a very religious old woman who lived down on the second floor, Sister Belle . . . something (he had never known her last name), who began to be concerned when she saw him so seldom, and never the old dog. Yet even she was not inclined to go up knocking on his door to inquire. She tried to get her husband to do it, but he refused. So instead she began to pray for the old man, fervently. She also asked God's guidance on how she should handle this situation, for she sensed something was radically wrong up in that dismal flat.

Thanksgiving Day came. Sister Belle had a big dinner down in her flat, with all her children and grandchildren there. She cooked the turkey herself and all the trimmings, and had everything ready to be served by five o'clock. It was dark by this time. Now she took down the biggest plate she could find, really a platter, and heaped it full of turkey and dressing with gravy, sweet potatoes, squash, succotash, and two big buttered rolls. She told her daughter where she was going and instructed her to put dinner on the table. Then she took the food upstairs and knocked on the old man's door.

"Who's that?" he said in a weak, croaky voice.

"The lady downstairs, sir. I've brought you up some Thanksgivin' dinner if you'd like to have it."

Old Matthew finally threw the bolt and cracked the door a little. He peeped out and squinted as if his eyes were not accustomed to the light. His face was hollow and sunken, and looked even worse without his dentures in. He opened the door wider now and stood peering at Sister Belle, then at the platter covered with a paper napkin.

She proffered her gift. "Here. I thought you might like to share Thanksgivin' dinner with us," she said. "The Lord provides for all, you know. Praise His name."

The old man took the plate with trembling hands but as if he still did not understand. He stood gaping at her.

"Are you sick, sir?"

"No," he said.

"We ain't seen you—or the dog—out recently. *He* ain't sick, is he?"

"Oh, no," the old man said quickly.

"Well, I pray for you'all," Sister Belle said. "Prayer changes things. It can move mountains. You pray for me too, hear? We all need it." She left and went back downstairs.

He closed and locked the door as if in a dream and took the food back to the kitchen. When he had put in his dentures he sat down at the table and began to eat ravenously, using no silverware, only his dirty fingers. "Ah, old dog, I can't give you none of this," he said. "It's too good." Later when he had finished and wiped his hands on the dish towel he went up front and sat down in the old armchair again. The television screen was black and silent now because it had burned out a tube two weeks before. The old man did not care and made no effort to get it repaired. His hands idly in his lap, he sat in the weak yellow light of the lamp at his elbow. But he did not sit long and soon went back to retire very early. He sat on the side of the bed and tugged off a shoe. "Where are you, old dog?" he said. "Huh? . . . where'n the hell are you? Still out at the city dump, I reckon. That's where I took you, ain't it? But Greenhaven Cemetery's only half a mile away. Hear that, old dog? We won't be far. Until we both rot." He finally undressed, put his clothes on a chair, and went to bed.

The week before Christmas they came in an ambulance and took him to Cook County Hospital. Sister Belle had supervised everything. She even brought her own pastor to the hospital to see and to pray with him. Not, as she frankly told him, to get him well again but to bring peace to his soul. With tongue in cheek he listened. He did not want to offend her and tried his best to go along with the program. And thanks to Sister Belle he died fairly content. (It was actually a kind of ennui.) He left enough money for his funeral expenses, but there were no mourners to go out to Greenhaven with him. Not even Sister Belle. Only the undertaker's functionaries were present. So it was at eleven o'clock on a cold morning three days into the new year that they buried him a half mile from the city dump.

Later, when the building owners took over the flat, to vacate and clean it up for new tenants, they first had to get rid of the few pieces of grimy furniture and other effects they found. It was all absolutely worthless. Moreover the black workmen were convinced it was contaminated and piled it all in the alley and burned it. Then they proceeded to scrub the place and freshly paint it. There were three of them.

"They say some old man and his dog lived here," the first said. "For years—just the two of 'em."

"Can't you tell?" another said. "No woman would've lived in this filth."

"Well, they're both dead," the third said, lifting a bucket of suds up onto the scaffold. "It's moot now."

"It's whut . . . ?"

"Moot. M-O-O-T. I heard a lawyer say that once."

"Say whut? Whut you mean?"

"I never looked it up but it's a legal word meanin' it don't matter no more. Or not to worry 'bout it. Or it's water over the dam—it's moot."

The first fellow, up on the scaffold, turned and laughed. "All right, Lawyer Willie, *moot*, then. Now let's get goin' and finish this nasty old place today, so we can start on that big beautiful job up on 14th Street in the mornin'."

"Right, man, right," Willie said.

Overnight Trip

The street lights and the lights from the store windows shone gauzily through the rainy mist, as Amos slouched up Michigan Boulevard, peering now and then across the Chicago river to the matriarchal old Wrigley building, solitary, stark-naked white, and wet, against its glaring floodlights bursting up from the south bank. For just an instant the Taj Mahal flashed to his mind out of a colorful travelogue movie, but right off he realized it was very, very different; it had a *soft* glow—with placid, waxen tints. Ducking his head, squinting, and turning up his coat collar at the same time, he leaned his long skinny Negroid frame shrinkingly into the weather.

All day long, at his linotype machine, he had been in low spirits, and the miserable night didn't help any. Sometime during the afternoon he had vaguely decided to take the bus home, instead of the El. That way he wouldn't have to transfer; and, too, there wasn't so much commotion on the bus. He could think. Lately, he was always looking for opportunities to isolate himself—in order to think, to persist in this constant mulling over in his mind of matters that had, so far, completely foiled him.

He stopped and waited at South Water Street where he'd

be sure of getting a seat—the ride out to 79th and King Drive was a long one. Soon he caught a No. 3 going south; all along Michigan Boulevard, down to the Illinois Central station at 12th Street, people were clambering aboard out of the near-freezing drizzle.

He settled back in his seat, tired; and, gazing out the window, his mind reverted to the thoughts that never seemed to leave him—slippery, confounding thoughts, and grimly anchored to the fate of his marriage. He thought of little else lately. But he never seemed to reach any solid conclusions—although he always started from the same point, the one premise he could be sure about: that he loved little Penny. To him, she was the near-perfect wife. But after that, his mind would stray off into connective dilemmas and motives—the whys and wherefores—and they were myriad and confused. She was many things to him: diminutive and shy, but straightforward and natural, too; so honestly herself, so lacking in cunning, and sweet—but, at times, thoughtful and uncommunicative. But, alas, it was the combination of these very qualities that had finally set up the extraordinary impulses tormenting his brain. For he now harbored a quiet, but fierce, urge to circumscribe and protect her—to shield her from what he considered a dangerous, seamy world. His rather set, channeled mentality could not see that the urge was fast growing into an obsession—even if suppressed, still a bizarre, whimsical, mad obsession. Actually, the soul-searching that occupied his days and nights was peripheral, for he could not bring himself to examine his odd purposes.

The big bus rocked and spattered along. He was now vaguely aware of the black woman sitting beside him, her eyes closed, nodding. Her chin occasionally dropped and rested on her chest, as she hugged a bulky, rumpled shopping bag on her lap. How wonderful, he thought, to be able to sleep on a bus.

His dismal day had begun that morning at breakfast when

Penny mentioned that her friend, Bobbie, had invited her to go down to St. Louis with her—on just an overnight trip. Although Penny didn't say so, he knew she wanted to go—despite his cautious reminder that they hadn't spent a night apart in their whole six years of marriage. After that he had adopted an uneasy nonchalance. But all day long now he had seethed inside— Bobbie was a pert, saucy, friendly girl, and pretty too, but a divorcee and, he suspected, had been around. He could not understand Penny's really fine intelligence—the antithesis of her seeming naiveté; nor, for that matter, her frustration, her yearning for children—and her repressed sexual longings so puzzled by his once-a-fortnight ineptness. All this eluded his narrow, hedge-like mind—to him, she was a little girl (an orphan of eighteen when he married her) who required his sheltering, his craft, always.

He was forever cueing her on the precautions she must take for her own personal safety when he was not present: never cross the street without first looking both ways; always pull down the shades in the bedroom and bathroom at night—all the way down; never, for any reason, be out of the house alone after dark; make sure the apartment doors are locked all during the day; and never, never, under any circumstances, open the door to a salesman. But, although visions of harm befalling her from *any* quarter were to him unnerving enough, the image of harm to her from a *man* filled him with cold terror, drove him to cement up his mind against the very thought. It was more than jealousy. To him she was inviolate. And more extraordinary still—and quite beyond his comprehension—was his dark intuition that she was inviolate even against himself. Those fortnightly transgressions, he so regarded them, dismayed and saddened him—made him feel a ravisher.

The bus left 43rd Street—as his seat-mate snored softly. Peering through the glass out into the wet night, he wondered what it was about life that made it so risky. You were always on the edge of trouble—at least, most of *his* life it had been like that. After graduation from high school, he had hopped bells and waited tables. Then along came the chance to learn linotyping. Being black, he knew the barriers existing then— from the union, as well as employers. But he went through it all—and succeeded; and for seven years now he'd had a job he prized—with a Chicago daily. And after he found little Penny and married her, he breathed easier, confiding to him- self that he was finally "out of the woods." But now he realized you never were. This was hard to accept—although he was thirty—for his teachings had been the very opposite. His mother, now long dead, used to say to him, "Keep on agoin' fou-werd, Amos, and look to Jesus, an' everything will come out all right." It was a mild shock to regard this as possibly untrue. Still—he felt that Penny loved him. She always said so—that is, whenever he asked her. But he always had to ask her. He guessed that was just her way.

It was 6:20 when finally he got off the bus at 79th Street, and walked north, homeward—he always neared home with a warm pang of expectancy. He knew Penny was there, quiet and self-possessed—sometimes faintly sardonic—in her tiny rose apron. When he felt himself walking faster, he resolutely slowed his gait. He wondered if he shouldn't have brought her something—assorted nuts, maybe, or some dates. But he could never be sure what she liked; she never said.

Their apartment was on the second floor, and after using his key, and going up, he wiped his feet vigorously on the mat out- side, and let himself in. The neat rooms were small and boxy— but there were soft colors everywhere; the modern furnishings still looked new, if rather miscellaneous, and the little sofa and two arm chairs were protected by plastic covers.

"Hi," he called toward the rear, pulling off his rubbers.

"Hi," the poised reply came back.

He walked into the bedroom and found Penny sitting on a

velvet hassock, a blue dress draped across her knees, and a needle and thread in her hand. "What're *you* up to?" he grinned, reaching into the closet for a coat hanger.

"I'm taking up the hem on this dress. Can't you see?" She looked up at him and laughed softly. Like himself, she was medium brown-skinned, but small, even for a woman, and very cute. After hanging up his hat and coat, he bent down and kissed her on the forehead. Then it hit him—the dress and the trip to St. Louis.

"Hungry?" she asked.

"Oh, so-so." He was moody now.

She got up and went to the dresser and stuck the needle in a pin cushion, before hanging the dress in the closet. Then she started for the kitchen, and as always, he followed, slumping in a chair at the kitchen table, and, in a show of unconcern, began eating from the bowl of potato chips.

"You'll spoil your dinner," she said.

"Okay." He watched her turn the oven on, and sensed her preoccupation. "What'd you do today?" he asked.

After a short, busy delay, she turned around to him. Well, she'd stayed up after he left—she couldn't sleep anymore; she did the kitchen floor, as he could see; that was first; then started cleaning the two clothes closets—and what a job *that* turned out to be; then took a bath; and later, called Bobbie; after that, watched the two o'clock movie—it was pretty good today, for a change; then she took a nap; and about 5:30, started dinner. She crossed in front of him to open the refrigerator.

Quickly his long arm shot out around her waist, pulling her back onto his lap; her feet dangled off the floor.

"Gimme a kiss," he whispered. She looked at him. "Come *on*, I said gimme a kiss." She turned her lips to his and closed her eyes, and he kissed her with abashed briefness. "Do you get lonesome sometimes—during the day?" he said.

She looked self-consciously over at the casserole just out of the oven. "Oh . . . not often."

After a silence he said, half to himself, "Maybe we ought to see the doctor again."

She swung her legs gently to and fro, and said nothing.

"Maybe next time would do it," he went on, still half in soliliquy. "Are you game?"

"Yes." But she faced him dubiously.

Then, as he kissed her dryly again, she suddenly with violence jerked her head and shoulders back from him, and viewed him sadly. "Oooooh, I want some kids so!" She closed her eyes with a little shiver.

"I pray every night," he said weakly.

"I *know*, but we don't give ourselves a chance!" The words came out first in exasperation, then pity. Conscious of her outburst, she slipped down off his knees, and pulled the refrigerator door open. When she took out the two salads and turned around again, he was staring gloomily at the door. "The rolls are almost ready." She was gentle now. "Go wash up."

He got up and followed her to the table and put his arm down around her shoulder. "D'you love me?" he said, and studied her profile.

"Sure."

"How d'you *know* you love me?"

"Oh, shoot . . . you just know things like that—you don't talk about 'em."

"I love *you*. Y'know *that*, don't you?"

"Yep," she grinned. He could see she was trying to be funny, but he caught the tenseness.

They finished a mostly silent meal. And afterwards, she lost no time in returning to the bedroom, and the dress, as, inevitably, he followed her. He sat in the bedroom chair, quietly smoking a big black pipe, and contemplating her. "What'd

Bobbie say about going to St. Louis?" He could stifle the question no longer.

"She's going day after tomorrow, Thursday—and back Friday night."

"Has she got some relatives down there or something?"

"No, she's going to see some lawyer that's handling a case for her father. I didn't get it all . . . something about her father's farm down in Missouri."

"D'you *want* to go?"

". . . I wouldn't mind. I've never been to St. Louis—just through there."

"Where would you stay?"

"At a hotel, Dopey," she laughed softly . . . . But then, after reflection, she said, "I don't just *have* to go—I didn't promise Bobbie for sure."

Her willing concession came so honestly, so childlike, it completely undermined him. Feelings of tenderness and remorse flooded him, and he longed to take her in his arms again. "Of *course* you can go," he said huskily. "If you want to . . . you can go."

At first she paused. Then tiny fires of elation jigged in her eyes. "I told Bobbie I wouldn't mind going—It'd be just the one night."

". . . Okay . . . ," he said, his voice now a dejected echo. "You'd better go pick up your ticket tomorrow."

"Oh, Bobbie'll get them!—I can pay her Thursday, on the train."

She sewed with purpose now, as he looked on helplessly. He hadn't expected such eagerness from her, and he tried to gulp the swelling in his throat. It was just a harmless overnight trip, he knew, but perhaps the beginning of something. She could like it. Next time she'd want to stay longer, maybe. He burned to seize her by the wrists, to wrestle her down, to beg her not to go. But he sat mute—ineffectual.

Thursday morning they were up before six o'clock. He sat on the side of the bed and rubbed his weary neck, waiting for Penny to clear the bathroom. He had pitched and tossed all night, and was jaded. If he'd had *his* way, this particular morning would have postponed itself—from day to day, perhaps— until he'd had a chance to think the whole thing out; for now he sat searching his past again, for reasons—he had a passion for reasons. The ache deep inside him—why? And why the fear? Was it punishment? What wrong had he done? But he could not make his plodding brain give answers.

He sighed and looked at his wristwatch—train time was 8:20; he was glad they wouldn't have to rush. They?—he realized it wasn't necessary for him to take her; he could put her in a cab. But he well knew he'd take her, in the end—even if it made him late for work.

Penny came out of the bathroom, in a robe too long for her, on her way to the kitchen to make coffee; she looked tired. As he entered the bathroom, he felt contrite for keeping her awake by his restlessness. He opened the door of the little white medicine cabinet to get a fresh razor blade, and saw her nail scissors on the bottom shelf; and there on the second shelf were two new powder puffs lying primly on a folded piece of pink Kleenex, next to a small can of tooth powder. He could never understand why she preferred tooth powder to tooth paste; it was probably due to that guff about the dentists using it; she *would* fall for a line like that; that's what worried him about her. In the left-hand corner of the second shelf there were a half dozen bobby pins, all placed in a careful row, and next to them were hand lotion, cold cream, and a lipstick. On the towel rack at his right he saw her spotless, bright-colored towels and wash cloths. He stood there holding the cabinet door open, studying the mute little articles, and reflecting how completely they all mirrored her personality—at least the part that could be mirrored; he felt he didn't understand the rest—

he'd never really got inside her mind. How he hoped she didn't feel trapped with him. He knew you couldn't keep a woman trapped for long—even a good woman.

As he shaved, his mind soared back over and beyond his present state, to their first meeting—at a church picnic in Dan Ryan Woods. She was living with her grandmother then. He remembered he'd asked her for a date that very first day, and had felt some surprise at her ready "Yes"—he put it down to inexperience. They had four straight dates in two weeks, and she appeared to like every minute of it. Then—he couldn't wangle a date with her for two months; the only reason she gave was that she wasn't dating for awhile. But after the two months, they started again. And within eight months they were married. That all this was six whole years ago didn't seem possible. He had seen, before their marriage, how crazy she was for pretty clothes—she had very few of them—and one bright April Saturday afternoon, when they were still newlyweds, he took her downtown to a department store and bought her a beautiful, banana-colored spring coat. He would never forget her happy, earnest eyes, and her struggle against her natural reserve, when telling him how she adored it. And on their way home, she asked him if they could get a bottle of sparkling Burgundy—her grandmother always had it at Christmas dinner, she said—and when they got home and drank it, they were both giddy, and she giggled a lot. He recalled that a seam in her stocking was twisted, and that she wanted to make love on the day-bed—they didn't own a real bed yet—and afterwards (including the nap) she had teased him for what she called "stalling." He was still a little frightened, reliving it.

It was snowing lightly when, at eight sharp, they arrived in a cab at 63rd Street station. He had insisted on coming, despite her quizzical look when he told her. They walked stoically through the main station building out onto a long concrete

platform that paralleled the tracks, where a small enclosure—
with window walls—provided shelter from the weather. He
was carrying her small off-white bag—the one from the two-
piece luggage set he had bought her for their honeymoon trip
to Detroit. They entered the enclosure and he set the bag down
on the concrete floor, and they took seats on a bench along the
wall and looked out at the lazily-falling snow—there was very
little of it on the ground and the housetops, for it was just beginning. Penny looked calm, but he sensed her excitement.
She wore a heavy grey coat and white gloves, but no hat, and
he noticed how the tiniest particles of snow had melted in her
hair.

"Gee, what a pretty snow," she said.

"Yeah." He was grave.

"Wonder if it's snowing in St. Louis?"

He did not answer right away; he took out his pipe and
knocked it hard against the hot radiator along the wall, and
patted his pockets for tobacco. "I wouldn't know, honey," he
finally said. "That's three hundred miles from here."

"Oh," she said.

They sat without talking; he smoked his pipe and she
watched the people entering. A blond sailor with a pimply
face came in, with his girl. There were no seats left—at least
twenty people were in the little enclosure now—and the two
stood in a corner, only six feet from Amos. The girl's thin coat
hung open down the front, so that, as they stood against the
wall, the sailor ran his arm inside around her waist and pulled
her to him, and they kissed wetly with open mouths. People
pretended not to see. Penny kept her eyes out the window, and
Amos sucked noisily at his pipe. A grinning black man with
bloodshot eyes, slouching against the wall, and still reeking of
his all-night liquor, ogled the couple. "Hey, Daddy-O," he
cackled, "cool it! *Cool* it, man!" Then he broke into a loud,
gravelly, drooling laugh. Amos got up and stalked to the win-

dow, as Penny stole one more fleet glance at the pair. Then she looked at her wristwatch—and then toward the door.

"Oh, *there's* Bobbie!" she cried. Amos turned around.

"Hi!" Bobbie laughed, out of breath, as she shouldered her way, with purse and bag, through the stiff-swinging door. Penny and Amos called "Hi" at the same time—"How's everything?" he asked bravely.

"Fine, Amos! Howya doing, honey?" she said to Penny, panting and setting her bag down. She was wearing a red coat and a little white hat.

"You made it!" Penny said happily. "I was getting worried."

"You know *me*, honey—and I thought I gave myself plenty of time. Well, I'm here, anyhow."

Amos watched her with a grudging respect. Here, he thought, was a little girl who had married a big bruiser of a man, the fullback type, but who, whenever they got into one of their frequent brawls, was suddenly transformed into a she-puma—scratching, clawing, pummelling, shrieking; giving far more than she had to take. And she was so lithe and feminine—so frilly! That's what to him was so wacky about it. She was slightly taller than Penny, and a lighter brown—with a perky, cheerful radiance that explained her delight in the splashy colors of her clothes. But he recoiled from the heavy black eyebrow pencil she used. To him that spoiled everything.

"I got our hotel reservation," she said to Penny "—at the Jefferson."

"Oh, swell!" Penny said, as Bobbie sat down on the bench beside her; the two were soon lost in a busy, heedless chatter, as Amos stood.

The fine snow kept sifting down, for there was practically no wind. The big radiator against the wall started pounding and hissing—to Amos the heat was suffocating; he was wretched.

"Don't forget to take in the newspapers," Penny finally

turned and said to him, glancing at Bobbie with a teasing little snicker.

"Okay, ma'm," he grinned. "Anything further?"

"Oh, I'll think up something else in a minute."

Suddenly the loud-speaker broke in raucously: "May we have your attention, please! Illinois Central train No. 21, *The Green Diamond*, for Springfield, St. Louis, and scheduled intermediate stops, is now approaching the platform. Please stand back of the white line, and watch your step as the train approaches!"

Penny had already grabbed up her bag off the floor, and Amos had to wrest it from her. Then he picked up Bobbie's bag, and slowly pushed outside ahead of them. All the people were coming out now, as the snow kept falling lightly. The giant orange and green Diesel unit came sliding in, as the rails and cross-ties settled heavily, sending tremors throughout the concrete platform. The bespectacled old engineer, wearing starched biege coveralls, sat two stories up, and looked bored as he eased the heavy coaches to a stop. The people were walking briskly down the platform toward the coaches, which looked nearly full already—most passengers had boarded downtown at the main station. When Amos and the girls reached their coach, he set the bags down for the porter.

"St. Louis?" the porter asked.

"Yes," Amos said. "So long, kids." He could barely speak.

Bobbie, now ahead, was climbing aboard, the porter just touching her elbow. "Bye-bye, Amos!" she cried. "See you tomorrow night!"

He did not hear her, as he bent down and took Penny in his arms. He had never seen her eyes so bright—like a ten-year-old child's—as she kissed him with embarrassment before the crowd. Then she hurried up the steps and, turning to wave, disappeared after Bobbie. He stood docilely aside. The ache had never been like this—he kept opening his eyes wider and wider, stretching them grotesquely to prevent the stinging, the brimming over. He dared not look.

But when all the passengers had boarded, his eyes searched the windows of Penny's coach. All the seats he could see were filled. Now the porter reached down and picked up his little portable step and swung aboard, and the train was moving—slowly, smoothly, silently, inexorably; her coach was slipping away. Then he saw her! She was leaning awkwardly over two seated people, waving to him, and smiling her childlike, artless, sad smile. He waved frantically just in time, as the stone station building ruthlessly cut off the view.

He stood there for a moment. And then he turned and slowly walked back toward the street. He knew she'd return tomorrow night, but that really she was gone.

An Untold Story

🎞 "Aw-w-w, that this too, too solid flesh wud melt, thaw, an' resolve itself into a *dew!* Or that th' Evah-lastin' had not fixed his canon 'gainst self-slaughtah! Aw, Gawd! Gawd! How weary, stale, flat, an' unprof'table seem t'me all th' uses uv this world! *Fie* on't! Aw, fie! 'Tis an unweeded garden, that grows t'seed! Thangs rank an' gross in nature possess ut merely!"

Lonnie paused now and stood flashing his wide gold-toothed smile. He set his glass of beer on the bar and stepped back proudly. "You cats know who that is?" he cried. The others only grinned.

"Naw, Lonnie, y'got *me!*"

"Shakespeare, man! Shakespeare! Hamlet!" His satin-ebony face glowed in the little tavern's murk. The short line of beer drinkers was caught in a rare moment of disablement. There was silence.

Lonnie gloated. "You-all don't know anythang about *that!*" Taking up his glass again and letting his eyes float ceiling-ward, he resumed:

"That it should come t'*this!* But two months dead!—nay, not s'much; not *two!* So eggcellent a king! That wuz, t'*this,*

Hy*pee*rian to a satter!"—His shrill voice carried outside into
the night—"So lovin' t'my mutha, that he might not beteem
th' winds uv *heaven* visit hu' face too roughly! *Heaven* 'n'
earth. Must I re*mem*bah?"

He stopped now. Eyes half-closed, head swaying, he again
spread his gold-capped smile.

"Cool it, Lonnie!" someone shouted, horse-laughing.

"Let him keep on, man!"

"Naw, naw," Lonnie said, serious now—"That's enough.
That stuff's way over your heads. Too deep fuh'ya. I learned
that in college."

"*Haw! College!* Christ, did'ja hear that!—Yeah, *barber*
college!"

"Naw," Lonnie said—"College."

Sidney, the car hiker—a black dwarf with a black greasy
conk scarf on his head—gripped his glass of beer and
screeched: "*Where?*—Somewhere down in Bip!"

"Yeah," said Lonnie. "It wuz down in Bip all right—but
it was a college right on."

"Where, ole buddy?"

"Mississippi."

"I told'ja!—I told'ja!" screamed Sidney, spinning half-
around on his bar stool like a dervish. "Didn't I tell'ya!—
Down in Bip!" He wailed, jackknifing with laughter.

"What college, Lon?" Jackson, the bartender, asked. Jackson was a big brown-skinned man with tree-trunk sideburns,
and invariably soft-spoken. "Y'never told us this before."

"There's a lotta thangs I never told you," Lonnie said, at
last smiling. "I went to Wirebridge State Training an' Industrial School."

"Hell!—don't sound like no college t'*me!*" scoffed Sidney.
"That's a *school!*"

"No, it ain't, either," Lonnie said. "It's a college. I wuz
studyin' fuh the ministry then."

A howl of laughter exploded in the low-hanging haze of cigarette smoke. Even Jackson, the bartender, grinned.

Lonnie was stubborn. "Well, it's a fact."

"*Whut's* a fact?" barked 'One Tittie' Powell, a scar-faced wine-o. "—thut you're a preacher, or thut you went t' college?"

More laughter. "Take it easy now, One Tittie!" warned Sidney—"You're fixin' t'git that *other* tittie cut off!"

"I didn't say I wuz a preacher," glowered Lonnie. "I said I went t'college."

"Oh, 'scuse *me!*" smirked One Tittie, clapping his hand to his mouth in mock apology.

Lonnie ignored him. "It wuz a college all right. Ole Professah Washington taught *Greek even!*—an' a lot of other thangs. *I* wuz in his literature class—Shakespeare. Je-*sus!* Did he know his Shakespeare! He could rattle it off all day an' all night—if you think *I* can go, Lord, you oughta heard *him!*" Then Lonnie laughed, showing his gold teeth.

The only light in the place came from the juke box, plus one weak bulb over the cash register; and, behind the bar, bartender Jackson's bulk loomed indistinct as he gave Lonnie an indulgent grin. He dragged on his cigarette and blew a plume of white smoke out at his few ghetto neighborhood patrons. The Friday night tavern TV showing of "Hondo and the Apache Kid" had just ended and the talk had been idle until Lonnie began his elocutions.

"Y'shoulda went on an' *been* a preacher, Lonnie," Sidney goaded, "—like you started out!"

Lonnie grinned again. "Yeah . . . I know. But when ole Professah Washington got inta th' immortal bard (Ah'm referrin' to Shakespeare, you-all) an' made him so powerful—oh, *so* powerful!—I forgot all about preachin'!"

Bradley, the Democratic precinct captain, swivelled around on his bar stool and crossed his legs. "Hell,"—he was smug—"we learned all about Shakespeare in high school."

Lonnie threw back his head and gave a contemptuous guffaw. "Man, whutayou talkin' about! Why, if you lived t'be a hundred years old, an' studied twenty-fo' hours a day, you could never learn 'all about' Shakespeare! He'll bust th' average man's skull wide open!—Lord, *wide open!*"

"How'd *you* ever learn anything 'bout him, then?" yapped Sidney.

"I just got through tellin' you! I studied under ole Professah Washington—th' master himself. We took up Hamlet in January—*January*, mind you—an' wuz supposed t'finish in three weeks. Ah, but we didn't. It wuz th' middle of April— *April!*—before ole Prof finally said we'd have t'get on t'somethin' else. He just shook his ole woolly white head an' said life wuz too short; that how could you evah find time t'take up somethin' else when you could nevah finish Hamlet. We studied it fuh four months near'bout—an' even *then* ole Prof didn't wanta quit!"

"Who'n th' hell wuz *Hamlet?* whined Ramsey Jenkins, the shivering paretic. His half-glass of beer trembled in his bony fingers as he squinted at Lonnie.

Bradley, the precinct captain, laughing, cut in: "He wuz a bad sonofabitch, Ramsey, when he had his sword, his rapier— as bad a sonofabitch as ever lived!"

Ramsey looked lost.

"Naw, naw," said Lonnie. "He could be gentle, too."

Ramsey's shaking hand mashed out his cigarette as he looked innocently first at Bradley, then at Lonnie.

"He wuz a *man*, Ramsey," Lonnie said with great feeling— "a man in a play; a play that Shakespeare wrote. An' he wuz a *flesh 'n' blood* man, too. Ole Prof used t'say that Shakespeare bid Hamlet *rise*, rise from th' printed white page, an' breathed inta him th' breath o' life!"

"It wuz a stage show, Ramsey," Bradley explained.

"An' *how!*" sneered Lonnie. "I guess it *wuz!*—just th' greatest evah put on by a livin' human!"

"Where'd *you* ever see it?"—Bradley was rude—"Down in Bip?"

"I nevah saw it at all. But I bet'cha I've *read* it a hundred times!"

"Any chicks in it?" whispered shivering Ramsey wistfully. All laughed—except Lonnie.

"Ramsey wants t'know if there's any *chicks* in it, Lonnie!"

Lonnie finally smiled. "Yeah, there's a chick. Yeah . . . a beautiful chick—Ophelia. Beautiful Ophelia . . . ." His voice trailed off in reverie.

"Y'*see* now, Ramsey?" someone said.

Jackson, the bartender, now began gathering in the empty beer bottles on the bar. "Don't you ginks never say I didn't give'ya nuthin'," he grinned.

"Whutaya mean, Pops?" cried Sidney, expectant, wide-eyed.

"This round's on th' cash register," Jackson answered.

"Oh, *no!* Oh, *no!*"

"Hey, now!"

"Jackson, mah boy!"

"Pops is poppin'!"

"Who'da thunk it!"

Jackson was already opening and setting up the cold bottles of beer on the bar. Eager Ramsey giggled excitedly as he reached for his bottle—resembling a scarecrow, he wore a soiled, clumsy suit over his wasted frame, and his shoe heels were miserably run-over. Suddenly he looked around for Lonnie—who stood apart, preoccupied. Ramsey climbed down from the bar stool, bottle and glass in hand, and, leering, approached Lonnie. "Ophelia was *fine*, eh, Lonnie?—fine awhile, I bet!"

Lonnie frowned—"Whutayou talkin' about? You drunk?"

"Drunk! . . . Drunk on this soap suds?"—Ramsey held up his trembling glass and tittered.

Lonnie gave him a dubious look.

"Ophelia, Lonnie!—*Ophelia!*" Ramsey pleaded, snivelling.

Lonnie half-turned toward the others at the bar. "I wuz not talkin' about Ophelia!" he said to Ramsey, but in a loud, high, attention-getting voice. Then he flashed his smile again. "I wuz talkin' about Hamlet!—*Hamlet, th' Dane!*" Then, ignoring Ramsey, he fell into an uproarious, contemptuous laugh.

"J-e-e-e-zuss Christ!" exploded One Tittie. "Are we goin' through this *agin!*" His scarred, bloated face showed a slight flush under the brown from his years of cheap green wine.

"He wuz gonna tell us about the little chick," Ramsey sighed in disappointment, stumbling back to the bar.

"Naw, I wuzn't, either," said Lonnie. "I said I wuz talkin' about Hamlet."

"Well, whut *about* him!" yelled One Tittie, his bland gray eyes (goat's eyes) staring. "Cain't you ever git *to* it!—get *done* with it!"

Lonnie stood leaning against the bar and said nothing. Finally he reached for his beer, but merely sipped it.

"*I* was interested," Jackson, the bartender presiding, said quietly to One Tittie. "He said Hamlet was a *man* . . . in a play."

One Tittie, breathing heavily, sat glowering at him.

Jackson wiped the bar with his wet rag, but returned One Tittie's stare. "That means somethin'," Jackson went on dryly, "—maybe somethin' kinda deep. That's th' trouble with a lotta people—they got hides so thick they can't pick-up on things like that. Then they git mad."

Lonnie's chin went up and he beamed.

One Tittie, smoldering but muddled, said nothing.

"Oh, it wuzn't nuthin' much." Lonnie was offhand now. "—I

wuz just tellin' about ole Prof, an' him sayin' that Shakespeare breathed th' breath o' life inta Hamlet, that's all."

"Aw-w-w, Lonnie!" Ramsey writhed in frustration.

"Shut up," Jackson said to him, and turned again to Lonnie.

"Well, y'see,"—Lonnie leaned forward now—"ole Prof used to dwell fuh days—*days*—on th' soliloquies, and———."

"Chr-i-i-i-st!" Sidney, the dwarf, howled. "Oh, God! . . . *whut?*"

Lonnie was patient. "Th' soliloquies were th' thangs Hamlet would say to him*self* . . . when he wuz all *by* himself—didn't none o' you-all evah talk to yourself?"

"Oh, yes, yes, yes, Lonnie!" sang Ramsey, ecstatically rubbing his palms together.

"Well, Hamlet did too sometimes—when he wuz mighty low and upset. One time there he wuz even thinkin' about committin' suicide. . . . 'To be, or *not* to be! *That* is th' question!'" Lonnie declaimed.

There was general silence. Jackson, the bartender, fingered a tiny glass of brandy.

"Yeah . . . ole Prof used t'recite that."—Lonnie was proud—"His ole black face would light up under his spectacles like a Christmas tree. And when he finished, he'd close th' book real softlike—like he didn't wanta hurt it. But he hadn't looked at that book once, not *once*—an' didn't need to. 'Ah, young men an' young women,' he'd say to us, 'th' soliloquies of Hamlet are th' most profound utterances in all poetry. Greater than th' Book of Job! Here we have th' deepest expressions of a troubled spirit—a soul in agitation.' Then th' ole man would take off his spectacles an' wipe 'em with his handkerchief—tryin' t'pull himself together."

"Yeah . . . tryin' t'pull hisself together," echoed Ramsey blithely.

"Shut up," grinned Bradley, the precinct captain.

"Aw, hell," Jackson glowered at them both.

But One Tittie's void, bodeful eyes studied Jackson.

"One day in class," Lonnie said, "ole Prof called on me, an' asked me just when th' play Hamlet wuz first produced. Hell, that wuz easy. I said sixteen hundred an' three. Well, he just smiled, an' looked around t'see if ev'rybody went along. Henry Skyles already had his damn hand up! He knew *ev'ry-thang*—so *he* thought! Well, Henry said none of us could be sure—that it wuz probably *before* sixteen hundred an' three. Some fool in th' back of the room laughed—because Henry an' I were the best in th' class. Prof raised his eyebrows, smiled again, an' gave his low little whistle; then he patted his foot on th' floor, an' looked around th' class. The *rest* of 'em didn't know, *that* wuz for sure! I wuz wonderin' now if ole Henry *had* me. Prof asked him why not sixteen hundred an' three. Henry said sixteen hundred an' three wuz th' year it wuz first *published*, imperfectly in quarto——."

"Whut th' God-damn-hell! . . . ," blurted One Tittie.

Jackson turned on him coldly. ". . . if you'd just let him talk."

Ramsey, on his bar stool, had finished his beer now and sat twisting and fidgeting.

"Lonnie," Bradley, the precinct captain, spoke up, "Hamlet's a story. Why don't you tell 'em the story. They'll understand *that*."

"*Hmmmmph!*" Lonnie scowled. "Th' story's only for th' unthinkin'—an' the unfeelin'. That's whut Prof said. Hell, *it* ain't nuthin', that is, compared to some uv th' deeper thangs. You just kinda hold onta th' story, in the back o' your mind, one-hand-like, while you're goin' in deeper—way deeper . . . inta th' other . . . ." Lonnie paused to clear his mind.

The beer drinkers—except churlish One Tittie—looked at each other.

"Lon, it *would* be better if you just went on an' told us th' story," Jackson, the bartender, now agreed. "Go ahead. And wuz *you* right, or wuz the other fella, Henry, right?"

". . . Henry wuz," Lonnie finally admitted. "He wuz really studyin' up on th' stuff—night an' day. I found out. Wuz ole Prof proud of him!—mighty proud. I started studyin' my head off then—grindin' an' grindin' away. Pretty soon ole Henry couldn't hold a candle to me. He never did ketch me down wrong after that! Now Prof wuz proud o' *me*. An' then . . . then back home in Memphis, my ole man got to drinkin' worse an' worse—with my little sisters right there in th' house. He wouldn't work, he wouldn't bring home any food, he wouldn't do nuthin'. So I had t'leave . . . I had t'leave Wirebridge, an' go on home. Finally, I brought m' sisters up here to Chicago, an' got a job. Pushin' a broom then wuz th' best I could get. 'Course I got a little better job now but it ain't much better."

"L-o-n-n-i-e," whined Ramsey, "th' little chick———."

". . . yeah," Lonnie mused, ". . . Ophelia."

"Why don't you go ahead now, Lon, an' tell us th' story," Jackson said.

Lonnie seemed not to hear. "After I dropped out, ole Prof wrote t'me—three or four times—an' said I wuz th' best Shakespeare student he evah had. Told me t'save my money an' hurry up an' come on back, just as soon as I could. Said it would be a shame if I didn't. Henry, he went on an' finished. Then he came up to Wisconsin, an' finished there. I saw his picture in *Jet* 'bout a year ago; he wuz teachin' English literature down at Fisk, in Nashville—that was Prof's ole school. When Prof passed, he willed all his books to Henry." Lonnie paused, smiled, cocked his head bravely, and fought tears. "*I* wuz th' one that shoulda had 'em."

There was silence.

Finally shivering Ramsey asked in awe: "Wuz Ophelia a pink-toe, Lonnie?"

Jackson glared at him, then turned to Lonnie. "Go on, Lon—tell us th' story. . . . Somethin's eatin' you. Maybe it'll help get it off your chest—whutaya bet?"

Lonnie sighed with impatience. "I said th' story ain't nuthin' . . . *nuthin'*. It's what's buried way down underneath th' story."—he reflected for a moment—". . . th' fucked-up world."

They sat in silence. Finally One Tittie swung around on his stool and stared down the short bar as if he had had enough. "He don't know th' God-damn story!" he breathed menacingly. "*Y'see?* You'kin stay here all night, and y'still won't git it!" he shouted. "'Cause *he don't know it!*"

Jackson, behind the bar, stood up,

Lonnie hung his head. ". . . Maybe I don't," he finally said. ". . . an' again maybe I *do*."

"He can tell it, or not," Jackson decreed. "—just as he sees fit. He don't have to . . . if he don't want to."

One Tittie now was coolly dead pan. "You girls mus' be sleepin' together," he said, his goat-eyes drilling Jackson.

Jackson froze. Then his big hands casually dragged down off the bar, as he half-turned behind him toward the little shelf beneath the cash register.

In the instant One Tittie's switch-blade was out and open. "G'wan an' reach fuh that God-damn rusty pistol! *G'wan!*"

Jackson continued bending around toward the little shelf.

One Tittie, scattering smashing bottles, vaulted, cleared the high bar, and drove the knife into Jackson's back.

Jackson let out a kind of bovine bellow, then groaned, as they crashed to the floor behind the bar; still stretching and clutching for his pistol, he broke wind. One Tittie, winding up now like a baseball pitcher, drove the knife home twice more, as Jackson screamed. Then One Tittie leaped up, stepped free of his victim, wheeled, and faced the others across the bar; he was crazed-eyed and waiting; finally he hurtled around the end of the bar and out of the door into the night.

They were all over and behind the bar at once, and pulled Jackson over onto his back and placed his legs out straight and close together. Lonnie was wringing his hands and jabbering softly, his mumbling resembling a witch doctor's incantations. ". . . git an ambulance! . . . aw, git an ambulance! . . . call th' police! . . . git him to th' hospital quick! . . . go git a doctor! . . . oh, Gawd! . . . hurry . . . *hurry up!*"

Jackson, prostrate, took a deep, deep breath and sighed heavily, his big eyes staring straight up, wide and surprised. He moved his lips as if to speak, as a big tear ran off his cheekbone. Then suddenly a universe of fright came in his eyes, before finally his jaw dropped and he was gone.

Lonnie fell on his knees beside him and clutched up the dead man's hand and, shaking as in zero cold, tried to speak to him. All the others leaned over into the huddle, craning in to see. A moment passed. Then Lonnie on his knees bent down low to the floor and, still trembling, peered into Jackson's popping, vacant eyes, but soon looked away.

Ramsey, the paretic, in a frenzy and chattering wildly to himself, lurched from the huddle. "It's turrible!—o-o-o-h, it's turrible! It's all *his* fault!"—he pointed a bony, accusatory finger down at Lonnie, who gazed around at them all without seeing or hearing. "He wouldn't tell it! He wouldn't tell us the story!"

After the Ball

Outside it was a cold bright February day, but inside, Abigail Rivers sat in her elegant bedroom primping for her father. She always dressed carefully for him, the distinguished high appeals court judge, recently widowed, who was coming to lunch today. Clad only in panty girdle, slip, and mules, Abby, as her friends called her, leaned forward before the dresser mirror plucking her eyebrows with silver tweezers. Besides, tomorrow night, Friday, was the ball—her new short chic red dress had been delivered only that morning—and she was thinking of how well she would look on this gala occasion. It was already past eleven o'clock now and the sun, streaming in at the windows of the lavish apartment, made all sorts of weird, geometric, rainbow configurations on the thick pile of the lemon carpet.

Abby was still, at forty-one, a beautiful woman, but she had been reminded of this fact for so long by everybody that she had come to believe what was really her luck was some signal achievement of her own. An only child, she had always been pleased with herself and the way she looked—with her smooth nut-brown complexion, shapely limbs, strong white teeth responsible for her sensual smile, and a high, intelligent hair line.

Also in many ways she resembled her mother, Gertrude—deceased only five months—and friends of the family often commented on it. Like Gertrude's, Abby's facial features seemed only semi-Negroid, somehow vaguely Caribbean, with perhaps a dash of French; there was the beautiful *cafe au lait* skin, the crested cheekbones, the explicit, piercing eyes, the protuberant (pouting) lips . . . the fleet, impatient, yet dazzling smile.

Always the passion of Abby's life had been her father, whom she sat preening for today. And now that even the youngest of her three children was away at a girls' school, the other two at colleges, and her busy husband, Charles, at this very hour aboard a Cleveland-bound plane on business—he'd be back in time for his social club's ball tomorrow night—Abby, alone at last, had immediately telephoned her father in his spacious, walnut-paneled chambers and invited him to come to lunch.

At such times she took keenest pleasure in looking her alluring best, as well-turned-out, exciting, as careful effort could make her. The Honorable Thaddeus Roland Toye, judge on the United States Court of Appeals in Chicago, Bachelor of Arts, Juris Doctor, holder of four honorary degrees, symphony trustee, was a man of gravely fastidious sensibilities and, wittingly or not, had influenced his daughter in the glamorous way in which she always wished to appear before him. He was also piercingly observant, nervous, fragile, of poetic temperament, and latently tyrannical, and would sit watching Abby's every movement, making mental, wistful comments in his inmost soul. "Papa," she would nervously laugh, "if I caught any other man looking at me like that, I wouldn't like it a bit—not even Charles!" The judge would only look puzzled, and then sigh, seeing nothing funny in her remark.

Yet for this ominously eccentric mystery enveloping him she adored him. She understood that his utter addiction to her was a fact she could depend on as long as he lived—which would be always, she had almost, in her own idolatry, brought herself to believe. So she felt it necessary, and proper, that he be given freest opportunity to admire her. She could conjure up his image in a flash, thinking of how he walked so erectly for a man of seventy-one, though he was only moderately tall. Yet despite his uncertain health and high blood pressure there was such elegance in his gait, an air of finest breeding in his clothing, his hammered gold cuff links, the cologne for men, his soft tannish color, and silken gray hair now thinning on top, that she could recall no rarer pleasure, no deeper inward thrill, than their recent walks together in the old neighborhood, sometimes, in the sadness just after her mother's death, hand in hand, in the crisp, bright October weather, maples towering overhead, leaves on the sidewalk swirling about their feet, and despite everything, her heart cascading joy.

Yet over the years there had been occasional ruptures in this idyllic relationship. The first occurred when she was sixteen. She had left the small Minnesota college where her parents had just sent her and run off and married a penniless black basketball star. Her parents' reaction, especially her father's, was one of shock and disbelief, and, in time, quiet outrage. They at once set about systematically to undo the marriage, the father warning the daughter, at last in desperation begging her, not to have a child. But all the alarm was unnecessary, for even without this opposition, only a miracle could have saved the marriage. Yet it struggled on for eleven months more—Abby leaving the boy twice but each time returning—until at last it was formally ended by divorce.

Afterwards she was sent no farther than the University of Chicago, her father's alma mater, so that now she'd be living at home. She took her studies seriously for almost three years, then strangely, and to the appalled consternation of her father, left the university before graduating. Her purpose again, it soon developed, was marriage—to Charles Rivers, a young black engineer and industrial designer, whom she, by sheerest chance, had met only two months before. Her mother liked Charles well enough but her father secretly loathed him, and accused Abby of instability, impulsiveness, even hinting strongly at perfidy. But Abby was impressed, awed, by her father's displeasure and, though unaware of it, had never loved him so much as now.

But in the ensuing years Charles Rivers had marvelously prospered. He had made his money not only in the engineering profession, but in canny real estate and other investments. And now, after almost twenty years of marriage, and three nearly grown children—Kenny, Caroline, and Susie—Abby found herself living an even more affluent life than she had lived with her parents. There were the three cars, the two maids, foreign travel, and recently Charles had moved his family into a large, luxurious condominium apartment on the thirty-sixth floor of exclusive Swearingen Towers, on the near Northside, with a grand, sweeping view of Lake Michigan. To placate her overweening ego now, Abby entertained lavishly. Her parties were among the most superbly catered and talked-about, and more than ever she was lionized, flattered, and sought after as one of the four or five reigning leaders of black society—an elusive enclave referred to by one impressed white society editor as Chicago's "*le haut monde noir.*"

Abby derived a jaded excitement from every minute of her present life-style, when she was not thinking about her father. And she thought of him often—constantly, some of her friends felt, for her extreme, bizarre feelings about him were well known to them all. There were few conversations with any of them in which she would not find some pretext for referring to him—to "Papa." Over luncheon cocktails, or at a women's brunch, or the Arts Club, she might be heard to say, "Papa's even put a little stereo-phonograph in his bedroom now and this month is playing all of his Haydn records—especially the string quartets." Or on the telephone to a friend, "Did you see Papa's picture in the *Daily News* yesterday? . . . about the opinion he wrote in the railroad strike injunction case? Did he slave on that case!" Or in the candlelight of a sumptuous mixed dinner party—where there were whites—she might say, "My father believes so strongly in the black revolution that he disqualifies himself from participation in many of these cases coming up to his court." (When in fact she knew, or suspected, the judge's views on the subject were, like her own, at best equivocal.) Or on an occasion like tomorrow night's ball, her invited guests—the Manns and the Sheppards—were already amused by the certainty that Abby would talk almost constantly about her father. It was her one predictable trait, her passion.

Judge Toye arrived for lunch at twenty minutes past noon. Abby met him in the entrance foyer of her apartment wearing a beautiful pink plaid suit, with a tiny magenta scarf at the throat, and her eyelids bearing just a trace of green eyeshadow. But they were eyes bright with happiness, and even before she took his overcoat she ran her arm around his fragile waist and smiled boyishly at him, saying, "Papa, you're getting better looking every day, do you know it?" Faintly smiling, whimsical, he handed her his hat and coat, then bent over stiffly and pulled off his overshoes. "Your hair's so pretty," she said, "and almost white. Papa, is that another new suit? The other day—remember?—you were wearing a beautiful dark striped suit, and English shoes! My, oh, my!— are you *elegant* these days! If Mama were here she'd be looking at you out of the corner of her eye with that skeptical, amused smile of hers—I can see her now. Wait a minute! . . . you're not getting ready to turn up here with some rich widow, are you?"

He gave her a brief, tentative, yet observant smile. "Not that I know of," he said.

Suddenly she closed her eyes and kissed him blindly, im- pulsively, on his little white mustache. "How're you getting along?" she whispered, and squeezed his hand, ". . . tell me."

"Oh, I'm doing all right, I guess," he said, and walked heedlessly ahead of her out of the foyer, slight hauteur in his step, into her elaborate, luxurious parlor.

"Want a drink, Papa?" she said happily.

"No, thanks . . . oh, maybe I will have a little sherry." He gazed at her as he sat down on the lush, oyster-white sofa. "When have you heard from the children? Caroline got over her cold all right, did she?"

"Yes, she's back at classes—they've had a terrible winter in Wisconsin, in Madison. But wait till you hear about Kenny."

"Yes?—ha, Kenny."

"He wants to move out of the dormitory and get an apart- ment, with a couple of other boys. He says he can study better. Charles had to go to Cleveland this morning on business, just overnight—the Pelican Club's dinner and ball is tomorrow night, you know—but he'll see Kenny while he's there and give him a hearing on this apartment business!"

The judge sighed. "Well, Kenny will soon be twenty."

"That's right, Papa. He thinks he's a full-fledged man right now, though. He's even grown a scrubby little beard since you saw him, and wears an Afro haircut. Ha!—oh, that Kenny!"

"Get my sherry, will you?"

"He's writing poetry, too, you know. 'Black' poetry, he calls it. He's very race-conscious—very race-proud."

"Well, my father wrote poetry when he was in the Yale Divinity School," the judge said. "It wasn't 'black' poetry, though—whatever that is." He sniffed testily, but soon sighed again—"Get my sherry, will you, please?"

Abby left and went into the adjacent dining area, almost all of which was visible from the parlor, as his eyes followed her. She took two small crystal goblets out of the huge Sheraton breakfront and poured their sherrys, saying, "My little Susie, bless her heart, gives me less trouble than any of them. And writes me long air-mail letters from Putney—always air-mails them, ha!"

The judge, all the while watching her, finally smiled.

"But, Papa, that's not what I wanted to talk to you about." She was returning to the parlor now, and gave him his sherry, then, her own in hand, sat down on the sofa beside him. "Do you know what Charles asked me the other evening?" she said—"He wanted to know why you don't come live with us now. We've got plenty of room here, certainly—even when the children are home."

The judge had sat up. ". . . Oh, I couldn't do that."

"Papa, stop being mulish! Charles mentioned it again this morning. . . . I'd said something about your going to bed at night in that big old house alone."

He looked away, shaking his head. "No, no, that wouldn't do."

"*Why* wouldn't it? . . . Oh, Papa, you shouldn't be living alone."

"I'm making out," he said, but in a tone of dejection. "I'm looking around for another cook, though. Della's getting too old—and crabby. Besides, she's wanted to quit ever since your mother died, I think—she was very fond of your mother. But it's too much for you to expect of me, to close up the house. And I wouldn't want to sell it—you wouldn't want me to."

Abby grew pensive. "No, I wouldn't want you to do that," she said. "As long as we've got that house at least it'll seem as though Mama's a little nearer. You're a brave man, Papa—how do you do it?"

Now he took a quick sip of his sherry and seemed not to hear her. ". . . That house need not be so dead . . . so lonely," he suddenly mused aloud. Then with a soft vehe-

mence—"It's *very* dead now." He stared at her—"I've thought
of how it was before you left . . . and how it would be if you
returned. . . ."

Abby turned to him, with a baffled look. ". . . if I . . . ."

"*Yes*"—again vehemently—"doesn't that make just as
much sense as my coming to live *here!* Ah . . . ." Suddenly
the spasm in his face was gone, giving way to a strange trance-
like expression.

". . . Papa, I don't understand you . . . ."

He only gazed at her now.

She stumbled on. ". . . Although our big old house, full
of memories and all that, is still a very nice place to live in,
Charles wouldn't think for a moment of moving out of here.
He'd wonder if I'd lost my mind if I suggested it."

"You are right, you *don't* understand me!" he said, and
coldly sipped his sherry.

She looked at him wide-eyed.

"You agree, don't you," he said, more temperately, "that
we should be together."

". . . Yes, Papa, yes!—why am I asking you to come
live here?"

"Oh, how *could* I?" he said impatiently. "Charles and I
could never live under the same roof."

"Apparently he doesn't think so. Oh, Papa! . . . ."

The judge glared. "Charles knows I'd be living in *his* house
then—subject to *his* jurisdiction." He jerked off his glasses and
cleaned them roughly with his breast pocket handkerchief.

"Oh, Papa, how you imagine things! You've never been
quite fair to Charles."

He looked at her for a moment, but did not answer. At last
he reached and nervously drained his sherry and set the glass
on the end table.

Abby put her own sherry aside now and got up, her face

drawn, distressed. "Come on," she said. "I've fixed some lunch for us—Lulu's off today."

Soon he followed her into the dining area, where she served each of them a small broiled lamb chop, buttered asparagus spears, a tiny water-cress salad, and garlic bread, with a chilled German rosé wine. They ate in silence.

Finally she looked at him dolefully and said, "Papa, I want you to promise me you'll think over what I've asked you. You shouldn't be living alone."

Leaning forward, his wrists on the edge of the table, he gazed at her. "You ignore *my* suggestion," he said, quivering with emotion. "A simple suggestion . . . the old house need not be so dead any more." He began masticating his food, then with a trembling hand touched his lips with his napkin, feigning composure.

"Papa, I'm *sure* I don't understand you!" Again her voice was full of distress. "Are you saying . . . are you saying I should leave my husband? . . . leave my children? . . . and . . . and come . . . ." She stopped. Then, ". . . is that what . . . ." She could not finish.

He was still watching her. At last he leaned across the table again and, almost tenderly, whispered it: "Abigail, I am saying that you should be *faithful to your destiny!*"

Gaping at him, she could not speak, as the final glimmerings of horror came on her face.

Suddenly the judge raised both hands to his head, putting his finger tips to his temples and pressing hard, as if to quell some violent disturbance inside. Then he made a painful grimace, before seeming almost to wilt in his chair.

Abby was oblivious. "*Papa! . . . Papa! . . . what are you saying? . . . !*"

He only gave a piteous little hacking cough and looked away. Finally, his hand groping, he extended his wine glass. ". . . more, please," he said hoarsely.

At last she poured more wine into his glass, still staring at him.

He took a quick swallow of it. "*You're* responsible!" he said, gulping, trembling. "I say, if you're shocked, you're responsible! But you're *not* shocked . . . no, no! . . . you're a mischievous, almost evil person. Your cruelty knows no bounds! . . . it's a sacrilege, really . . . *inhuman!* . . . oh!" He threw up his hands, then seemed to wilt again. ". . . Ah, yes," he said finally, in resignation—"You've abandoned me now, and I accept it. But, oh Abby, for my weakness, which knowingly or not, you have nourished, have pity on me! Don't think *too* harshly of me, but have pity . . . have pity . . . ." His voice faltered, then died away to a whisper, almost a whimper.

Abby could say nothing. Her eyes were filled with tears of revelation, wonder . . . horror.

Afterwards, she served them cranshaw melon and black coffee, and they finished their meal in silence. When, at one forty-five, he prepared to go, he looked old and tired, almost haggard, as he feebly stooped to put on his overshoes. Abby, her eyelashes still wet, was silent, and seemed clumsy, unsure of herself, as she helped him with his overcoat. When he had gone, she stood in the middle of her parlor for a long, long time, trying hard to understand what really had happened. Finally she sat down on the sofa and cried again a little, but for the moment her tears caused her no pain. There was only confusion, doubt, irresolution, and she quickly got up and dried her face, then smoked a long, lacquer-tipped cigarette.

Friday evening, the reception, dinner, and ball were resplendent affairs. At seven-thirty it was snowing lightly as the guests began to arrive at the Continental Plaza Hotel. At the main entrance, uniformed doormen met the big shiny black cars pulling up under the canopy and disgorging their occu-

pants—the women radiant, bejeweled, and dripping furs, with
filmy scarves thrown over their wigs or fresh coiffures against
the falling snow. In the Grand Cotillion Room, the pre-ball
reception was just beginning and would last for an hour, after
which dinner would be served in the north wing of the room,
where there was also a sleek floor for later dancing.

Abby and Charles arrived at eight, Charles tall, brown, still
athletic-looking in his tuxedo. They checked their wraps—
Abby had worn her chinchilla coat—and entered the noisy
cocktail party and reception. She was beautiful in her new
short red dress, but was plainly wretched and preoccupied.
Yesterday the pain had finally returned with a vengeance and
she had slept hardly at all that night and had brooded and
moped all day today. The luncheon had changed everything.
Now it was her wild, terrible thoughts, her agony, that monopolized her mind. Moreover, the ordeal had changed slowly,
metamorphosed, into a strange, numbing fear which grew by
the hour. Had her father been right in what he had said? she
continually asked herself. *Was* she responsible? . . . *was*
she evil? . . . and, most excruciating of all, *had* she abandoned him? Her own uncertainty shocked her and soon the
old dread returned with its inevitable glimpses of horror that
had kept her awake all night.

Although it was not overly large, the Grand Cotillion Room
was truly grand. Its art and statuary gave it elegance, while
its low crystal-chandeliered ceiling preserved its intimacy. A
strolling trio of musicians—violin, accordion, and bass—
moved among the two hundred guests, playing old and new
hit tunes, as the busy cocktail waiters plied everyone with a
variety of drinks. Almost all the guests had arrived now and
the cocktail-party noise had considerably increased. The host
Pelican Club, of which Charles was a member, was a very
snooty organization, and always gave a snooty ball—an in-
vitation was a badge of social prowess. Abby soon rounded up

her four guests, the Solomon Manns and Jack Sheppards, and, drinks in hand, they all stood in a group talking.

But her mind, in a painful reverie, was elsewhere. Was it true, she persisted in wondering, that she had abandoned her father? If so, how could she possibly have brought herself to do it? . . . *no matter what.* The thought made her eyes sting—he was disillusioned, bitter, and utterly alone now, and was sure she had abandoned him; had even, ruefully, said he accepted it. At this, her remorse rose and swelled in her throat, producing an inward sob. Yet how could she do his bidding, now knowing, understanding, his inmost macabre, desolate mind? For then she would become an acquiescing mental partner. And what of her family, her *children?* . . . again she was shocked, to the point of doubting her own sanity. Now anguish was so plain on her face that Charles was looking curiously at her. At once she raised her drink and gave him her dazzling smile. *"Salud!"* she said.

The Manns, Sheppards, and Rivers were old friends. Well-to-do Solomon Mann, thin and very dark, owned a printing and engraving company, while Jack Sheppard was managing partner in a firm of black certified public accountants. "Let's leave this awful crush!" Abby said to them distressfully over the noise—"Let's take our drinks to our table." Soon they left the reception area, went forward, and sat down comfortably at Charles' table. Surrounding them, the white linen-covered tables were arranged around the dance floor in a broad horseshoe, each table with its own floral centerpiece and six matching *Louis Quinze* chairs. Now others began leaving the cocktail party and coming in to their tables, for the reception was almost over. Soon the strolling musicians began moving among the guests again. "Oh, doesn't the little violinist play beautifully!" exclaimed Abby, trying frantically to seem animated, a sudden, wild fire in her eyes.

Yet she could not even briefly free her thoughts of her calamity. She looked on the crisis, however, as finally narrowing itself now, converging, becoming sharper in outline, and perhaps dissipating some of her confusion. She had had intimations of this earlier in the evening whenever she thought of her father's one telling accusation—her abandonment of him. It was to this charge she was most sensitive, vulnerable, before it the most pathetically weak, because of the strange, manic love she bore him—ironically, a love so powerful, so bordering on paranoia, it had become both blind and pitiably helpless, making her in the process its victim also. Could it be conceivably true, she asked herself for the *nth* time, tortured by the possibility, that she had abandoned him? She was rational enough to see it depended on what abandonment meant, yet knew she was not guilty in any real sense. Then, if in any, in what sense? With a sinking feeling, she realized he viewed their situation in a more demanding, literal light. But this somehow only deepened, intensified, her flood of pity for him in his confessed condition. No matter, she told herself, what aberrant thoughts his mind, so foreign to her now, had harbored, how could she forsake him? At the moment she would not give herself an answer, yet her will was slowly, tortuously, moving toward what was for her an inescapable state of fulfillment.

Just then, olive-skinned Dorothy Gilman, a friend of Abby's, was passing the table. When she saw Abby she smiled happily, stopped, and the women all talked for a moment. As she was leaving, she routinely inquired of Judge Toye. Abby froze. *"Oh, Papa's fine!"* she quickly smiled, showing her dazzling teeth. Then, contrary to everyone's expectations, she dropped the subject at once, as Ruth Solomon and Edith Sheppard looked incredulously at each other.

When the last stragglers from the reception came in to their tables, they found that the cocktail noise had preceded them, although the dinner waiters, in their wing collars and little

maroon tailcoats, were already entering with the soup. Later
there was filet mignon with claret, as Abby tried hard to keep
up with the fun and talk at her table. Yet her mind was freer
now, her decision really made. What before had been tentative
had become final and absolute. Now her thoughts dealt purely
with planning—she was already thinking of how she would
prevail upon her father to get rid of the old leather sofa in the
solarium, where it had been gathering dust almost since her
girlhood; she would install more cheerful furniture there.
But nothing much could be done about the huge, dark, old-
fashioned kitchen, except possibly to replace its crumbling
walltile and below that lay some bright now linoleum. And
her mother's room? . . . she caught her breath, conscious of
the feeling of discomfort; the room's closet space was terribly
cramped, inadequate, she thought nonetheless; especially for
a large, a very large, wardrobe . . . like her own. This must
be remedied. And Mama's clothes? . . . there was no other
way, at last they must go to the Salvation Army. But the
thought jarred her, as the knife of guilt went into her heart.
She sat merely picking at her food now.

It was dessert time, and the strolling trio was still moving
among the tables, although already some young black musicians, comprising the ten-piece dance band, had now made
their appearance at the upper end of the dance floor and were
setting up their instruments and equipment, preparing for the
dancing soon to follow. Abby still ate mechanically and wondered how she would tell Charles, explain to the family, especially to Susie, who would at once discuss the matter at length
in a series of air-mail letters—the thought of Susie brought a
mute cry in her throat. Yet the answer came quickly—she
would not tell them. It would be *her* secret, locked inside herself—unknown even to her father. *No* one would know until
time came to act. She felt so tolerant now, and tender, toward
her father, and sought more than ever to tear from her mind

the horror and desolation of yesterday's luncheon. She craved to exculpate him and made herself wonder what he'd meant by what he'd said . . . what had he *really* meant? Continually searching for ways to acquit him, or at least to raise huge doubts, she was soon glad to feel herself slipping again into total confusion. She wanted to feel responsibility only for her own thoughts and deeds now—not his. She would no longer try to go inside his mind; it was too unique, too complex a mechanism for her ever accurately to read. She felt warned— she might *mis*-read it, and do him a colossal injustice . . . if she hadn't already made this unthinkable mistake. Suddenly again her heart was flooded with the tenderest pity for him— to her, the wisest, best, and greatest of men. He needed her. Then she confessed it—she needed him. Yes, yes—she would return! . . . gladly, and with a penitent heart. She would return to that house, *their house*, even if it had to be accomplished gradually—begun, say, by staying weekends, or maybe at first, only every other weekend; then *every* weekend and more . . . until . . . later . . . perhaps a little later . . . then . . . then . . . . She could drive her reckless thoughts no farther, yet knew now she could only do what she must.

Suddenly the dance music started—loud, agitated, groovey. The young band was playing an advanced, frantic type of Motown beat, especially in the bass and thudding drums. Charles, laughing, pulled Abby up, led her to the dance floor, and they danced. By the time of the second set, the floor was jam-packed and the band was giving its all—beads of perspiration already stood on the foreheads of some of the men dancing, and the beautifully-gowned women seemed trying both to maintain their dignity and recapture their youth. The dancing continued for almost an hour and Abby danced with the other men at her table and Charles the women. Her unalterable decision made, she began to feel for the first time a vague lifting of the dead weight that had earlier borne her down. She talked and laughed with her guests and seemed suddenly warm, spirited, genial—almost her old captivating self again.

During a twenty-minute intermission in the dancing, a brief ceremony took place. An award was conferred on the club member who during the past year had made some notable contribution in his chosen field or profession—this year it was a victorious civil rights lawyer. Immediately following, the club's newly-elected slate of officers was formally installed—in earlier years often by Judge Toye, as Abby too-well remembered—and then for a few minutes everyone relaxed, awaiting the final hour of dancing.

The intermission was almost over, and Charles, Abby, and their guests were still seated at their table, when Charles saw John Gaston, a fellow club member, approaching—leading a hotel attendant, a uniformed, blond young man, toward them. "Charles," Gaston said, nodding toward the attendant, "he's got a telephone call for you."

Charles looked at the two men—then across the table at Abby, who too had heard. "Who would be calling me here?" he laughed to them all, as he got up. He left with the attendant, and Abby's eyes followed them over the rich red carpet and out of sight.

"This way, sir," the attendant said, as they passed through the reception area and out of the Grand Cotillion Room. Just outside, in the red-carpeted hall and to the left of the marble colonnade, he pointed out to Charles a French telephone next to a great gilt mirror. Charles tipped him a dollar, picked up the phone, and soon learned he was talking to some administrative person, a young woman, at Wesley Memorial Hospital.

"You're Mr. Rivers . . . ?" she said brightly. ". . . Judge Toye's son-in-law? Judge Toye is in the hospital. He was brought here earlier in the evening—ill."

"Is that true?" But Charles' mind was not adjusting. He

swallowed. ". . . Ill? . . . I can be right over there—I will. I'm not far from you. I appreciate your locating me. What's the nature of his illness? . . . is it serious?"

"He's unconscious. The doctors are with him now—he may have suffered a stroke, from what they say."

"Can you imagine? . . . I'll be right over . . . ." Charles was vaguely hanging up, already wondering how he would tell Abby, and dreading having to do it. Or should he tell her at all . . . right now? He should go to the hospital by himself . . . tell her later—how long would it take? He still stood at the phone, trying to make up his mind. No, no, that wouldn't do, he thought—he couldn't go off and leave her without explaining what was up, where he was going.

He went back into the Grand Cotillion Room, to their table, and told them immediately—trying to keep his voice steady. "I've got to go to Wesley Hospital," he said. "The judge is ill. They've taken him there."

Abby stood up. Then sat down at once. "What's the matter with Papa?" she said—at first all but politely. ". . . What's . . ."—then her voice thinned, became almost a plea. Charles hesitated. Now a distraught, wild look came on her face as if she would scream. But soon she controlled herself and leaned back in her chair, looking searchingly at Charles. The Manns and Sheppards leaned forward. Just then the dance music started up again, and Abby almost shrieked it—"*What's the matter with him, Charles?*"

"They think he's had a stroke." Charles spoke over the crashing music. "He's unconscious."

"Oh, God!" she breathed.

Everyone around them now was getting up to dance.

"I'm going to the hospital," Charles said. "It's just down on Superior Street."

"I'm going with you, Charles!" Abby's voice was strange, hollow, as she stood up again. Their guests got up too. "I know you'll understand," she finally said to them—"Papa's ill . . . ." Seeming almost in a dream now, she said it as if informing someone who had just walked up.

But the Manns and Sheppards, themselves concerned, protested they could not possibly enjoy the rest of the evening knowing the judge was ill—they would go home. All six went out, got their wraps, and left the hotel. It was still snowing lightly as Charles got the car and drove Abby directly to the hospital.

They found the judge in a private room in a coma. A young doctor told them he had suffered a massive cerebral hemorrhage, that his condition was frankly grave.

Della, the judge's old cook, still in her sweater and galoshes, sat at the foot of the bed like a glum, omniscient sentinel. Abby, too stunned to cry, merely stood over the bed, staring down incredulously into her father's face. Under the white covers up to his arm pits, he lay on his back with his eyes closed, his breathing measured and easy, as if he were asleep. Stolid, philosophical, sometimes harsh, old Della sat shaking her head and half-talking to herself, perhaps praying. "It took me almost an hour t'raise a doctor," she soon muttered sadly— "and longer'n that to get an ambulance."

"Was the judge at home when it happened?" Charles asked.

"Indeed he was."

"Had he complained?"

Della gave him a level gaze. "The judge *never* complained." Then for a moment she was silent. "Yet somethin' was worryin' him," she said. "I could see it—worryin' him bad. He wasn't himself . . . hadn't been for a couple of days—yesterday, particularly . . . up in his room he was walkin' the floor all the time I was cookin' his dinner, and later ate just like a bird."

Charles took off his overcoat and hung it and his Homburg in the closet—as Abby still stood staring down dry-eyed at her father.

"This evenin' I'd just served him his dessert," Della said, "when he put his hand up and gripped his forehead, like suddenly he'd got a terrible bad headache. Then he just slumped over in his chair, and that was it."

Abby exhaled audibly, almost in a groan, and her face was drawn and hard. Soon Charles took her coat from her as he would a child's and hung it in the closet, leaving her to stand over her father in her short chic red dress. The judge's delicate hands—tan-blanched, veins standing high—lay on top of the covers, as she reached and touched his forehead with the back of her hand, then stared down into his peaceful face again, oblivious of everything around her. Della and Charles could only look on, but finally Charles, sighing nervously, went over and sat in the chair against the wall. It was eleven twenty-five and the room was very quiet.

But in a few minutes Charles, restless, impatient, got up again. "I'm going to find some doctors around here," he said— "I want to see what they're doing for Papa, what treatment they've got in mind for him. They don't seem to be doing anything now—I'm going to go have a talk with somebody."

Della shook her head irascibly. "Doctors!" she said— "There's been a room full of 'em in here, ever since I brought him here."

"Do they know who he is?" Charles said.

"Indeed they do—I told 'em in a hurry. There's been plenty of doctors, and plenty of nurses, and all kinds of machines in here. They've done everything they could."

"I'm going to go try to phone a doctor I know, at his home," Charles said—"Dr. Reichmann. He's supposed to be very good on something like this—strokes. We've got to call in somebody for consultation on Papa—right away." Soon he left the room and went down the hall toward the elevators.

"Wastin' his time and that doctor's too," Della grumbled as he left. Then her face lengthened in sorrow again.

Abby still stood over the judge. His breathing was so peaceful it could barely be detected.

Finally Della spoke in a mournful, resigned voice. "Abby, let's pray. Let's get down on our knees right here and pray. I've talked to all the doctors, young and old. Not one of 'em give him till mornin'. Doctor Jesus is the only one that can save him now."

But Abby had become almost as rigid as if she had turned to stone, and her staring eyes, trained on her father's face, shone with a fanatic's luster.

"*Abby!* . . . *Abby!*" Della cried, suddenly scooting forward in her chair, ". . . Open up that hard, bitter, Godless heart of yours and let the Lord come into it! . . . Get down on your knees and pray for your father!"

Abby only stared stolidly now into the judge's face. "It's too late," she finally said absently in a hoarse whisper, half to Della, half to her father. ". . . too late . . . ." At last a few tears came down her cheeks and dropped off the point of her chin, but at once she stopped crying and seemed to become even more stark, unyielding, her eyes dazzling in their strange insanity. The room was deathly quiet and Della sat gaping in awe.

Minutes passed.

"Why was he so crazy about you?" Della said. ". . . Ah, a papa's love—I never saw anything like it."

Abby seemed deaf, inanimate.

Della gazed out the window onto the lights of the city. "Your mama herself used to wonder," she said. "And worry, too, sometimes. Ah, Lord—bless her heart. . . ."

Silence.

"Well, he's goin' to leave you now," Della said. "You've got to face it. You're blessed, though, with a good husband—and three *wonderful* children. You ought to thank God for that."

Abby's eyes had not left her father's face.

A Gift

Cora didn't mind going to a lawyer's office half as much as she did to a doctor's. A lawyer didn't keep a big office full of people waiting for hours, and probably the worst you'd hear from *him* was that you didn't have a case—you weren't always getting the sweats, or that dull ache in the crater of your stomach. But then right away, sitting in the lawyer's tiny outer office with the two other clients, she remembered she wasn't there on a picnic, exactly. She breathed a solemn little sigh and continued thumbing through the old *Life* magazine she'd found in the chair. A hot, dusty beam of sunlight filtered through the window toward her feet, spotlighting the frayed hole in the carpet; and soon the newsboy clumped in and tossed the afternoon paper on the table.

The office of Thaddeus M. Campbell, attorney and counsellor-at-law, had no receptionist; the waiting clients went in to him in the order in which they had come, and it was Cora's turn next. The two other clients, both women, were chewing gum and biding their time. Finally, the one who had come in last—she was squat, very bow-legged and, like Cora, getting on in years—said, nodding her head toward the inner office, "The lawyer's *in* there, ain't he?"

"Yeah, he's in there. He ain't been back long, though," the younger woman said, looking for confirmation at Cora, who nodded politely and smiled.

"He's mostly in court in the mornin's," the bow-legged woman said, in a know-it-all manner. "Got more business'n he can take care of."

Cora and the younger woman looked pleasant and said nothing.

"Who's in there with him?" asked Bow-legs.

"Some girl," the younger woman finally said, shrugging.

"Uh-huh, I thought so. Divorce, probably. He gets a lot of them. These young kids'll marry at the drop of a hat, y'know; an' get divorced the same way—babies or no babies." She crossed her leg and put a cigarette in her mouth. "He kinda likes these young chicks, too," she cackled softly, leaning forward and nodding again toward the inner office, where voices could now be heard and shadows seen moving behind the frosted-glass door.

The door opened, and ebony-hued Mr. Campbell ushered out a gimlet-eyed brown girl, about twenty. He looked surprised, and a little flustered, to see the three women there, although two of them had been waiting when the girl went in. Then a broad, sheepish smile rippled his face: "Now, who's next, ladies?" Bow-legs' shoulders shook with pent-up hilarity.

Cora looked thin as she stood up and gently tugged her dress away from her warm body. "I think I'm next, Lawyer." She looked around at the other women.

"All rightie! Step right in," said Mr. Campbell. He was average-sized, in his late fifties, and now rather wilted from the humidity, in his gray suit and white shirt. Cora stepped shyly by him to go in.

The dinky outer office gave no clue whatever to the appearance of his private office, which was large and comfortable—although dusty in places—and showed off high, book-lined walls. There was also the impression, from the cluttered accumulation of papers and files, that he had occupied the premises for years. Hanging rather askew on the wall behind his desk was a bamboo-framed motto (a warning): 'A Lawyer's *Time* Is His Only Stock-in-Trade.'

Mr. Campbell deftly closed the door behind Cora and pointed to a red leather arm chair at the side of his desk. "Have a seat right here, little lady." He patted the back of the chair with his dark finger tips.

Cora sat down on the front half of the chair and held herself erect, her small hands folded across the white purse in her lap, as Mr. Campbell stepped around behind the desk and sat down in his swivel chair. He reached across the desk blotter for his pen, and poised it over an open ledger, as Cora noted the big Masonic ring on his finger.

"And now, let's see—your name?" He was twisting his hips in the chair to get comfortable.

"Cora Jones."

"Missus?"—He was writing.

"Yes, it is," said Cora with a wisp of a smile—but her brown face was drained and wan. Missus!—she knew *she* didn't look like any frumpy old maid!

After he took down her address and telephone number, he reached forward with careful pomposity to return the pen to its desk holder. Then he reared back. "And now, Mrs. Jones, let's talk." His elaborate preparations amused her and partly relieved her tensions, as did his Stygian, smiling face—a face neatly concave, with the lower lip thick and heavy-hanging and baring a red lining glistening with saliva.

"By the way—," he suddenly said, "have you been in before?"

"No."

"Well—I just wondered."

"You spoke one time at our church—on Women's Day," Cora said. "Root Street Baptist."

Mr. Campbell threw back his head in an ivory buck-toothed laugh. "Well! I remember that! How *was* my talk?—pretty good?"

"*I* thought so," Cora laughed.

Then her smiles dissolved. "Lawyer, I came to see you about havin' my will made out."

"Well—you *did?*" Mr. Campbell, only now finishing his laugh, nodded with approval. "Your last will and testament, eh?—hereby revoking all former wills and codicils by you heretofore made!" His finger tips mirthfully drummed the desk blotter, as Cora gave a faint little uncomprehending smile. "Well," he said, "before we get into the technicalities of the thing, tell me a little about yourself—your situation. That always helps, y'know—we get a better picture. A lawyer has to have a pretty clear—."

"Lawyer," Cora cut in, "my picture ain't hard to get. I just want to will what I got to my husband." She surprised herself.

"Oh . . . ," said Mr. Campbell, his spirits blunted. He drummed the blotter again, thoughtfully. "Any children?"

Cora hesitated—. "Yes, I got two boys . . . by my first husband. But they don't figure in this—they're both grown, with families. They don't even live in Chicago." She was irked. She didn't see what *they* had to do with it. Everything she had was going to Albert—the way they'd treated him all these years! . . . and they hadn't been decent enough to come when she was in the hospital, and knowing she was all by herself after Albert's trouble. Well, Albert had been nicer to her in five minutes than their father was the whole time before she got fed up and walked out. "A will's all I need, then, ain't it?" Cora said to Mr. Campbell.

"Well now, Mrs. Jones, that all depends . . . it all depends. Is there real estate?"

". . . Like a house? Yes, I got a house."

"What else?" probed Mr. Campbell, on the initiative again.

"Just a bank account—and I got a few war bonds."

"Whose name is the bank account in?"

"Mine."

"Well, a joint account would almost take care of your situation." Mr. Campbell was smug now. "Why, yes . . . as to the cash certainly—why don't you and your husband handle it that way?"

Cora stalled and strove for coolness. "Albert . . . he's away right now."

Mr. Campbell looked puzzled. "For long?" he asked.

There was an uncertain silence. Then she sighed, "Lawyer—he's in Statesville."

"Oh-h-h . . . ," Mr. Campbell breathed, leaning forward. "Well . . . isn't that something." He swivelled his chair around and gazed out the window at the big Shell Oil sign across the street. "When'll he be back?" he finally asked.

"I don't know, Lawyer. I wish I did. He ain't up for parole for two years yet."

Mr. Campbell swivelled back and faced her. "Well, that's not too bad—it could be a whole lot worse." Cora knew he itched to know what Albert had done. Finally he leaned forward again and, in an anxious, coaxing whisper, asked, "What happened?"

"He shot a man."

Mr. Campbell's eyebrows went up. "Well!"

Now Cora suddenly burned to speak out—it had been months since she had talked to anyone about Albert. Her eyes became thin slits. "Yes, Lawyer, he shot a good-for-nuthin' whiskey-head that wasn't fit to shine his shoes, and—."

"Oh, my!" Mr. Campbell shook his head in commiseration.

She ignored him. "—and *I* was partly to blame!"

He did not interrupt again.

"A bunch of the rattiest people you ever saw in your life moved in back of us—across the alley. They'd stay up all hours of the night, drinkin', and playin' that old low-down music so loud, and usin' all kind of bad language—just carryin' on somethin' terrible! In the wintertime it wasn't so bad; but in the summer, with the windows up, and all that carousin' going on, you just couldn't sleep to save your life. Albert didn't like it a bit. He didn't say much, though—just set there in his sock feet and read his newspapers. But *I* was always after him about it—all the time—it got on my nerves so bad . . . . Well anyhow, one Thursday night late, they got so loud Albert couldn't take it any more. He jumped up outa the bed and put his pants on over his pajamas. I didn't see him put his pistol in his pocket—but he did. And that fixed it, Lawyer—that fixed it. He went out through the back and crossed the alley and knocked on their door, and asked them in a nice way to quit makin' so much noise—so people could sleep. Then one of them drunk wine-os called him that awful name. Lawyer, if you only knew how Albert hates that word! He always did! . . . Mother . . . so-in-so. *You* know. I wasn't there, but I know what happened then! Albert just went out of his head—whipped out his pistol and shot at him . . . hit him in the leg, the knee." Cora bent forward, gripping her purse. "But Lawyer . . . do you know—in a week he died. *Died!* They tried Albert, then—for killing him. Poor Albert . . . when he had to leave, it was awful! I wanted to kill myself." Her face was hard now, with sunken eyes.

Mr. Campbell could only sit and look on. Finally he stirred and slowly shook his head. "What a tough break—an awful tough break . . . ." They sat in silence. "It could've been a lot worse, though," he said after a moment, "—a longer sentence. The rest of his time'll go in a hurry; you watch."

Then Cora said quite evenly, "Lawyer, I'm sick."

Mr. Campbell only stared.

She was phlegmatic. "I was operated on last winter . . . it's incurable—I've lost thirty pounds already. The doctors don't give me long."

The shock partially opened Mr. Campbell's mouth. He did not try to speak.

"I've been goin' to see Albert every time the people down there'll let me. But he gets so upset about me bein' sick, he's almost crazy. Thank God I didn't tell him *all* the doctors said. He wants to get out so bad—to take care of me; thinks I'd get well right away if he was home to look after me. I don't know what's goin' to happen to him—I'm so scared he'll mess up his chances for parole, worryin' about me. Me goin' down there does more harm than good now. He don't know it, but this past week was the last time. I made up my mind . . . and said goodbye." Her lip quivered, but she controlled herself.

Mr. Campbell gaped.

Then Cora looked at him as if to arouse him. "When Albert does come home, Lawyer, I won't be there. That's why I had to come and see *you*."

"I wish I could help you . . . I wish I could."

"You can, Lawyer, you can! Make out the will!"

Mr. Campbell sighed. ". . . Okay, Mrs. Jones . . . I'll make it out. I'll take care of it."

When, later, Cora left Mr. Campbell's office, she walked west on 63rd Street, all but oblivious of the grinding clatter of the "el" trains overhead and the strident human noises around her. The afternoon sun glared down on the dry pavement and the parked cars along the street, and, passing a furniture store, she noticed the baseball game on the big TV set in the window. She thought of Albert and how he liked to watch the ball games—and wrestling and boxing too—at home on their television. She wondered what he'd do when he walked into a house full of dusty furniture and grimy curtains, the refrigerator bare, and the gas and electricity cut off. He'd probably just sit down—helpless. She'd seen him do it before, when he was miserable. But before, *she'd* always been there, to smooth things out, fix things up; sometimes he seemed to her more like a son. But now, he'd just sit down. There was one thing, though: he wouldn't be penniless. She'd just seen to that.

When she reached Cottage Grove Avenue, the big corner drug store made her want a frothy, cooling malted milk. She went inside and climbed up onto one of the little revolving seats at the soda fountain and, waiting, studied herself in the long stretch of mirror—she was fascinated by mirrors lately. She saw that the little white hat went well with her green dress. And she'd just had her hair done the day before, and it looked nice, she thought. Her nails were so much better too, since she'd been away from the job. Finally the counter boy came and took her order, and began scooping out the ice cream for the malted.

It was then Cora saw the woman in the mirror—over at the cosmetics counter . . . Belle Williams? It sure looked like Belle! Cora furtively watched her. She couldn't be sure until the woman turned her head and gave a side view. It *was* Belle! Cora plunged her eyes to the counter. Oh, Lord!—she couldn't take *her* today! Some other day, maybe—but not today! Old mouthy Belle! Cora hadn't seen her in over a year. At one time they had both belonged to the Women's Club at Root Street Baptist, and for awhile old Belle and Albert sang in the choir together. Cora felt needles of exasperation recalling how Belle had started the gossip around church about Albert and Mattie Clark. Mattie also sang in the choir then. It didn't seem almost five whole years ago!—but it was. For Cora it had been the low point of her marriage; had made her wonder if marrying a man eight years her junior hadn't been a sad miscalculation.

The counter boy poured the malted and shoved the straws toward Cora, as she glanced in the mirror again. Belle was still there. Cora was distraught. The two hadn't met since Cora's illness and she knew Belle would stare at her thinness and ask a lot of silly questions; because Belle, herself, was silly—and evil too, sometimes. She was certainly evil when she went around talking about Albert and Mattie—("Why, that chippy's runnin' after Sister Cora's husband, and'll tell you in a minute she loves him—yes, honey, *loves* him—and always will! An' don't care who knows it!") Cora's heart was leaden, recalling it. She had made her own little private investigation at the time, and found that Albert *was* driving Mattie home from the choir practice far too regularly. She was furious at first, then heartsick—Mattie was Albert's age, or younger, and twice divorced. And it was during one of Albert's crazy spells—when he sometimes did things nobody could understand. He'd had these brain storms before—several times during their fourteen years of marriage—but they'd been mostly about things that didn't matter.

But she had made no scenes, kept a poker face, and watched his day-to-day reactions. That Mattie's love was not returned she was almost certain; and later on, she had figured it out at least to her own satisfaction: Albert had at first been stumped completely by Mattie's boldness—it was all so new to him; then he was a little frightened; but flattered too—Cora always knew he had a trace of conceit. But, in the end, she felt he had come through okay—untouched. At any rate, she liked to think he had. Now she risked another glance in the soda fountain mirror. Belle was not in sight—but the place was large. Then she saw her—at the cash register near the door, paying for her merchandise. Cora felt a sighing sense of deliverance.

She sat and sucked the thick malted up through the big straw and remembered how she used to fear gaining weight; that seemed ages ago. She hoped Albert would be able to get ahold of himself, to snap out of it—if he hadn't already ruined his chances for parole. But when finally he did come home— the thought made her eyes sting—what would become of him?

Would he go back to his old life as a drifter because there was nobody to encourage him, to brag on him? A maze of doubts and fears tussled in her mind. She sat on the little soda fountain seat, engulfed in her thoughts, seeming to have turned to stone. Innocently the malted milk straw slipped from her lips back into the glass, as she stared in the mirror. Oh, no!—No! Oh, Jesus!—No! That would never work! Never! Those things had happened too long, long ago. She was just all mixed up from seeing Belle Williams, that was all; from being taken back into the stone-dead past.

Her purse slipped off her lap onto the floor, and she got down and picked it up, absently brushing it off as she sat down again. But her taste for the malted was gone, and she pushed it away. How addled could she get? she kept asking herself. Was her sickness affecting her mind?—somehow this thought too would not leave her. She took a dollar bill from her purse, reached for the check, and climbed down off the seat again. As she walked toward the cashier, she was followed by the counter boy's curious stare.

After paying her check, she walked out into the street in a blind befuddlement and started south on Cottage Grove. She kept telling herself she would never go off on a wild goose chase after somebody that couldn't possibly be located, somebody she hadn't seen—or even heard of—in almost four years. But the goading of the thought would give her no peace—soon she was grudgingly conceding Mattie probably wasn't the *worst* person in the world; and maybe, like everybody else, had her better side, too. She remembered how Mattie, a beautician, used to send four or five of the poorest church kids to camp every summer, and how whenever Jimmie Stokes, the church camp director, gave his report to the deacon board, he always praised her; how she used to help out her two sisters (gruffly, sometimes) with needed cash toward bringing up their snotty-nosed broods; for Mattie was childless. Cora began to wonder

if Mattie's hardness wasn't really a cover-up for something—
a soft heart, maybe—and she was startled to find she hoped
it was.

But walking the streets wouldn't bring the answers, Cora
told herself. She must go home. Maybe there she could think
it all out. She turned around and walked back to the corner she
had just left, and crossed over to the west side of Cottage
Grove—for the southbound bus. The traffic was heavy and
noisy as she darted across, and she began to feel tired.

At the bus stop there was a brown-skinned girl standing
waiting, with a small baby in her arms. Whenever Cora glanced
at the baby, its glittering eyes were watching her. But today
she did not cluck and coo at it, as ordinarily she would have.
Instead, she stole sly glances of unconscious envy at the young
mother. But soon Mattie was back in her mind. And she found
herself thinking of the little beauty shop Mattie had operated,
years before, away back down near 36th and State. She'd had
her hair done there many times, and remembered it well. But
she also knew about the new slum clearance projects in that
area—sometimes little businesses like Mattie's had to keep on
the move, a step ahead of the excavators; and then she might
not even be in business at all any more. Cora felt jaded; and
turned now to gaze at the bright-eyed baby again. Ah, but
maybe Jimmie Stokes had kept in touch with Mattie . . .
she'd bet Jimmie *had!* He was probably up in Michigan now,
though—at the church camp.

She hurriedly left the mother and baby, and re-crossed Cottage Grove. When she entered the drug store again and walked
back past the cigarettes, the greeting cards, and electric toast-
ers, toward the telephone booths, she felt a sharp new purpose,
a buoyant urgency. She threw open the big telephone directory
and, after a search for the number, stepped into the booth,
inserted her dime, dialed, and waited.

A child finally answered—. "Hello."

". . . Hello . . . is Mr. Stokes in the city?"

"Yes'm—He's out in the back yard." Cora's pulse faltered.

". . . Can I please speak to him, then?" she said.

"Yes'm."

She felt nerves in her shoulder blades tighten. How would she ask him? What would he think of *her*, of all people, asking about Mattie Clark!—she was certain he, like all the others at church, knew the talk about Albert and Mattie. He'd probably think she was nutty or something. Then in the phone she heard a door slam as someone on the other end approached. She panicked. Her free right hand shot over and eased down the hook, and desperately held it down. Finally, she returned the phone to the hook, and left the booth.

She was weak now, and wanted to sit down. But she would not return to the soda fountain. Instead she again stood over the telephone directory, and pretended looking up another number, absently turning the pages as hapless moments passed. But the stubborn, resilient purpose inside her had not abated; it was active; she knew its promptings. Where could she find someone acquainted with Mattie!—somebody that didn't know the whole story. Members of the church wouldn't do . . . ah, what of Reverend Thomas! *He* might have seen her lately! You could trust Reverend Thomas. Cora easily found his telephone number; and stepped back into the booth, dropped another dime in the slot, and dialed. She could hear the number ringing—four, five, six times . . . . But after the tenth ring, and no answer, she hung up. Soon she was back in the street.

As she crossed Cottage Grove once more, to the bus stop, she was furious with herself for not going home the first time; only she shrank from the thought of that house. But her bus was coming now, and she had to run to catch it. She took a seat near the front and sank down exhausted; it was no use—Albert would make it somehow; he'd *have* to; nobody'd ever accused him of being a weakling; he only needed a little gentle guidance once in awhile, a show of interest, that was all. But as she thought it, she knew it wasn't true. Albert would always need help; she well knew he hadn't amounted to much before their marriage; had been the jack-of-all-trades type—even a prize fighter; then had drifted from job to job—until she first met him when he started at the canning factory where she worked.

The bus lurched on out Cottage Grove. She felt a languor now from the deadening fatigue; she would stretch out on the sofa awhile when she got home; and tonight she'd write Albert. Hadn't he gained weight since he'd been away!—didn't they ever get any exercise down there? She liked him better slender. He was reading a book too, now and then, he'd told her—she remembered at home when he wouldn't look at one, but devoured all newspapers; would even tear out editorials he liked, after reading them to her, and carry them around in his bulging wallet. But the wallet never bulged with money, she recalled. Until they married, he'd never had a real home; she felt that was one reason he appreciated her. And she knew he did—despite all the talk about Mattie. He'd never said an unkind word to her in his life—and his Valentine cards were almost a foot square. After all, what *was* love? Some people were different. That was *his* way.

The hot bus seemed to be stopping at every cross street, discharging and receiving passengers. But she knew it would eventually take her home, and she was miserable; any reminder of that house and Albert's homecoming always shocked her. It was at that instant Mattie's bold image swept back into her consciousness. She did not hesitate. She jumped up and yanked the signal cord. The bus driver glowered at her in the mirror and refused to make so sudden a stop. But when finally she was let off, her eyes roved the street in both directions for a cab. Seeing none, she started walking back north. She had gone almost a block before she sighted a yellow cab coming south, and ran out to the curb to flag it.

"I want to go to 36th and State," she told the black driver as she climbed in panting.

Fifteen minutes later the cab, proceeding north on State Street, approached 39th. Cora felt it was a ceremony she was going through now, for she saw the radical changes in the area—the new low-cost housing, and the straight white sidewalks criss-crossing the fresh green lawns. Even the old street car tracks were asphalted over, and there were only the big new CTA buses.

As they passed 38th Street, the cab driver half-turned around to her and said, "Thirty-sixth block, did you say?"

"Yes."

"What number?"

". . . I don't know. When we get there, go slow. I won't be gettin' out—I just want to see somethin'."

The driver said no more, and drove on. Cora now noticed that many of the older buildings still in sound condition had been left standing, and were in use. Mattie's little beauty shop had been on the right, just north of 36th—on the ground floor, front, of a three-story brick. Her pulse pounded at the thought—before a wave of despair went over her. But the cab kept going—it was passing 37th now, and she stared ahead through the windshield to 36th. Nothing seemed changed.

When they reached 36th, the driver slowed. "Yes . . . along in here," she said, peering out the right side. Time seemed to stop.

Then her startled heart tripped and raced away. There it was! The same building. The same store-front. The same plate glass window, bearing the same flourished, faded lettering:

MATTIE'S *CHEZ POMPADOUR*
Mattie Clark, proprietress

"Right here! Right here!" she cried—her voice was croaky.

"Here it is!"

The driver stopped, and backed up thirty feet, directly in front of the building. She was already in her purse for money, and pressed two dollars in his hand.

"You don't want me to wait fuh you?" the driver asked, faintly disappointed.

"Oh, no!"—Cora seemed surprised at the question. Then, as she grappled with the door handle, he reached back and opened the door for her, and she scrambled out.

But as the cab drove off, she felt abandoned. Panic crept up her thin legs into her body, and she stood unable to move. How would Mattie take it? She'd certainly be shocked—maybe mad. Or she'd just laugh at Cora . . . . No, she wouldn't laugh—nobody would do that. But there'd be customers in there, and she'd have to take Mattie off to one side. She started walking toward the door now—slowly, stiffly, in a numbing fright. As she came closer, she took in deep, deep breaths. And when she could go no farther, she opened the door.

The stench of oily, frying hair struck her flush in the face— two beauty operators in pink smocks were busy with their hot straightening combs. But the shop was air-conditioned; and two women customers sat in wicker arm chairs along the wall, waiting their turn and watching the ball game on the TV set, while a roly-poly yellow woman got a manicure. Cora's anxious eyes searched the room for Mattie.

The operator at the first chair—a wiry, little, black girl— broke off gossiping with her customer to look at Cora and smile, pointing over to an empty wicker chair. "Have a seat, honey," she said, "—right over there."

Cora, in a tumult of confusion, started toward the chair— but caught herself.

". . . Is Mattie in?" she smiled, embarrassed.

"Oh, no, honey!" the girl said—. "Mattie's in California. Her and her husband went on their vacation."

Cora's mouth fell open. ". . . Oh . . . ." The blood went from her face. ". . . husband . . . ." Then in the instant she flashed a desperately brilliant metallic smile—"*Oh, I see!* . . . I see! Well, good for her! Ain't that nice! Well, thanks, anyhow . . . thank you!" She was backing toward the door.

"They won't be gone long, though!" the girl laughed, "—when Mattie's money runs out! Just give 'em one more week! Ha-ha-ha-ha!"

But Cora had hurried out into the street.

The Beach Umbrella

The Thirty-first Street beach lay dazzling under a sky so blue that Lake Michigan ran to the horizon like a sheet of sapphire silk, studded with little barbed white sequins for sails; and the heavy surface of the water lapped gently at the boulder "sea wall" which had been cut into, graded, and sanded to make the beach. Saturday afternoons were always frenzied: three black lifeguards, giants in sunglasses, preened in their towers and chaperoned the bathers—adults, teen-agers, and children—who were going through every physical gyration of which the human body is capable. Some dove, swam, some hollered, rode inner tubes, or merely stood waistdeep and pummeled the water; others—on the beach—sprinted, did handsprings and somersaults, sucked Eskimo pies, or just buried their children in the sand. Then there were the lollers— extended in their languor under a garish variety of beach umbrellas.

Elijah lolled too—on his stomach in the white sand, his chin cupped in his palm; but under no umbrella. He had none. By habit, though, he stared in awe at those who did, and sometimes meddled in their conversation: "It's gonna be gettin' *hot* pretty soon—if it ain't careful," he said to a Bantu-looking fellow and his girl sitting nearby with an older woman. The temperature was then in the nineties. The fellow managed a negligent smile. "Yeah," he said, and persisted in listening to the women. Buoyant still, Elijah watched them. But soon his gaze wavered, and then moved on to other lollers of interest. Finally he got up, stretched, brushed sand from his swimming trunks, and scanned the beach for a new spot. He started walking.

He was not tall. And he appeared to walk on his toes—his walnut-colored legs were bowed and skinny and made him hobble like a jerky little spider. Next he plopped down near two men and two girls—they were hilarious about something— sitting beneath a big purple-and-white umbrella. The girls, chocolate brown and shapely, emitted squeals of laughter at the wisecracks of the men. Elijah was enchanted. All summer long the rambunctious gaiety of the beach had fastened on him a curious charm, a hex, that brought him gawking and twiddling to the lake each Saturday. The rest of the week, save Sunday, he worked. But Myrtle, his wife, detested the sport and stayed away. Randall, the boy, had been only twice and then without little Susan, who during the summer was her mother's own midget reflection. But Elijah came regularly, especially whenever Myrtle was being evil, which he felt now was almost always. She was getting worse, too—if that was possible. The woman was money-*crazy*.

"You gotta sharp-lookin' umbrella there!" he cut in on the two laughing couples. They studied him—the abruptly silent way. Then the big-shouldered fellow smiled and lifted his eyes to their spangled roof. "Yeah? . . . Thanks," he said. Elijah carried on: "I see a lot of 'em out here this summer—much more'n last year." The fellow meditated on this, but was non-committal. The others went on gabbing, mostly with their hands. Elijah, squinting in the hot sun, watched them. He didn't see how they could be married; they cut the fool too much, acted like they'd itched to get together for weeks and just now made it. He pondered going back in the water, but he'd already had an hour of that. His eyes traveled the sweltering beach. Funny about his folks; they were every shape and color a God-made human could be. Here was a real sample of variety—pink white to jetty black. Could you any longer call that a *race* of people? It was a complicated complication—for some real educated guy to figure out. Then another thought slowly bore in on him: the beach umbrellas blooming across the sand attracted people—slews of friends, buddies; and gals, too. Wherever the loudest-racket tore the air, a big red, or green, or yellowish umbrella—bordered with white fringe maybe—flowered in the middle of it all and gave shade to the happy good-timers.

Take, for instance, that tropical-looking pea-green umbrella over there, with the Bikini-ed brown chicks under it, and the portable radio jumping. A real beach party! He got up, stole over, and eased down in the sand at the fringe of the jubilation—two big thermos jugs sat in the shade and everybody had a paper cup in hand as the explosions of buffoonery carried out to the water. Chief provoker of mirth was a bulging-eyed old gal in a white bathing suit who, encumbered by big flabby overripe thighs, cavorted and pranced in the sand. When, perspiring from the heat, she finally fagged out, she flopped down almost on top of him. So far, he had gone unnoticed. But now, as he craned in at closer range, she brought him up: "Whatta *you* want, Pops?" She grinned, but with a touch of hostility.

Pops! Where'd she get that stuff? He was only forty-one, not a day older than that boozy bag. But he smiled. "Nothin'," he said brightly, "but you sure got one goin' here." He turned and viewed the noise-makers.

"An' you wanta get in on it!" she wrangled.

"Oh, I was just lookin'—."

"—You was just lookin'. Yeah, you was just lookin' at them young chicks there!" She roared a laugh and pointed at the sexy-looking girls under the umbrella.

Elijah grinned weakly.

"Beat it!" she catcalled, and turned back to the party.

He sat like a rock—the hell with her. But soon he relented, and wandered down to the water's edge—remote now from all inhospitality—to sit in the sand and hug his raised knees. Far out, the sailboats were pinned to the horizon and, despite all the close-in fuss, the wide miles of lake lay impassive under a blazing calm; far south and east down the long-curving lake shore, miles in the distance, the smoky haze of the Whiting plant of the Youngstown Sheet and Tube Company hung ominously in an otherwise bright sky. And so it was that he turned back and viewed the beach again—and suddenly caught his craving. Weren't they something—the umbrellas! The flashy colors of them! And the swank! No wonder folks ganged round them. Yes . . . yes, he too must have one. The thought came slow and final, and scared him. For there stood Myrtle in his mind. She nagged him now night and day, and it was always money that got her started; there was never enough--for Susan's shoes, Randy's overcoat, for new kitchen linoleum, Venetian blinds, for a better car than the old Chevy. "I just don't understand you!" she had said only night before last. "Have you got any plans at all for your family? You got a family, you know. If you could only bear to pull yourself away from that deaf old tightwad out at that warehouse, and go get yourself a *real* job . . . . But no! Not *you!*"

She was talking about old man Schroeder, who owned the warehouse where he worked. Yes, the pay could be better, but it still wasn't as bad as she made out. Myrtle could be such a fool sometimes. He had been with the old man nine years now; had started out as a freight handler, but worked up to doing inventories and a little paper work. True, the business had been going down recently, for the old man's sight and hearing were failing and his key people had left. Now he depended on *him*, Elijah—who of late wore a necktie on the job, and made his inventory rounds with a ball-point pen and clipboard. The old man was friendlier, too—almost "hat in hand" to him. He liked everything about the job now—except the pay. And that was only because of Myrtle. She just wanted so much; even talked of moving out of their rented apartment and buying out in the Chatham area. But one thing had to be said for her: she never griped about anything for herself; only for the family, the kids. Every payday he endorsed his check and handed it over to her, and got back in return only gasoline and cigarette money. And this could get pretty tiresome. About six weeks ago he'd gotten a thirty-dollar-a-month raise out of the old man, but that had only made her madder than ever. He'd thought about looking for another job all right; but where would he go to get another white-collar job? There weren't many of them for him. *She* wouldn't care if he went back to the steel mills, back to pouring that white-hot ore out at Youngstown Sheet and Tube. It would be okay with *her*—so long as his pay check was fat. But that kind of work was no good, undignified; coming home on the bus you were always so tired you went to sleep in your seat, with your lunch pail in your lap.

Just then two wet boys, chasing each other across the sand, raced by him into the water. The cold spray on his skin made him jump, jolting him out of his thoughts. He turned and slowly scanned the beach again. The umbrellas were brighter, gayer, bolder than ever—each a hiving center of playful people. He stood up finally, took a long last look, and then started back to the spot where he had parked the Chevy.

The following Monday evening was hot and humid as Elijah sat at home in their plain living room and pretended to read the newspaper; the windows were up, but not the slightest breeze came through the screens to stir Myrtle's fluffy curtains. At the moment she and nine-year-old Susan were in the kitchen finishing the dinner dishes. For twenty minutes now he had sat waiting for the furtive chance to speak to Randall. Randall, at twelve, was a serious, industrious boy, and did deliveries and odd jobs for the neighborhood grocer. Soon he came through—intent, absorbed—on his way back to the grocery store for another hour's work.

"Gotta go back, eh, Randy?" Elijah said.

"Yes, sir." He was tall for his age, and wore glasses. He paused with his hand on the doorknob.

Elijah hesitated. Better wait, he thought—wait till he comes back. But Myrtle might be around then. Better ask him now. But Randall had opened the door. "See you later, Dad," he said—and left.

Elijah, shaken, again raised the newspaper and tried to read. He should have called him back, he knew, but he had lost his nerve—because he couldn't tell how Randy would take it. Fifteen dollars was nothing though, really—Randy probably had fifty or sixty stashed away somewhere in his room. Then he thought of Myrtle, and waves of fright went over him—to be even thinking about a beach umbrella was bad enough; and to buy one, especially now, would be to her some kind of crime; but to borrow even a part of the money for it from Randy . . . well, Myrtle would go out of her mind. He had never lied to his family before. This would be the first time. And he had thought about it all day long. During the morning, at the warehouse, he had gotten out the two big mail-order catalogues, to look at the beach umbrellas; but the ones shown were all so small and dinky-looking he was contemptuous. So at noon he drove the Chevy out to a sporting-goods store on West Sixty-Third Street. There he found a gorgeous assortment of yard and beach umbrellas. And there he found his prize. A beauty, a big beauty, with wide red and white stripes, and a white fringe. But oh the price! Twenty-three dollars! And he with nine.

"What's the matter with you?" Myrtle had walked in the room. She was thin, and medium brown-skinned with a saddle of freckles across her nose, and looked harried in her sleeveless housedress with her hair unkempt.

Startled, he lowered the newspaper. "Nothing," he said.

"How can you read looking *over* the paper?"

"Was I?"

Not bothering to answer, she sank in a chair. "Susie," she called back into the kitchen, "bring my cigarettes in here, will you, baby?"

Soon Susan, chubby and solemn, with the mist of perspiration on her forehead, came in with the cigarettes. "Only three left, Mama," she said, peering into the pack.

"Okay," Myrtle sighed, taking the cigarettes. Susan started out. "Now, scour the sink good, honey—and then go take your bath. You'll feel cooler."

Before looking at him again, Myrtle lit a cigarette. "School starts in three weeks, she said, with a forlorn shake of her head. "Do you realize that?"

"Yeah? . . . Jesus, time flies." He could not look at her.

"Susie needs dresses, and a couple of pairs of *good* shoes—and she'll need a coat before it gets cold."

"Yeah, I know." He patted the arm of the chair.

"Randy—bless his heart—has already made enough to get most of *his* things. That boy's something; he's all business—I've never seen anything like it." She took a drag on her cigarette. "And old man Schroeder giving you a thirty-dollar raise! What was you thinkin' about? What'd you *say* to him?"

He did not answer at first. Finally he said, "Thirty dollars are thirty dollars, Myrtle. *You* know business is slow."

"*I'll* say it is! And there won't be any business before long—

and then where'll you be? I tell you over and over again, you better start looking for something *now!* I been preachin' it to you for a year."

He said nothing.

"Ford and International Harvester are hiring every man they can lay their hands on! And the mills out in Gary and Whiting are going full blast—you see the red sky every night. The men make *good* money."

"They earn every nickel of it, too," he said in gloom.

"But they *get* it! Bring it home! It spends! Does that mean anything to you? Do you know what some of them make? Well, ask Hawthorne—or ask Sonny Milton. Sonny's wife says his checks some weeks run as high as a hundred sixty, hundred eighty, dollars. One week! Take-home pay!"

"Yeah? . . . And Sonny told me he wished he had a job like mine."

Myrtle threw back her head with a bitter gasp. "Oh-h-h, God! Did you tell him what you made? Did you tell him that?"

Suddenly Susan came back into the muggy living room. She went straight to her mother and stood as if expecting an award. Myrtle absently patted her on the side of the head. "Now, go and run your bath water, honey," she said.

Elijah smiled at Susan. "Susie," he said, "d'you know your tummy is stickin' way out—you didn't eat too much, did you?" He laughed.

Susan turned and observed him; then looked at her mother. "No," she finally said.

"Go on, now, baby," Myrtle said. Susan left the room.

Myrtle resumed. "Well, there's no use going through all this again. It's plain as the nose on your face. You got a family—a good family, *I* think. The only question is, do you wanta get off your hind end and do somethin' for it. It's just that simple."

Elijah looked at her. "You can talk real crazy sometimes, Myrtle."

"I think it's that old man!" she cried, her freckles contorted. "He's got you answering the phone, and taking inventory— wearing a necktie and all that. You wearing a necktie and your son mopping in a grocery store, so he can buy his own clothes." She snatched up her cigarettes, and walked out of the room.

His eyes did not follow her, but remained off in space. Finally he got up and went back into the kitchen. Over the stove the plaster was thinly cracked, and, in spots, the linoleum had worn through the pattern; but everything was immaculate. He opened the refrigerator, poured a glass of cold water, and sat down at the kitchen table. He felt strange and weak, and sat for a long time sipping the water.

Then after a while he heard Randall's key in the front door, sending tremors of dread through him. When Randall came into the kitchen, he seemed to him as tall as himself; his glasses were steamy from the humidity outside, and his hands were dirty.

"Hi, Dad," he said gravely without looking at him, and opened the refrigerator door.

Elijah chuckled. "Your mother'll get after you about going in there without washing your hands."

But Randall took out the water pitcher and closed the door.

Elijah watched him. Now was the time to ask him. His heart was hammering. Go on—now! But instead he heard his husky voice saying, "What'd they have you doing over at the grocery tonight?"

Randall was drinking the glass of water. When he finished he said, "Refilling shelves."

"Pretty hot job tonight, eh?"

"It wasn't so bad." Randall was matter-of-fact as he set the empty glass over the sink, and paused before leaving.

"Well . . . you're doing fine, son. Fine. Your mother sure

is proud of you . . . ." Purpose had lodged in his throat.

The praise embarrassed Randall. "Okay, Dad," he said, and edged from the kitchen.

Elijah slumped back in his chair, near prostration. He tried to clear his mind of every particle of thought, but the images became only more jumbled, oppressive to the point of panic. Then before long Myrtle came into the kitchen—ignoring him. But she seemed not so hostile now as coldly impassive, exhibiting a bravado he had not seen before. He got up and went back into the living room and turned on the television. As the TV-screen lawmen galloped before him, he sat oblivious, admitting the failure of his will. If only he could have gotten Randall to himself long enough—but everything had been so sudden, abrupt; he couldn't just ask him out of the clear blue. Besides, around him, Randall always seemed so busy, too busy to talk. He couldn't understand that; he had never mistreated the boy, never whipped him in his life; had shaken him a time or two, but that was long ago, when he was little.

He sat and watched the finish of the half-hour TV show. Myrtle was in the bedroom now. He slouched in his chair, lacking the resolve to get up and turn off the television.

Suddenly he was on his feet.

Leaving the television on, he went back to Randall's room in the rear. The door was open and Randall was asleep, lying on his back on the bed, perspiring, still dressed except for his shoes and glasses. He stood over the bed and looked at him. He was a good boy; his own son. But how strange—he thought for the first time—there was no resemblance between them. None whatsoever. Randy had a few of his mother's freckles on his thin brown face, but he could see none of himself in the boy. Then his musings were scattered by the return of his fear. He dreaded waking him. And he might be cross. If he didn't hurry, though, Myrtle or Susie might come strolling out any minute. His bones seemed rubbery from the strain. Finally

he bent down and touched Randall's shoulder. The boy did
not move a muscle, except to open his eyes. Elijah smiled at
him. And he slowly sat up.

"Sorry, Randy—to wake you up like this."

"What's the matter?" Randall rubbed his eyes.

Elijah bent down again, but did not whisper. "Say, can you
let me have fifteen bucks—till I get my check? . . . I need to
get some things—and I'm a little short this time." He could
hardly bring the words up.

Randall gave him a slow, queer look.

"I'll get my check a week from Friday," Elijah said, ". . .
and I'll give it back to you then—sure."

Now instinctively Randall glanced toward the door, and
Elijah knew Myrtle had crossed his thoughts. "You don't have
to mention anything to your mother," he said with casual
suddenness.

Randall got up slowly off the bed, and, in his socks, walked
to the little table where he did his homework. He pulled the
drawer out, fished far in the back a moment, and brought
out a white business envelope secured by a rubber band. Holding the envelope close to his stomach, he took out first a ten-
dollar bill, and then a five, and, sighing, handed them over.

"Thanks, old man," Elijah quivered, folding the money.
"You'll get this back the day I get my check. . . . That's for
sure.

"Okay," Randall finally said.

Elijah started out. Then he could see Myrtle on payday—
her hand extended for his check. He hesitated, and looked at
Randall, as if to speak. But he slipped the money in his trousers
pocket and hurried from the room.

The following Saturday at the beach did not begin bright
and sunny. By noon it was hot, but the sky was overcast and
angry, the air heavy. There was no certainty whatever of a

crowd, raucous or otherwise, and this was Elijah's chief concern as, shortly before twelve o'clock, he drove up in the Chevy and parked in the bumpy, graveled stretch of high ground that looked down eastward over the lake and was used for a parking lot. He climbed out of the car, glancing at the lake and clouds, and prayed in his heart it would not rain—the water was murky and restless, and only a handful of bathers had showed. But it was early yet. He stood beside the car and watched a bulbous, brown-skinned woman, in bathing suit and enormous straw hat, lugging a lunch basket down toward the beach, followed by her brood of children. And a fellow in swimming trunks, apparently the father, took a towel and sandals from his new Buick and called petulantly to his family to "just wait a minute, please." In another car, two women sat waiting, as yet fully clothed and undecided about going swimming. While down at the water's edge there was the usual cluster of dripping boys who, brash and boisterous, swarmed to the beach every day in fair weather or foul.

Elijah took off his shirt, peeled his trousers from over his swimming trunks, and started collecting the paraphernalia from the back seat of the car: a frayed pink rug filched from the house, a towel, sunglasses, cigarettes, a thermos jug filled with cold lemonade he had made himself, and a dozen paper cups. All this he stacked on the front fender. Then he went around to the rear and opened the trunk. Ah, there it lay— encased in a long, slim package trussed with heavy twine, and barely fitting athwart the spare tire. He felt prickles of excitement as he took the knife from the tool bag, cut the twine, and pulled the wrapping paper away. Red and white stripes sprang at him. It was even more gorgeous than when it had first seduced him in the store. The white fringe gave it style; the wide red fillets were cardinal and stark, and the white stripes glared. Now he opened it over his head, for the full thrill of its colors, and looked around to see if anyone else agreed. Finally after a while he gathered up all his equipment and headed down for the beach, his short, nubby legs seeming more bowed than ever under the weight of their cargo.

When he reached the sand, a choice of location became a pressing matter. That was why he had come early. From past observation it was clear that the center of gaiety shifted from day to day; last Saturday it might have been nearer the water, this Saturday, well back; or up, or down, the beach a ways. He must pick the site with care, for he could not move about the way he did when he had no umbrella; it was too noticeable. He finally took a spot as near the center of the beach as he could estimate, and dropped his gear in the sand. He knelt down and spread the pink rug, then moved the thermos jug over onto it, and folded the towel and placed it with the paper cups, sunglasses, and cigarettes down beside the jug. Now he went to find a heavy stone or brick to drive down the spike for the hollow umbrella stem to fit over. So it was not until the umbrella was finally up that he again had time for anxiety about the weather. His whole morning's effort had been an act of faith, for, as yet, there was no sun, although now and then a few azure breaks appeared in the thinning cloud mass. But before very long this brighter texture of the sky began to grow and spread by slow degrees, and his hopes quickened. Finally he sat down under the umbrella, lit a cigarette, and waited.

It was not long before two small boys came by—on their way to the water. He grinned, and called to them, "Hey, fellas, been in yet?"—their bathing suits were dry.

They stopped, and observed him. Then one of them smiled, and shook his head.

Elijah laughed. "Well, whatta you waitin' for? Go on in there and get them suits wet!" Both boys gave him silent smiles. And they lingered. He thought this a good omen—it had been different the Saturday before.

Once or twice the sun burst through the weakening clouds. He forgot the boys now in watching the skies, and soon they moved on. His anxiety was not detectable from his lazy posture under the umbrella, with his dwarfish, gnarled legs extended and his bare heels on the little rug. But then soon the clouds began to fade in earnest, seeming not to move away laterally, but slowly to recede into a lucent haze, until at last the sun came through hot and bright. He squinted at the sky and felt delivered. They would come, the folks would come!—were coming now; the beach would soon be swarming. Two other umbrellas were up already, and the diving board thronged with wet, acrobatic boys. The lifeguards were in their towers now, and still another launched his yellow rowboat. And up on the Outer Drive, the cars, one by one, were turning into the parking lot. The sun was bringing them out all right; soon he'd be in the middle of a field day. He felt a low-key, welling excitement, for the water was blue, and far out the sails were starched and white.

Soon he saw the two little boys coming back. They were soaked. Their mother—a thin, brown girl in a yellow bathing suit—was with them now, and the boys were pointing to his umbrella. She seemed dignified for her youth, as she gave him a shy glance and then smiled at the boys.

"Ah, ha!" he cried to the boys. "You've been in *now* all right!" And then laughing to her, "I was kiddin' them awhile ago about their dry bathing suits."

She smiled at the boys again. "They like for me to be with them when they go in," she said.

"I got some lemonade here," he said abruptly, slapping the thermos jug. "Why don't you have some?" His voice was anxious.

She hesitated.

He jumped up. "Come on, sit down." He smiled at her and stepped aside.

Still she hesitated. But her eager boys pressed close behind her. Finally she smiled and sat down under the umbrella.

"You fellas can sit down under there too—in the shade," he said to the boys, and pointed under the umbrella. The boys flopped down quickly in the shady sand. He started at once serving them cold lemonade in the paper cups.

"Whew! I thought it was goin' to rain there for a while," he said, making conversation after passing out the lemonade. He had squatted on the sand and lit another cigarette. "Then there wouldn't a been much goin' on. But it turned out fine after all—there'll be a mob here before long."

She sipped the lemonade, but said little. He felt she had sat down only because of the boys, for she merely smiled and gave short answers to his questions. He learned the boys' names, Melvin and James; their ages, seven and nine; and that they were still frightened by the water. But he wanted to ask *her* name, and inquire about her husband. But he could not capture the courage.

Now the sun was hot and the sand was hot. And an orange-and-white umbrella was going up right beside them—two fellows and a girl. When the fellow who had been kneeling to drive the umbrella spike in the sand stood up, he was string-bean tall, and black, with his glistening hair freshly processed. The girl was a lighter brown, and wore a lilac bathing suit, and, although her legs were thin, she was pleasant enough to look at. The second fellow was medium, really, in height, but short beside his tall, black friend. He was yellow-skinned, and fast getting bald, although still in his early thirties. Both men sported little shoestring mustaches.

Elijah watched them in silence as long as he could. "You picked the right spot all right!" he laughed at last, putting on his sunglasses.

"How come, man?" The tall, black fellow grinned, showing his mouthful of gold teeth.

"You see *every*body here!" happily rejoined Elijah. "They all come here!"

"Man, I been coming here for years," the fellow reproved, and sat down in his khaki swimming trunks to take off his shoes. Then he stood up. "But right now, in the water I goes." He looked down at the girl. "How 'bout you, Lois, baby?"

"No, Caesar," she smiled, "not yet; I'm gonna sit here awhile and relax."

"Okay, then—you just sit right there and relax. And Little Joe"—he turned and grinned to his shorter friend—"you sit there an' relax right along with her. You all can talk with this gentleman here"—he nodded at Elijah—"an' his nice wife." Then, pleased with himself, he trotted off toward the water.

The young mother looked at Elijah, as if he should have hastened to correct him. But somehow he had not wanted to. Yet too, Caesar's remark seemed to amuse her, for she soon smiled. Elijah felt the pain of relief—he did not want her to go; he glanced at her with a furtive laugh, and then they both laughed. The boys had finished their lemonade now, and were digging in the sand. Lois and Little Joe were busy talking.

Elijah was not quite sure what he should say to the mother. He did not understand her, was afraid of boring her, was desperate to keep her interested. As she sat looking out over the lake, he watched her. She was not pretty; and she was too thin. But he thought she had poise; he liked the way she treated her boys—tender, but casual; how different from Myrtle's frantic herding.

Soon she turned to the boys. "Want to go back in the water?" she laughed.

The boys looked at each other, and then at her. "Okay," James said finally, in resignation.

"Here, have some more lemonade," Elijah cut in.

The boys, rescued for the moment, quickly extended their

cups. He poured them more lemonade, as she looked on smiling.

Now he turned to Lois and Little Joe sitting under their orange-and-white umbrella. "How 'bout some good ole cold lemonade?" he asked with a mushy smile. "I got plenty of cups." He felt he must get something going.

Lois smiled back, "No, thanks," she said, fluttering her long eyelashes, "not right now."

He looked anxiously at Little Joe.

"*I'll* take a cup!" said Little Joe, and turned and laughed to Lois: "Hand me that bag there, will you?" He pointed to her beach bag in the sand. She passed it to him, and he reached in and pulled out a pint of gin. "We'll have some *real* lemonade," he vowed, with a daredevilish grin.

Lois squealed with pretended embarrassment. "Oh, *Joe!*"

Elijah's eyes were big now; he was thinking of the police. But he handed Little Joe a cup and poured the lemonade, to which Joe added gin. Then Joe, grinning, thrust the bottle at Elijah. "How 'bout yourself, chief?" he said.

Elijah, shaking his head, leaned forward and whispered, "You ain't supposed to drink on the beach, y'know."

"*This* ain't a drink, man—it's a taste!" said Little Joe, laughing and waving the bottle around toward the young mother. "How 'bout a little taste for your wife here?" he said to Elijah.

The mother laughed and threw up both her hands. "No, not for me!"

Little Joe gave her a rakish grin. "What'sa matter? You '*fraid* of that guy?" He jerked his thumb toward Elijah. "You 'fraid of gettin' a whippin', eh?"

"No, not exactly," she laughed.

Elijah was so elated with her his relief burst up in hysterical laughter. His laugh became strident and hoarse and he could not stop. The boys gaped at him, and then at their mother.

When finally he recovered, Little Joe asked him, "Whut's so funny 'bout *that?*" Then Little Joe grinned at the mother. "You beat *him* up sometimes, eh?"

This started Elijah's hysterics all over again. The mother looked concerned now, and embarrassed; her laugh was nervous and shadowed. Little Joe glanced at Lois, laughed, and shrugged his shoulders. When Elijah finally got control of himself again he looked spent and demoralized.

Lois now tried to divert attention by starting a conversation with the boys. But the mother showed signs of restlessness and seemed ready to go. At this moment Caesar returned. Glistening beads of water ran off his long, black body; and his hair was unprocessed now. He surveyed the group and then flashed a wide, gold-toothed grin. "One big, happy family, like I said." Then he spied the paper cup in Little Joe's hand. "Whut you got there, man?"

Little Joe looked down into his cup with a playful smirk. "Lemonade, lover boy, lemonade."

"Don't hand me that jive, Joey. You ain't never had any straight lemonade in your life."

This again brought uproarious laughter from Elijah. "I got the straight lemonade *here!*" He beat the thermos jug with his hand. "Come on—have some!" He reached for a paper cup.

"Why, sure," said poised Caesar. He held out the cup and received the lemonade. "Now, gimme that gin," he said to Little Joe. Joe handed over the gin, and Caesar poured three fingers into the lemonade and sat down in the sand with his legs crossed under him. Soon he turned to the two boys, as their mother watched him with amusement. "Say, ain't you boys goin' in any more? Why don't you tell your daddy there to take you in?" He nodded toward Elijah.

Little Melvin frowned at him. "My daddy's workin'," he said.

Caesar's eyebrows shot up. "Ooooh, la, la!" he crooned.

"Hey, now!" And he turned and looked at the mother and then at Elijah, and gave a clownish little snigger.

Lois tittered before feigning exasperation at him. "There you go again," she said, "talkin' when you shoulda been listening."

Elijah laughed along with the rest. But he felt deflated. Then he glanced at the mother, who was laughing too. He could detect in her no sign of dismay. Why then had she gone along with the gag in the first place, he thought—if now she didn't hate to see it punctured?

"*Hold the phone!*" softly exclaimed Little Joe. "*Whut is this?*" He was staring over his shoulder. Three women, young, brown, and worldly-looking, wandered toward them, carrying an assortment of beach paraphernalia and looking for a likely spot. They wore very scant bathing suits, and were followed, but slowly, by an older woman with big, unsightly thighs. Elijah recognized her at once. She was the old gal who, the Saturday before, had chased him away from her beach party. She wore the same white bathing suit, and one of her girls carried the pea-green umbrella.

Caesar forgot his whereabouts ogling the girls. The older woman, observing this, paused to survey the situation. "How 'bout along in here?" she finally said to one of the girls. The girl carrying the thermos jug set it in the sand so close to Caesar it nearly touched him. He was rapturous. The girl with the umbrella had no chance to put it up, for Caesar and Little Joe instantly encumbered her with help. Another girl turned on their radio, and grinning, feverish Little Joe started snapping his fingers to the music's beat.

Within a half hour, a boisterous party was in progress. The little radio, perched on a hump of sand, blared out hot jazz, as the older woman—whose name turned out to be Hattie—passed around some cold, rum-spiked punch; and before long she went into her dancing-prancing act—to the riotous delight of all, especially Elijah. Hattie did not remember him from the Saturday past, and he was glad, for everything was so different today! As different as milk and ink. He knew no one realized it, but this was *his* party really—the wildest, craziest, funniest, and best he had ever seen or heard of. Nobody had been near the water—except Caesar, and the mother and boys much earlier. It appeared Lois was Caesar's girl friend, and she was hence more capable of reserve in face of the come-on antics of Opal, Billie, and Quanita—Hattie's girls. But Little Joe, to Caesar's tortured envy, was both free and aggressive. Even the young mother, who now volunteered her name to be Mrs. Green, got frolicsome, and twice jabbed Little Joe in the ribs.

Finally Caesar proposed they all go in the water. This met with instant, tipsy acclaim; and Little Joe, his yellow face contorted from laughing, jumped up, grabbed Billie's hand, and made off with her across the sand. But Hattie would not budge. Full of rum, and stubborn, she sat sprawled with her flaccid thighs spread in an obscene V, and her eyes half shut. Now she yelled at her departing girls: "You all watch out, now! Dont'cha go in too far. . . . Just wade! None o' you can swim a lick!"

Elijah now was beyond happiness. He felt a floating, manic glee. He sprang up and jerked Mrs. Green splashing into the water, followed by her somewhat less ecstatic boys. Caesar had to paddle about with Lois and leave Little Joe unassisted to caper with Billie, Opal, and Quanita. Billie was the prettiest of the three, and, despite Hattie's contrary statement, she could swim; and Little Joe, after taking her out in deeper water, waved back to Caesar in triumph. The sun was brazen now, and the beach and lake thronged with a variegated humanity. Elijah, a strong, but awkward, country-style swimmer, gave Mrs. Green a lesson in floating on her back, and, though she too could swim, he often felt obligated to place both his arms under her young body and buoy her up.

And sometimes he would purposely let her sink to her chin, whereupon she would feign a happy fright and utter faint simian screeches. Opal and Quanita sat in the shallows and kicked up their heels at Caesar, who, fully occupied with Lois, was a grinning water-threshing study in frustration.

Thus the party went—on and on—till nearly four o'clock. Elijah had not known the world afforded such joy; his homely face was a wet festoon of beams and smiles. He went from girl to girl, insisting she learn to float on his outstretched arms. Once begrudgingly Caesar admonished him, "Man, you gonna *drown* one o' them pretty chicks in a minute." And Little Joe bestowed his highest accolade by calling him "lover boy," as Elijah nearly strangled from laughter.

At last, they looked up to see old Hattie as she reeled down to the water's edge, coming to fetch her girls. Both Caesar and Little Joe ran out of the water to meet her, seized her by the wrists, and, despite her struggles and curses, dragged her in. "Turn me loose! You big galoots!" she yelled and gasped as the water hit her. She was in knee-deep before she wriggled and fought herself free and lurched out of the water. Her breath reeked of rum. Little Joe ran and caught her again, but she lunged backwards, and free, with such force she sat down in the wet sand with a thud. She roared a laugh now, and spread her arms for help, as her girls came sprinting and splashing out of the water and tugged her to her feet. Her eyes narrowed to vengeful, grinning slits as she turned on Caesar and Little Joe: "*I* know whut you two're up to!" She flashed a glance around toward her girls. "I been watchin' both o' you studs! Yeah, yeah, but your eyes may shine, an' your teeth may grit . . . ." She went limp in a sneering, raucous laugh. Everybody laughed now—except Lois and Mrs. Green.

They had all come out of the water now, and soon the whole group returned to their three beach umbrellas. Hattie's girls immediately prepared to break camp. They took down their pea-green umbrella, folded some wet towels, and donned their beach sandals, as Hattie still bantered Caesar and Little Joe.

"Well, you sure had *yourself* a ball today," she said to Little Joe, who was sitting in the sand.

"Comin' back next Saturday?" asked grinning Little Joe.

"I jus' might at that," surmised Hattie. "We wuz here last Saturday."

"Good! Good!" Elijah broke in. "Let's *all* come back—next Saturday!" He searched every face.

"*I'll* be here," chimed Little Joe, grinning to Caesar. Captive Caesar glanced at Lois, and said nothing.

Lois and Mrs. Green were silent. Hattie, insulted, looked at them and started swelling up. "Never mind," she said pointedly to Elijah, "you jus' come on anyhow. You'll run into a slew o' folks lookin' for a good time. You don't need no *certain* people." But a little later, she and her girls all said friendly goodbyes and walked off across the sand.

The party now took a sudden downturn. All Elijah's efforts at resuscitation seemed unavailing. The westering sun was dipping toward the distant buildings of the city, and many of the bathers were leaving. Caesar and Little Joe had become bored; and Mrs. Green's boys, whining to go, kept a reproachful eye on their mother.

"Here, you boys, take some more lemonade," Elijah said quickly, reaching for the thermos jug. "Only got a little left—better get while gettin's good!" He laughed. The boys shook their heads.

On Lois he tried cajolery. Smiling, and pointing to her wet, but trim bathing suit, he asked, "What color would you say that is?"

"Lilac," said Lois, now standing.

"It sure is pretty! Prettiest on the beach!" he whispered.

Lois gave him a weak smile. Then she reached down for her beach bag, and looked at Caesar.

Caesar stood up, "Let's cut," he turned and said to Little Joe, and began taking down their orange-and-white umbrella.

Elijah was desolate. "Whatta you goin' for? It's gettin' cooler! Now's the time to *enjoy* the beach!"

"I've got to go home," Lois said.

Mrs. Green got up now; her boys had started off already. "Just a minute, Melvin," she called, frowning. Then, smiling, she turned and thanked Elijah.

He whirled around to them all. "Are we comin' back next Saturday? Come on—let's all come back! Wasn't it great! It was *great!* Don't you think? Whatta you say?" He looked now at Lois and Mrs. Green.

"We'll see," Lois said smiling. "Maybe."

"Can *you* come?" He turned to Mrs. Green.

"I'm not sure," she said. "I'll try."

"Fine! Oh, that's fine!" He turned on Caesar and Little Joe. "I'll be lookin' for you guys, hear?"

"Okay, chief," grinned Little Joe. "An' put somethin' in that lemonade, will ya?"

Everybody laughed . . . and soon they were gone.

Elijah slowly crawled back under his umbrella, although the sun's heat was almost spent. He looked about him. There was only one umbrella on the spot now, his own; where before there had been three. Cigarette butts and paper cups lay strewn where Hattie's girls had sat, and the sandy imprint of Caesar's enormous street shoes marked his site. Mrs. Green had dropped a bobby pin. He too was caught up now by a sudden urge to go. It was hard to bear much longer—the lonesomeness. And most of the people were leaving anyway. He stirred and fidgeted in the sand, and finally started an inventory of his belongings. . . . Then his thoughts flew home, and he reconsidered. Funny—he hadn't thought of home all afternoon. Where had the time gone anyhow? . . . It seemed he'd just pulled up in the Chevy and unloaded his gear; now it was time to go home again. Then the image of solemn Randy suddenly formed in his mind, sending waves of guilt through him. He forgot where he was as the duties of his existence leapt on his back—where would he ever get Randy's fifteen dollars? He felt squarely confronted by a great blank void. It was an awful thing he had done—all for a day at the beach . . . with some sporting girls. He thought of his family and felt tiny—and him itching to come back next Saturday! Maybe Myrtle was right about him after all. Lord, if she knew what he had done. . . .

He sat there for a long time. Most of the people were gone now. The lake was quiet save for a few boys still in the water. And the sun, red like blood, had settled on the dark silhouettes of the housetops across the city. He sat beneath the umbrella just as he had at one o'clock . . . and the thought smote him. He was jolted. Then dubious. But there it was—quivering, vital, swelling inside his skull like an unwanted fetus. So this was it! He mutinied inside. So he must sell it . . . his *umbrella.* Sell it for anything—only as long as it was enough to pay back Randy. For fifteen dollars even, if necessary. He was dogged; he couldn't do it; that wasn't the answer anyway. But the thought clawed and clung to him, rebuking and coaxing him by turns, until it finally became conviction. He must do it; it was the right thing to do; the only thing to do. Maybe then the awful weight would lift, the dull commotion in his stomach cease. He got up and started collecting his belongings; placed the thermos jug, sunglasses, towel, cigarettes, and little rug together in a neat pile, to be carried to the Chevy later. Then he turned to face his umbrella. Its red and white stripes stood defiant against the wide, churned-up sand. He stood for a moment mooning at it. Then he carefully let it down and, carrying it in his right hand, went off across the sand.

The sun now had gone down behind the vast city in a shower of crimson-golden glints, and on the beach only a few stragglers remained. For his first prospects, he approached two teen-age boys, but suddenly realizing they had no money, he turned away and went over to an old woman, squat and black, in street clothes—a spectator—who stood gazing eastward out across the lake. She held in her hand a little black book, with red-edged pages, which looked like the *New Testament*. He smiled at her. "Wanna buy a nice new beach umbrella?" He held out the collapsed umbrella toward her.

She gave him a beatific smile, but shook her head. "No, son," she said, "that ain't what *I* want." And she turned to gaze out on the lake again.

For a moment he still held the umbrella out, with a question mark on his face. "Okay, then," he finally said, and went on.

Next he hurried to the water's edge, where he saw a man and two women preparing to leave. "Wanna buy a nice new beach umbrella?" His voice sounded high-pitched, as he opened the umbrella over his head. "It's brand-new. I'll sell it for fifteen dollars—it cost a lot more'n that."

The man was hostile, and glared. Finally he said, "Whatta you take me for—a fool?"

Elijah looked bewildered, and made no answer. He observed the man for a moment. Finally he let the umbrella down. As he moved away, he heard the man say to the women, "It's hot—he stole it somewhere."

Close by, another man sat alone in the sand. Elijah started toward him. The man wore trousers, but was stripped to the waist, and bent over intent on some task in his lap. When Elijah reached him, he looked up from half a hatful of cigarette butts he was breaking open for the tobacco he collected in a little paper bag. He grinned at Elijah, who meant now to pass on.

"No, I ain't interested either, buddy," the man insisted as

Elijah passed him. "Not me. I jus' got *outa* jail las' week—an' ain't goin' back for no umbrella." He laughed, as Elijah kept on.

Now he saw three women, still in their bathing suits, sitting together near the diving board. They were the only people he had not yet tried—except the one lifeguard left. As he approached them, he saw that all three wore glasses and were sedate. Some schoolteachers maybe, he thought, or office workers. They were talking—until they saw him coming; then they stopped. One of them was plump, but a smooth dark brown, and sat with a towel around her shoulders. Elijah addressed them through her: "Wanna buy a nice beach umbrella?" And again he opened the umbrella over his head.

"Gee! It's beautiful," the plump woman said to the others. "But where'd you get?" she suddenly asked Elijah, polite mistrust entering her voice.

"I bought it—just this week."

The three women looked at each other. "Why do you want to sell it so soon, then?" a second woman said.

Elijah grinned. "I need the money."

"Well!" The plump woman was exasperated. "*No*, we don't want it." And they turned from him. He stood for a while, watching them; finally he let the umbrella down and moved on.

Only the lifeguard was left. He was a huge youngster, not over twenty, and brawny and black, as he bent over cleaning out his beached rowboat. Elijah approached him so suddenly he looked up startled.

"Would you be interested in this umbrella?" Elijah said, and proffered the umbrella. "It's brand-new—I just bought it Tuesday. I'll sell it cheap." There was urgency in his voice.

The lifeguard gave him a queer stare; and then peered off toward the Outer Drive, as if looking for help. "You're lucky as hell," he finally said. "The cops just now cruised by—up on the Drive. I'd have turned you in so quick it'd made your head swim. Now you get the hell outa here." He was menacing.

Elijah was angry. "Whatta you mean? I *bought* this umbrella—it's mine."

The lifeguard took a step toward him. "I said you better get the hell outa here! An' I mean it! *You thievin' bastard, you!*"

Elijah, frightened now, gave ground. He turned and walked away a few steps; and then slowed up, as if an adequate answer had hit him. He stood for a moment. But finally he walked on, the umbrella drooping in his hand.

He walked up the gravelly slope now toward the Chevy, forgetting his little pile of belongings left in the sand. When he reached the car, and opened the trunk, he remembered; and went back down and gathered them up. He returned, threw them in the trunk and, without dressing, went around and climbed under the steering wheel. He was scared, shaken; and before starting the motor sat looking out on the lake. It was seven o'clock; the sky was waning pale, the beach forsaken, leaving a sense of perfect stillness and approaching night; the only sound was a gentle lapping of the water against the sand—one moderate *hallo-o-o-o* would have carried across to Michigan. He looked down at the beach. Where were they all now—the funny, proud, laughing people? Eating their dinners, he supposed, in a variety of homes. And all the beautiful umbrellas—where were they? Without their colors the beach was so deserted. Ah, the beach . . . after pouring hot ore all week out at the Youngstown Sheet and Tube. he would probably be too fagged out for the beach. But maybe he wouldn't—who knew? It was great while it lasted . . . great. And his umbrella . . . he didn't know what he'd do with that . . . he might never need it again. He'd keep it, though— and see. Ha! . . . hadn't he sweat to get it! . . . and they thought he had stolen it . . . stolen it . . . ah . . . and maybe they were right. He sat for a few moments longer. Finally he started the motor, and took the old Chevy out onto the Drive in the pink-hued twilight. But down on the beach the sun was still shining.

The Amoralists

It was late November. The low sun was setting in a purple haze, the air was cold, and, back out to the east, clouds were looming across Lake Michigan as if the first real snow could hit the city before morning. The man and woman walked along the sidewalk together in the approaching dusk.

"Although I'm tired," she said, "I needed this walk just to get out of that house. I'll be glad to get back to the hotel, though, and more than glad when it's all over and I can go home. I've never gotten used to deaths and funerals."

"I've got to be back in New York Friday evening without fail," he said. "But with the funeral at eleven Friday I can get from the cemetery out to O'Hare for a two-thirty flight okay, I think."

The woman, tall, spare, patrician enough, yet somehow dourly horsefaced, shuddered. "You know," she said, "it's almost as if we can't rush away fast enough."

Impassive, he did not answer. He too was tall, spare. And proud, at times dyspeptic. His hair was quite gray.

"Have we been wrong or right?" she said, turning to him as they walked. "I've thought about it a lot and can't make up my mind."

"I'm an amoralist," he said. "So was Nell. For me it's not enough to ask whether something's wrong or right. Wrong for whom? Right for whom? 'For whom' is important. Crucial, in fact. It certainly was to her."

"Yes. In her great days."

"She saw whatever she did as right, for her. Otherwise she wouldn't do it. Making that one decision was all that mattered to her. She didn't care a hang about us as her brother or sister. It meant nothing, absolutely nothing, to her. Of course, it didn't work out well in the end, but it wasn't her fault. She just ran into bad luck. Generally, though, that type of instinct pays off." They were passing a block of handsome brownstone duplexes. The sun seemed sinking faster now, into a bank of dark clouds. Soon the lights would .be coming on.

"Then I must ask myself," she said, touching her lank, silver hair, "if turning my back on her in her last dreadful days was right for me. I haven't *felt* right about it, that I know." She gave a theatrical sigh.

"Whenever you get that feeling, think, in her great days, as you call them, of her contempt for your husband, and therefore for you. She'd married John Stowe IV, you see, and that made a difference. She had to consider the Stowe family and her standing in it. Think of those two despicable children of hers and how they abused yours. Heartlessly, is the only word. Remember how that little vixen Judy used to treat your Sarah? You can't forget that. It might have been more understandable if your husband, your children, my wife, my boy Stan, weren't all wonderful, intelligent people. They are, they were then. Only they didn't figure in her scheme of wants, so she wrote them off. But this was right, for her. Think of those things once in a while and you'll see that what you did was right too, for you." He sniffed testily.

She gave another theatrical sigh.

"I'm an amoralist," he said again. "You see that."

"Yes, but does it strip you of all feeling for her, in her final days?"

"Not necessarily," he said at once. "It all depends on the point I've got to look at her situation from. You can bet, though, it's not the same as hers was. Sure, if I've got to assume her point of view, then I've got to feel compassion for her. But an amoralist doesn't make that mistake. He carefully selects his own point of self-projection, so to speak. He must. From my point, then, because of some of the things I've just reminded you about, all this bad history and so on, I felt *enough* compassion for her. Let's put it that way. Certainly more than she ever did for us, or for ours." They walked on in silence for a while.

"I find little to argue about in what you say," she finally said. "It was a bad time for us. Often one of humiliation before our so-called friends. Dotty Dillon never missed an opportunity to tell me about Nell's fancy little parties whenever she'd hear about one, knowing very well I hadn't been there. It was this sort of thing that finally drove us away from here. I prevailed on Chad."

"Remember," he said smugly, "I had preceded you."

"Yes, I'm sure your leaving helped make up Chad's mind, although in the end he preferred Denver to New York. But of course the point is we all got out of Chicago, were fed up. We've liked Denver, the children especially. Chad too has done well enough."

"He's done very well. This must have been galling to Nell, in her sudden widowhood and when her luck had run out."

"She never showed contrition, though."

"Of course not. She didn't feel any. She'd done her damnedest and failed, and died bitter but unrepentant. I wonder where she got that streak? Neither Dad nor Mother was like that. We didn't get it, you or I. But, as I say, I don't judge her. Others may, not I." He walked erectly, hands rammed in his topcoat pockets.

They encountered occasional pedestrians on the sidewalk and after another two blocks came to a big drugstore which was new and brightly lighted. They went on, obliviously. Triumphant in their final victory. The sun was down behind all the apartment buildings now, leaving a dull glow in the sky. Farther on they saw a few people hurrying home. One large Lucullian gentleman carried a white paper bag in his arm from which, among other things, a loaf of French bread and a bottle of wine protruded.

The tall pair continued walking as far as the boulevard. Then they stopped. "This is far enough, don't you think?" he said.

"Yes, let's go back."

They turned around and started walking in the opposite direction. It was almost dark.

"There's practically nothing to probate, you know," he said. "This won't surprise anybody, though. Not her former friends, anyway, who'd long since abandoned her."

"That must have been the hardest experience for her of all, those terrible people."

"Were they terrible, now?" he said. "From their point of view, she was just no longer useful, had no particular appeal to them, especially after her husband died so suddenly. What an untimely death that was. As I've said, sheer bad luck for her. Also there wasn't the estate she'd had every reason to expect, and what there was didn't last long in her foolish attempts at living in her former style. So it's only natural that after it became known that she'd been reduced to a bare existence, the people she'd already been seeing less and less of repudiated her outright. Even Judy, finally. And her boy Walter. Were they all terrible? You see, I must ask you my old question again: Terrible from whose standpoint? From Nell's, yes, certainly. But in any universal sense? I think not. To us, even? No." Both walked on in silence again, gloating.

Full darkness had come now. Soon they approached the mouth of an alley. Just as they got opposite it, a crazed black ran out at them with a knife in his hand. Ragged, filthy, his eyes bloodshot and wild, whispering the vilest obscenities, he put the long blade to the man's stomach. "Git up that alley, botha you! *Quick!* I'll let yoh guts out on the sidewalk! You bettah believe it! Go on! I won't be hungry tonight, I bet!" He turned to the blanched woman. "Bitch, you scream and I'll cut yoh head off!" The man gasped, glanced at his sister, and looked around helplessly. The nearest pedestrian was across the street and had not seen. They retreated before the knife up into the alley as the black, cursing, then breathing hard, urged them on. Ahead, half a block up the alley, there was a city light high atop a steel pole. Well before they reached it the black stopped, jerked the woman's purse from her with his free left hand, and stuffed it in his coat pocket. "Now gimme yoh money!" he said to the man, all the while reaching under the topcoat and patting the man's left hip pocket. Soon he had the wallet out.

"Take the money," the man said in a dry, quavering voice, "but leave me the wallet. There's nothing else in it of any value to you."

The black replied with a flood of obscenities and thrust the wallet in his own pocket. "I oughta kill botha you muthafuckas, that's whut I oughta do!" he said. "I still wouldn't be even!" Then he ran up the alley toward the high light and had soon passed the light and disappeared in the darkness beyond.

The woman began crying. Her brother, his face chalk white, took her by the elbow and led her out of the alley back to the lighted street. She became hysterical and passersby paused to look as he tried to calm her. He escorted her up the street until they came to the big drugstore again. He took her inside where, shaking, softly crying, she waited while he went into a telephone booth and called the police.

So it was not until almost four hours later, when a light snow had begun to fall, that they found themselves back at their hotel. In the interim they had ridden with the police scouring the area in search of a suspect. They saw none. They had then been taken down to central police headquarters to look at photographs and had later attended a lineup. To no avail. Finally a young policeman brought them to their hotel in a squad car. They went up to her room where they stood for a time staring out the window onto the lights of the city and the scant falling snow.

"The young policeman was nice, wasn't he?" she finally said.

He seemed not to hear her. "It could have been far worse," he breathed, sitting down. "He could have hurt us, even killed us. That knife."

"Why did he have to use such awful language?" she said. "Why did he call us such filthy names?" She shuddered again.

"He was crazy, I think. Insane, criminally insane, maybe. Or he could have been a narcotics addict. That's why it was a dangerous situation. Sure, he could have killed us."

"Oh, heavens. And he said he was hungry."

"People like that should be removed from society." He glared at her. "Just any way. Removed absolutely."

"Oh my, yes," she said. "How I hate to call Chad. He'll be so upset."

"Don't call him. Wait until you get home. In the morning I'll call my bank at home and arrange for some money for us here. My credit cards, everything, were in the wallet. Brutes like that should be removed from the midst of other people.

How can you have a society with animals in it like that?" He ground his teeth.

"It's awful," she said, starting to shake again.

He got up and went to the telephone. "I'll call room service for some food. We ought to eat something."

"I guess so," she said. "His face was so hacked up it looked like he'd been in a hundred knife fights, didn't it? I'll never forget it. Faces, especially expressions on faces, seem to linger with me forever. I've always been like that. I'll never forget his. It was awful. Tragic, in a way."

"Bosh!"

"It was. But I was almost afraid he might try to assault me, assault me sexually."

"What are you talking about!"

"Really. And I'd have screamed and he would surely have killed me then."

"Our society is a festering sore," he said. "Whom does it exist for? Certainly not for us, people like us. What do you want to eat?"

"Nothing at all heavy. Perhaps only scrambled eggs, and some toast. And Sanka."

"I think I'll have a ground sirloin sandwich." He telephoned and ordered the food. "It's largely the courts," he said "What do judges care for the rights of the decent citizen? Although they'll profess otherwise, very little. We need an overhaul of our system of justice. Completely."

"The police were so considerate tonight, weren't they? One was colored."

"The police are efficient. But who supports them? Few, very few."

"I've never been called such names," she said.

"Oh, why, of course you haven't! My God! You never even knew there was such language. And nobody else but those animals."

"He seemed to get some kind of satisfaction out of calling us all those horrible, filthy names."

"Brute! Animal!" he said.

"They do live like animals, don't they?"

"Worse, worse!"

They were mostly silent now until the food came. The food seemed to calm them some. The man was less petulant. "Why would they insist on having a wake for Nell?" he said before biting into his sandwich.

"Heaven knows. I wonder how many people will show up. Judy and Walter, of course, belatedly. But who else?" She took a forkful of eggs and dabbed her lips with her napkin.

"I have no idea," he said.

"I only want to get home, to Chad. I know the wake tomorrow night and the funeral the following morning will seem an eternity, an ordeal. Oh, I wish I didn't feel merely like I was going through the motions for Nell. I wish I felt something more." Another sigh.

"We can't dictate such things," he said. "I never try. Neither did she."

"Did you notice the expression on her face lying there in the funeral parlor? You see, I'm always remembering things about faces. Hers wasn't a bit reposeful, like dead people's are supposed to be. Can't a mortician do something about that? Don't they have some way of changing the expression? It was so bitter. Can't they?"

"I don't know," he said brusquely.

"Oh, I feel so badly." A last exaggerated sigh.

When they had finished their meal they sat for a while staring in space. Gloating. Finally he said good night and went to his room. He had seen that outside it was snowing in earnest now and he was thinking he might have to buy some overshoes before he got home.

The March

Earlier in the day the weather forecast had said "cold but sunny," but now in the late afternoon the sky was murky and ominously changing as the sun sank slowly among dragon clouds of red. Winter had come in earnest to Chicago in time for Christmas, now three days past, and a great quilt of snow, already dingy from the smog, covered everything, including the west stretch of Bowen Avenue ahead of Wilma walking home. A minute ago she had left the Cottage Grove Avenue bus with the usual four blocks to go to reach her flat, but this evening it was without that awareness of tedious distance she always had when on weekdays she came home from work. Today was Sunday and, returning from the Union Station where she had just seen Archie, her stripling son of eighteen, off to the army, she was glumly oblivious of all such physical phenomena as weather and distance. After she had kissed him good-bye and watched him, gangling-tall and black, carrying his small piece of luggage through the train gate, she—herself only thirty-five—had felt the utter deflation, the sudden void, of her existence, and had moped out of the station. He had *wanted* to go!—the thought made her eyes sting. Less than a year ago a boy still with his old newspaper route, now a draftee, gone—eventually to Vietnam.

She passed a vacant lot now where two cars, rusty snow-thatched relics, had been abandoned until the first thaw would come, and where a shivering dog searched and sniffed in the rubble for food. Also there extended down the street ahead of her twin rows of straggly, run-down, three-flat buildings, with their dwellers' cars parked bumper to bumper out front. She walked on, unmindful. But about a block and a half from home she encountered the two Sewell boys, neighbors, out playing in the dirty snow with the new football they had got for Christmas. "Hi," she finally grinned to them, and kept walking. Rudie, the older and a clodhopper, heaved the ball out in the street to his little brother Phineas before calling to her: "There was a fire next door to you—the firetrucks just left." She stopped and gaped down the sidewalk in the direction of her flat. "... No kiddin'," she said—"which building? ... where Mrs. Jenkins lives, I bet." "Yeah," Rudie panted—"it was only in one bedroom, though. They put it out quick." She speculated that Cleet, Mrs. Jenkins' worthless son, had drunkenly set fire to his mattress again—one night last summer she had heard her rail at him that he'd be better off dead—but, uncaring, Wilma walked on, her mind monopolized by her own calamity. At the train gate Archie's face had been only a sweet, smug mask, she thought. She had watched him, tried to catch some clue to his true feelings, but had failed. Yet she remembered a trace of something in his face she did not like: its resemblance to his father's—John Taylor, a one-year husband, whereabouts long since unknown. Her surname now was Daniels. But even in this lay at least a part of her misery—she was going home to Harry Daniels. There would be only the two of them in the now-drab, monotonous apartment.

She entered the vestibule of their building, went slowly up the steps to the third floor, and, using two keys, let herself in. Her husband, a walnut-black, slovenly, heavy-featured man of fifty, sat in the living room watching a pro football game on television. He barely looked up as she entered, but soon he grinned and said in his rasping voice, "I can sure see *you* ain't feelin' so hot, hon—did Archie get off all right?" "Yeah." She made herself smile, and continued through to the bedroom—the smile dissolving at once—where she took off her hat and coat and futilely viewed herself in the dresser mirror. Archie's train was rolling eastward now, she knew—to Fort Dix, New Jersey, where he'd get his basic training. And she recalled how, in a rarely talkative moment, he had said he hoped later to get to go to the big Marine amphibious training base at Camp Lejeune, North Carolina. It was all so incredible to her—he had wanted to go. The thought kept recurring and was like a knife in her heart. And she was somehow furious with him—how could he forget those twelve awful years between her two marriages when alone she had fought for their survival? She sat down on the side of the bed, her hands in her lap, and again gazed absently into the mirror. She was average in height and size, with a smooth brown lantern-jawed face that gave her a kind of homely attractiveness. Soon she was admitting to herself she had known for at least three months Archie would have to go. Yet she'd still at the last moment been unprepared. And although he'd had to leave, why had he wanted to go? He had seemed quietly excited, eager. She was sure it was not because of his stepfather, with whom he got along well enough. Nor had she herself run him away with saccharine displays of love and attention, acts she had always avoided from fear of making him into a mama's boy.

She got up now and went into Archie's bedroom. The first

objects she saw were his gym shoes, thrown carelessly on the floor just inside the closet. There would be no more basketball now for a while, she knew, picking up the shoes and placing them above her head on the shelf. Yet his clothes were hung neatly on hangers, and his schoolbooks—he had graduated from high school the past June—were stacked against the closet wall with the two pairs of street shoes he had left behind resting on top. But the bed was poorly made, and she punched and kneaded the pillow and tightened the blanket. Soon she sat down on his bed and cried a little.

Later at dinner in the kitchen, her husband Harry, who had been drinking bourbon while he watched the football game, was uncommonly voluble, even for him. He gnawed a lamb chop, licked his fingers, and talked in his hoarse voice: "That screwball Cleet Jenkins next door damn near burned their place down again. . . . Had three fire trucks out front while ago. Somethin' oughta be done about him—they oughta draft him and send him straight to Vietnam. It'd be good riddance. But, no, they don't want *him*. They wanta nice, clean-cut boy like Archie—so Cleet can stay round here organizing peace marches. Last summer it was open-housing marches, now they're marchin' against the war."

Wilma was grim. "Who wants war? *I* don't."

"Nobody does, hon—nobody. But we've always had 'em, ain't we?—and probably always will. They can march till their feet fall off, but they ain't goin' to change *that*. No, sir. Hell, what good is marchin'?"

Wilma thought about it and secretly, grudgingly, agreed.

Much of Harry's face was greasy from the chops now—even the big Masonic ring on his finger had an added glisten. Outside it was dark, and Wilma's head spun and ears rang from the stiff drink she'd had while cooking dinner. But she was determined not to start crying again. Soon Harry, who

had been watching her, said, "You'll get used to Archie bein'
gone, hon—the first week'r two might be a little rough, but
you'll snap out of it then, see? Ain't that right?"

She finally bridled at the inanity of his talk, "I ain't *never*
going to get used to him being gone," she said. Harry gave
her an apprehensive look and for a while ate in silence. But
soon her anger ebbed as she thought of how her marriage to
him, a widower, had taken off her the awful weight of her long
struggle to survive. He operated a gasoline service station
and since their marriage had told her if she liked she could
quit her job as a garment worker and just take care of the
house. But she had turned the offer down in order not to
further jeopardize the small independence left to her and
Archie—she knew she would never have married him except
for Archie and what he needed as a growing teenager.

"What movies are on TV tonight?" she finally said, and
smiled.

Harry beamed. "There's a Nazi spy picture on Channel
Seven. Let's see it, hon. Leave the damn dishes in the sink."
When they had finished eating they got up from the kitchen
table and she cleared the dishes and stacked them under the
tap. He had already returned to the living room and was
tuning in the television, when the doorbell rang.

It was the two Sewell boys—Rudie and Phineas. "What's
up, boys?" Harry said to them the moment he opened the
door. Outside in the street the temperature was only five
above zero and they looked cold. Rudie was about thirteen,
but Phineas, only ten, was plainly freezing—he wore a
quilted parka with an oversize hood that almost hid his
solemn yellow face. Rudie clutched a sheaf of leaflets in both
hands. "We're passin' these around to everybody," he said,
". . . for Cleet. They're about the march New Year's Day."
He handed a leaflet to Harry, who glanced at it and immediately bristled. "I know 'bout it already," he rasped. "Does

your daddy know what you boys're up to, takin' this stuff around for Cleet?—does he?" Rudie looked at him. "... No, sir," he finally said. Little Phineas spoke up in defense: "Cleet paid us—he give us a dollar." "That don't make it no better," Harry said. "Come in here and close that door and let me see the rest of them pluggers." He went to the mantelpiece and got his glasses. The boys had closed the door and were standing in the middle of the room, when Wilma came in.

"Hi, Rudie," she said glumly, "hi, Phineas. What're you two doin' out in the street at night in all this cold?—my goodness."

"They're doin' Cleet Jenkins' dirty work, that's what," Harry said, "... why, this is against the government"—he was studying a leaflet—"why, sure it is. It calls Johnson a murderer. Cleet could be arrested for this, d'you know that? You're passin' out literature attackin' the president—and the government. You boys might could be arrested for this yourselves, d'you know it?" The boys were wide-eyed, hushed.

"Here, Rudie, let me see one of those," Wilma said, and took a leaflet. It read:

MARCH FOR PEACE IN VIETNAM

RALLY!   WAR PROTEST RALLY!   RALLY!

ON NEW YEAR'S DAY

Join the thousands of protesters who will MARCH! Then hear the speeches about the cruel hoax of our NEGRO BOYS fighting and dying in Vietnam. Find out why Johnson is murdering our nonwhite brothers in North Vietnam, who only want to be left alone in peace. Why are we sending NEGRO BOYS thousands of miles across the sea to fight for so-called DEMOCRACY when these same boys never shared in it right here at home? Hear all the outstanding speakers at Temple Hall on 47th Street im-

mediately after the big march—3 o'clock, New Year's
Day! The march forms at 1 PM at 35th and South Parkway (in front of the World War I Negro Soldiers' Monu-
ment) and proceeds south to Temple Hall. Come out (dress
warmly) and be counted on in this great cause—the cause
of PEACE! It is time to act. NOW!

BRING OUR NEGRO BOYS HOME!

Sponsored by the Southside Chapter, Chicago League for
Peace in Vietnam.

"See what I mean?" Harry said to her the moment she
had finished reading—"Now, what kinda stuff is that, hon?"
He turned to the boys—"Here, let me have them bills,
Rudie. Somebody oughta give that Cleet a good whippin' for
sendin' a couple of kids out at night in the cold to do
somethin' he ain't got the guts to do himself, or that he was
too dadbloom drunk to do—layin' up there today lettin' his
mother's place go up in smoke. Here, let me have 'em."
Rudie, eyes still wide in his tawny face, surrendered the
leaflets and Harry tossed them on the sofa, some slipping to
the floor. "Now, you boys go on home where you oughta be,
where it's warm—I really oughta call your daddy." The boys
stood looking at him as he went to the door, and soon he
ushered them out. When he had thrown the night lock, he
went back to the sofa, gathered up all the leaflets, and
dropped them in the wastebasket beneath the mantelpiece.

"What've you got against Cleet?" Wilma said forlornly,
turning her back to pick up her cigarettes. "I don't know if
you shoulda done that, Harry. It ain't none of your business,
is it, what Cleet does? Or those boys, either—you ain't their
father."

The television had been on all the time and Harry turned
it off and sat down in his chair. "You forget, hon, I was a
father once," he said. "My boy Ernest, my only child in the

world, started out a good boy. Like Archie is now. But what happened? Why, he got to runnin' around with a bunch of them hopheads and hippies, like Cleet Jenkins, and now he's in his grave, ain't he? If it wasn't for them he'd be alive tonight. He might even be a college graduate by now, who knows? Even my own life mighta been different. But, no, I had to watch him go down, and it was an awful thing to see, I'll tell you—*me*, his father. His mother bein' dead, he was my responsibility, but I didn't have a chance with him after he started runnin' around with that crowd of scum. I tried everything in the world to help him—everything. But he wouldn't listen. He didn't want my help—he didn't want *any* help. He didn't care—he didn't care whether he lived or died. Sometimes I think he wanted to die. He hated life and woulda liked to wrecked the whole world maybe. *That's* what that ratty outfit done for him. It was a bad experience for me, I'll tell you—bad, bad. I sure wouldn't wanta have to go through it again. So, hon, maybe you ought not to feel so bad about Archie after all—it might really be a blessing he had to go."

Wilma gaped at him. "A blessing! My God, are you crazy? I raised that boy from the time I brought him wet into the world. Tonight's the first night in his life we ain't slept under the same roof—the first night! And you talk about a bless- ing—Christ!" She stared at him with blazing eyes, and added, "I don't give a damn about nothing—about the government, about Johnson, the law, or nothing. I just want my boy back!"

Harry was pouting now. He set his brow and heavy lips in an injured frown and kept his eyes in the far corner. Suddenly he turned and glared at her—"Okay! You miss *your* son and I miss *mine!*"

Wilma gave a futile sigh and left the room.

Later, about nine forty-five, the doorbell rang again.

Almost at once Harry—he was still alone in the living room, but drinking more bourbon now and watching another television show—heard a man's wild footsteps vaulting up the stairs three steps at a time. He was almost certain who it was and, experiencing the tiniest fear, kept his seat. Soon there was a volley of sharp raps on the door. Finally he got up, went to the door, and, as expected, opened it to Cleet Jenkins—a tall, bespectacled, cadaverous youth of about twenty-four. Cleet, although wearing a huge, ill-fitting overcoat, was bareheaded and wore his hair long, au naturel African style—it was so thick, woolly, and matted that at the sides it dangled in little grapes. He seemed by now, though, to have sobered up, but was clearly jittery and overwrought.

"The Sewell kids said you took their leaflets away from them, Mr. Daniels," he said, jutting his long, wasted frame across the threshold—"I want them back. I want them back right away. You have a nerve."

On impulse Harry made a sudden move to shut the door in his face, but Cleet deftly inserted his foot, and Harry at last grunted disgustedly—"Come in, damn it, come in. All right, I took 'em and probably saved you from goin' to the penitentiary—they called the president of the United States a murderer, didn't they? *Didn't* they? There's gotta be a law somewhere against that—you and all your education oughta be able to figure that out."

Cleet, breathing excitedly, had already stepped into the room and closed the door. "I said you have a nerve, Mr. Daniels"—his eyes now were thin slits—"Give me my leaflets. They're mine, my property. Such cheek—God."

Then Harry smelled Cleet's stale whiskey breath, and suddenly remembering Cleet's compulsive, almost manic, craze for liquor, he turned cunning to distract him. "If you'll set down a minute, Cleet," he grinned, "and have a little drink with me, I'll explain to you what happened—set down there."

"No, no!—I don't have time, I don't have time!" Cleet backed against the door, but the mention of whiskey seemed to have so goaded his excitement that he now painfully wrung his hands as he talked and glanced furtively about the room as if hoping he might sight the bottle. "Those leaflets should have been out long ago!" he began agonizing loudly—"but you interfered. And you had no right. Now I've got to go around tonight yet and put them out myself. Give them to me, Mr. Daniels. No more of your rude—your uninformed—talk, either. Come on, come on!"

"Now, keep your shirt on, Cleet. Don't you wanta little taste of that sour mash there before you go? Huh?" Harry chuckled and gestured vaguely toward the bottle and ice on the other side of his chair. Just as Cleet was staring at him in tortured indecision, Wilma, who had heard, walked into the room again.

Harry at once straightened up. "Hon, I been tryin' to get Cleet here to see what I'm drivin' at about them damn handbills he's sendin' around and—"

"You don't havta offer him liquor to do it, do you?" she said, then turned to Cleet and pointed—"Your bills're there in the wastebasket. They're okay—we didn't destroy 'em." She went over and picked all the leaflets out of the wastebasket and handed them to Cleet.

Harry was riled. "Yeah," he said to Cleet, "take them damn things outa here. I don't want Uncle Sam on me like he's sure'n hell goin' to be on you—no, sir." He stepped to the door—"Yeah, take 'em and *git*." Cleet glared at him, but left and went down the steps, clutching the leaflets in two fistfuls.

Wilma disdainfully ignored Harry now, returned to the

bedroom, and began preparing for bed. But by the time she went into the bathroom to brush her teeth she was angry and desperate—she thought of the coming months that must be endured in this house without Archie and was slowly gripped by panic. She felt encircled by events. And each time she thought of Archie on a train plowing into the night and putting hundreds of miles between them, she wanted to cry again, then stubbornly refused herself the luxury. What to do? . . . what *could* she do?—she knew from now on these questions would plague her, give her no rest. For a moment she had the notion of writing Washington—she didn't know specifically whom, maybe the president—to explain her plight, how she needed her son. But what kind of need was it? she thought—certainly not economic. Archie hadn't been her financial support, and that was what mattered in Washington. Moreover, she was married to a man who could support her, and even had a job herself. Anyhow, she knew her need for Archie couldn't be put into words, couldn't be written. It was a need of the heart. And even though he had served as a merciful antidote to Harry, even this meant little when measured against this need.

She returned to her bedroom now, and as she undressed and put on her pajamas, she began speculating on the length of the war—maybe it would be over before too long, she thought. Then Archie would come home. What could she do to help end it and bring this about? She finally thought of Cleet, his leaflets, the New Year's Day march, and was unimpressed. Could these people, and others like them, really have any effect on how long the war would last? She did not know and was only puzzled. They were all probably a bunch of kooks like Harry always said . . . but *were* they?—she realized her deficiencies in judging matters of this kind. She only knew she didn't go for the bit in the leaflets calling President

Johnson a murderer—this man who had done so much for Negroes. But, she thought, even if the president did end the war, overnight, there was the problem of Archie's own ideas about coming home. He had seemed anxious to go, she reminded herself for the nth time. Would he be as eager to return? Doubts about this always racked her, and again she was somehow furious with him. Yet Archie was not a callous boy, she knew—he would not deliberately hurt her. But he was involved with his own life now. Where did this leave her? With Harry, she thought—and shuddered.

Soon Harry, the remainder of a drink in his hand, came into the bedroom. Reeking of whiskey, he was morose and began undressing in silence. He dropped a shoe to the floor, then muttered half to himself: "I shoulda kicked his ass down them stairs, that's what I *shoulda* done." Wilma frowned quizzically at him but said nothing. Finally he turned to her and said hoarsely, "And you, you takin' up for him almost like he was Archie, almost like he was your own son."

"That ain't so, Harry, and you know it—you just didn't have no business taking his handbills away from those kids, that's all. You was wrong."

"I was wrong, eh? Next you'll be out in the street marchin' with 'em—you'll be doin' that next."

She glanced carelessly at him, but curled her lip. "Maybe I will, at that—that's a thought."

He drained the drink and set the glass down hard. "Uh-huh, and when you do, you better keep *on* marchin'. Don't come back here—'cause you'll sure'n hell get put back out in the street, damn quick. You better think 'bout that. I ain't kiddin'. If you think I am, try me out." He dropped the other shoe on the floor.

She did not reply, but, sobered, thoughtful, climbed into bed and lay on her side with her back to him.

He glared at her back for a full minute, then said, "Yeah, you're gettin' some of the same medicine now *I* been gettin' all along. Only your boy ain't dead—*yet.*"

She spun over on her back and leaped out of bed. "You lousy bastard, you—don't you say that again!"

Harry grinned drunkenly. "Whatsa matter?—can't you take it?" he rasped. "Why, don't you know Archie ain't comin' back—why, hell, you saw him today for the last time. He'll be back, all right—in a metal box."

Aghast, she stood in front of him in her pajamas. "Harry, I knowed all along the kind of guy you was—sneakin', and mean, and all that—but I never knowed you was like *this.* God, I never knowed it—why, you're crazy. . . . How could you say such a thing to me? You're nuts—the devil in hell's got into you. Why, you dirty son of a bitch, you."

She left him and went for the night into Archie's room. Much later into the night, still sitting in the dark on Archie's bed, she reflected on her life. She knew it was her last night in this house, that she was utterly alone now, and that on New Year's Day it would do no good to march.

Yet, she thought, what was left her . . . but to march?

Macabre

"Neat" and "unobtrusive" are the words, I guess, best to describe the new girl they had hired in our Chicago office. She was black (of race, not color—her color was sort of an unclear tannish brown) but the fact of her race caused not a ripple, for we already had four black girls out of twenty-five or so. Most everyone liked these girls and when Doris came she was well enough received. She seemed to take this for granted, as she should have, and went about her duties— mostly just typing, no dictation as yet—in, as I say, quite an unobtrusive way. I wasn't high enough in the company (wholesalers of art supplies) to have my own private secretary, so most of the time I used a couple of girls, white, who'd been made available to me for dictation, using one about as much as the other. One day Alicia, the Italian girl, took a sick day, and the other, Katie, was doing some work for Jack Broyles, my very competitive colleague, but sidekick. I wanted to dictate and was sent Doris.

When she entered my cramped, cluttered little office I was impressed, as I've also indicated, by her neatness. She was not a pretty girl, nor very shapely—rather straight slight legs, high derriere—but I could see she spent time and effort on her appearance, and to good effect. Her dress was short, as was the fashion, but when she sat down to the right of my desk she made no attempt to tug the dress toward her knees, as Katie and Alicia generally did, but merely pressed her knees together and placed her shorthand pad down on them. Her pencil ready, she exhaled (I thought) a little nervously. It could have been a sigh. I was a little ill at ease myself, in fact maybe irritated; for I had a lot of work to get out before catching a plane that evening for Denver on company business. I wasn't sure—because she was new—that she'd be able to turn out the amount of work either of the other girls, accustomed to our office's rather brisk routine, could have, so I too perhaps sighed as I began dictating a tardy, and somewhat lengthy memorandum to Gerald Lawler, the company officer to whom I reported. At this, my trace of a sigh, Doris seemed really to tense—she sat very stiffly, hunching, shrinking her shoulders as if the room were freezing. Finally, after the memo, I dictated three letters, then asked her to go type what I'd given her, by which time I'd have more. She said "Yes, sir" and went out—unobtrusively. Looking back on it, I perhaps should have taken time to be a little more pleasant with her, smiled occasionally, put her at ease, but I'd never done this with the other girls. Besides, I was very busy.

Considering the work I'd given her, she wasn't gone too long, and brought back the memo and letters well within the time Katie or Alicia might have, and placed them on my desk before me. Her face was still a vacant mask, and this, I must say, also irritated me a little, although I wasn't at all sure she was really being difficult. I told her I wasn't quite ready yet to continue but would call her in a few minutes. She left again. What I really wanted, of course, was an opportunity to see what kind of work she had done before I dictated more. I leafed through the typed pages. They were immaculate. And the typing was good indeed, the spacing, indentation, and paragraphing beyond any but the fussiest criticism. I began to read the first page of the memo then. The sixth word in the fifth line stopped me . . . "advertisement." I had not dictated that, but "divertissement." Three lines farther my eye collided with "descending." I had said "dissenting." In the very next line I saw "casual"—I had dictated "causal." The last line of the page had "stick" instead of "stitch" and "makeup" for "macabre." (!) I didn't even begin the next page, but picked up the phone and called Marge Beall, our office manager. Marge and I after work occasionally had several martinis together (and I do mean several) in our favorite lounge—mostly when her husband was out of town—but, so far, that had been all.

"When will Jack Broyles be through with Katie?" I said to her—rather hotly, I'm afraid. "This girl you sent me either can't take dictation or she's hard of hearing, one. Or illiterate. She gets so many words wrong."

"Who'd I send you?"

"That new girl . . . Doris."

"Oh, Doris. . . . Why, you old Confederate, you," Marge laughed. "Isn't her work okay?"

I'm from Georgia but took this sally, this playful gratuity, and its implication, at least without overt reaction. "Of course her work's not okay," I said. "Who tested *her*? . . . Send me someone else, Marge—quick. I've got a lot of work to do."

"I can't, Reggie—not right now. There is no one. Katie'll be tied up for another hour or more. Why don't you have Doris type the work over?—you write in the correct words and have her do it over. I won't send you her again if you don't like her."

"I don't care who you send me as long as she can take dictation." I was slightly petulant now. I hung up and called Doris in again.

"Doris," I said, "pull up a chair and let's go over this stuff I gave you—you've got quite a few words wrong. What I'll do is write in the corrections and then you can retype this work." She directed toward me what I thought at first was a wary look, but afterward I concluded it was dry fear. She pulled up the chair beside mine and eased into it. "If I dictate too fast for you," I said—in the most agreeable, understanding way I knew—"feel free to stop me and tell me. Or if I use a word you don't know, stop me and I'll spell it. Okay?" I looked at her.

"Yes, sir," she said, but almost inaudibly.

I pulled the memo over before us and picked up a pencil. "Now, this word here should be 'divertissement'—that's the word I used." I crossed out "advertisement" and wrote in "divertissement." "Are you familiar with the word?"

Looking blankly at the page, not the word, she exhaled heavily again. "No, sir," she said.

"And this word here," I said—"it's 'dissenting,' not 'descending.'" She watched me write in the correction. I next changed her "casual" and "stick," respectively, to my "causal" and "stitch." Then I came to her expression "makeup"—for my word "macabre." To be truthful, I was a little unhappy with myself, contrite, for not having originally spelled the word for her, without making her ask me. For I doubted very seriously if either Alicia or Katie knew the word. Yet they most assuredly would have stopped me and got it right. Instead Doris had used a word she very well knew was wrong, rather than ask me to spell the correct one. Brushing aside all my contrition now, I thought this not only stupid of her but a little devious. I was unhappy with *her* now. I crossed out "makeup" and brusquely wrote in "macabre." "How did you ever come to use 'makeup?'" I said, smiling testily—"The two words don't sound *anything at all* alike."

She looked at me for a moment, then glanced furtively

away as she spoke. "The words I didn't know I tried to look up in the dictionary. . . . Some of them I couldn't find. . . ."

"Of course you couldn't—you can't locate words in the dictionary you can't spell. 'Macabre' is an unusual word anyhow—maybe I shouldn't have used it, because it's generally meant to describe something gruesome, perhaps some miserable, appalling, condition of life; while in this memo I was simply referring to the properties of certain paints—artists' paints and oils, and so on; not anything about real life. After this, Doris, just have me spell any word you're not sure about. I won't mind—it will save a lot of time."

She didn't look at me but gazed vaguely at the memo before us. "Yes, sir," she said.

I spent the next twenty minutes going through the rest of the memo and the three letters with her. There were so many inaccurate, bizarre, substitutions for the words I had dictated that I, besides being exasperated, was at a loss to understand how she could have tested well enough to be hired as a stenographer. As a typist, yes—a stenographer, no. For it was apparent her education was so deficient she had hardly any vocabulary at all. But really, at the moment, this fact was at best only dismaying to me—my job output was suffering. When I had finally finished with all the corrections, she took the corrected pages and redid them, and had them back on my desk even before I went to lunch. The job was perfect—perfect. Nevertheless, I was much happier that afternoon when Katie returned to me and I was able to finish all the work I had to do before leaving for O'Hare Airport.

I was in Denver three days. I returned home Friday evening but of course wasn't back on the job until Monday morning. Almost at once Marge came to my little office and asked me, in a curious, a slightly concerned way, really, what had happened—between Doris and me. I told her. And in my innocence I was very accurate, very complete. Yet I was unable to figure out quite what she was driving at. Then she said Doris had not returned after that day of our encounter, and that the day following had phoned in that she was resigning. No more than that . . . just resigning. I was surprised to hear it, naturally; maybe disappointed, and gaped at Marge for a moment. But I knew I had not treated the girl any differently than I would have any girl in our office under similar circumstances. One thing, though, did upset me—definitely. Marge, only *half*-kidding this time, had called me a "Confederate" again—"You unregenerate old Confederate, you," she'd said. I didn't like it a bit this time and I know I showed it. Sure, I'm from the South and no doubt that's why I took such offense at the insinuation I had mistreated the girl in some way, and because of race. I'm an educated man. And a compassionate man. I *know* this. And I take the greatest pains to be correct, indeed meticulous, about these matters of . . . of race. Although I do admit I'm no fuzzy bleeding heart either. But somehow Marge's remark, under the circumstances, offended me terribly and I sulked the rest of the day.

Around four o'clock that afternoon she phoned me—although her office is only about seventy-five feet from mine—and asked me if I'd buy her a drink when we left the office. She meant at our favorite spot, Terry's Lounge. Although I was sore at her, I wanted, really, to do it. I wanted a drink. I needed to talk. I also knew her husband had probably left town that day—he worked for a city-based public utility company yet had to travel a lot—or else she wouldn't have been able to stop for several martinis on the way home. But I wasn't sure whether or not I would take her—I told her only that I'd let her know by five. I knew I wanted to do it, though, and finally called Carrie, my wife, and said I couldn't get home for dinner—which created no problems for Carrie, who had her superpious mother (a real Christer) and our teenage (flit-to-be) son, Armand, there to eat with. Thus the way was cleared.

Terry, the owner of this small lounge, was a great little Irishman (although cocky when drinking Calvados) and greeted Marge and me with beaming, avuncular embraces— he thought himself all-wise in all matters clandestine. Because of its weird lighting, the place was always in a kind of half-murky gloaming, and Terry practically had to lead us to a booth, where (outside it had been snowing) he insisted on helping Marge off with her boots.

Our first pair of martinis were always straight up, with a lemon twist. Thereafter we customarily ordered them on the rocks, with an anchovy olive. Terry's man, Joe, was on tonight. Joe made the drinks huge and dry. "Why do we keep coming here?" Marge said, then took a sip of the first drink and chased it with water. She smiled: "This is the first time I've been brazen enough to actually ask you to bring me here. But you've been peeved at me all day."

"Well . . . oh, well, forget it," I finally said, and lit her cigarette. She was a plump blonde of thirty-six or so, and too short, but her face was candid and attractive. "You *were* a little raw with me," I added, however.

"I was nothing of the kind, Reggie—I've called you all those names before . . . 'Reb' . . . 'Dixiecrat' . . . 'Redneck' . . . 'Confederate.' And most of the time it's been when we were both drunk. . . . You only laughed. But, God, this morning you looked like you wanted to kill me. I know why, of course."

"Your saying that this morning, under the circumstances, was at least thoughtless. I'd told you what had happened between the girl and me, and I gave you a very truthful account. Tell me this, how would you have handled her any differently?—and do me the favor of being as truthful as I've been."

"I would have made the girl feel wanted," Marge said simply.

"I didn't make her feel *unwanted.*"

"Not consciously, no. Yet you somehow really socked it to her. By the whole incident you told her she was practically illiterate but that because of your magnanimity she would be tolerated."

I was furious. I knew I'd better keep quiet now or be sorry later. And I could think of so many telling, dispositive arguments—like: you can't run a business or a country on sentiment and with incompetents. I did say, "You're nuts . . . *nuts.*"

"Look, Reggie, the girl is a product of ghetto schools. Solid black. She's a high school graduate, sure, but from a *ghetto* high school—you've simply got to make allowances for that. Such· a person has first got to be made to feel wanted—till she can be taught, taught *on the job.* Sure, it's hard. It's exasperating. I've already failed with four girls. But I've won with four others, too. A five hundred batting average isn't so bad. Yes, it was *I* who tested her—*I* who hired her."

"I did make allowances," I said, "and deported myself as a gentleman—I treated her like the lady she is. Marge, I tell you, you're nuts."

"I hope you don't think *you're* the first to call me nuts." Her eyes flashed angrily—she had finished her second of Joe's martinis now and it was working; she was getting a little mean as she spoke—"A girl fresh out of the ghetto doesn't know the word 'macabre' and you make a big deal out of it. Jesus, Reggie."

I was determined now not to quarrel with her and later after ordering our third martini I somehow laughed, leaned across, and whispered to her: "Marge . . . *Marge* . . . let's not fight—let's make love." I surprised myself. It was the first time I'd made a real pass at her.

She looked at me, startled. But at last she smiled wearily. "No, so far, I've managed to be faithful to my husband," she said, "... whatever that is. God!—men are so insensitive ... ha, so *'macabre.'* "

This plummeted me into a long, morose silence. I was truly hurt again, for this time I could feel her disappointment with me; really, her disdain—not about the pass I'd made, not that; but about what she construed as my bigotry. And I knew I was *not* a bigot. Besides, I thought her a starry-eyed, impractical visionary now—who had, moreover, been callously unfair to me. I regretted I hadn't gone straight home from the office. Neither of us talked now. That Doris! ... Oh, that darned Doris, I thought. I *knew* I had done no wrong. She couldn't do the work ... she was helpless. What was I to do?—compliment her for this? Yet, I was hurting. I felt a deep, knifing pain.

By the time we had finished three of Joe's martinis apiece, we were both a little woozy. I'd had enough and wanted some convenient way to break up this murderous tête-à-tête. Soon I said (lying): "You know what I'll do? Tomorrow I'll go find that girl and bring her back." I grinned unsteadily at Marge.

"That would be the decent thing to do," she said without batting an eye. Yet I could tell she was half drunk. She reached down now and began putting on her boots. Then she got up and unsteadily put on her coat and in a moment strolled ahead of me toward the door, while I stopped and paid Terry and tipped Joe.

When we crossed the street in the snow and got in my car, she watched me with a strange, almost hysterical look. "Where are we going?" she said, now in a quavering, lachrymose voice I'd never heard before. . . . Yet it was essentially conciliatory, at least at the moment—or triumphant, or something . . . oh, it's impossible to describe it. I do believe she *felt* me changing—I had somehow become the object of a near instantaneous metamorphosis, and although I wasn't immediately conscious of it myself (it was subliminal, you see), she had sensed it at once. But perhaps it was both instantaneous and gradual—in a word, pervasive? . . . yes. I was in its throes for almost a week of tortured hell—a cruddy time I'll never forget. Yet sort of an immolation, I guess. Quite a period, to put it mildly. But isn't all this incidental? Or is it? It is too terrible to speak of—this metastasis, this five-day mutation. I can only compare it to King John rolling on the floor and chewing straw at Runnymede, or to Saul stricken down en route to Damascus. But in the car that night I did not deign to reply to her question, and started the motor and drove off in the general direction of her house.

A howling wind had come up. It got under the snowdrifts and, lifting them up, hurled them in great spiraling mini-cyclones that rocked my new Dodge on the Kennedy Expressway. Marge seemed to shiver now, and cuddled closer to me as I drove. "Take me to a motel, Reggie," she said—"now." Again, the eerie quaver.

Instead I took her home and let her out.

But within the week, by Friday, I had located the girl, Doris, and persuaded her to return to the office and work for me. Then one evening after work, soon—very soon—thereafter, I took Marge to Terry's Lounge again and later to the beautiful Su Casa motel. It had all turned out so exhilaratingly. I felt so whole—and after such a hairbreadth escape. The great British physiologist Sir Charles Sherrington has described pain as "the psychical adjunct of an imperative protective reflex." Ha, or more simply, pain is what the victim perceives in his mind after he has touched a hot stove.

The Frog Hunters

There were of course always the mosquitoes. But now a thin warm rain was falling and the air was oppressively dank so close to the little lake, the lead-colored lake. The rain had kept the boys indoors all afternoon and the camp barracks-dorm was bedlam as they played cards, shot craps, swatted carnivorous insects, wrestled each other onto the pine floor, and, in the case of at least one of them, tried to read a book. There were twenty-three in all, ranging narrowly in age from twelve to fifteen, and Camp Bosen had been their lot, their cruel fate, for five weeks of each of the past three summers. In the midst of this madhouse now Raymond half reclined on his bunk bed reading a salacious paperback which had finally come to him (it was *his* turn!) after already being carried around and read by six or seven of the hornier boys.

"Ray, you got to the place yet where she's panting and telling him, 'Lay me! Lay me, Clarence! Hurry up, lay me!' Huh?" Francis Flanigan, pimply-faced and brazen, asked, tittering.

"Not yet," grinned Raymond shyly, kneading his rather pointed towhead.

"Why don't *you* hurry up with that book?" Specs Dottweiler ranted at Raymond, "*I* get it next!"

"Me, after that!" It was little Hershel Reichman, barely twelve, speaking up for himself.

"I'll be finished with it by dinnertime," Raymond said.

" 'Hurry up, Clarence! Lay me, lay me!' " still echoed Francis Flanigan in a high, faked, womanish voice. It was he who had bought the book in the first place, read it, then begun its circulation among the pure, but brightly eager, campers. Fifteen years old, and a natural leader—also a natural sensualist—he had kept them awake night after night after lights-out describing (in pruriently minute detail) his own actual and imagined exploits, some with sly sybaritic overtones.

Now Ned Cavitt, one of the two men who had brought them up to camp this year, and who was in charge (so to speak—his *wards* were in charge), made his way through the melee to say something in a low voice to Raymond. Raymond, studying his face, was obviously sobered by the news he heard: His mother, according to Cavitt, had phoned from the city (Chicago) to say that tomorrow she and her sister were driving through—so she said—on their way up to Madison (Wisconsin) and planned to drop Raymond off some clean clothes. It would be all right, wouldn't it? she had asked Cavitt. Cavitt, busy, harried, a mercurial person anyway, a father of five himself, had hesitated. "Sure," he had finally said, "but it could bring Ray a little ribbing from the others, you know. A 'mama's boy' is the worst thing a kid can be called up here. When you get here, though, I'll have him come over to my hutment. Then make it. brief, will you? Okay, Mrs. Gibson." Thus it was agreed between them.

Just hearing all this silly strategy, the involved protocol, made Raymond gloomy—almost as much so as this reminder of the submerged hell that had reigned at home for six months. But anything could remind him of this. And although when he'd left, it hadn't quite reached critical proportions, he wondered now if the crisis hadn't come at last. Why else would his mother (Rita) be coming away up here? He needed no clean clothes—Rita knew the boys had laundry service not far from here. What then was brewing? Raymond, though sensitive and shy, was perceptive beyond his fifteen years, but although he'd tried he could not unravel all the tangled complexities of this strange malaise at home. He could not quite make up his mind whether the difficulty, the basic trouble, stemmed from causes *other than* the fact that Rita was white and his stepfather (Luther) black. He sighed and told Cavitt "Okay," that he'd wait for Rita's phone call. Cavitt left.

Raymond lay back on his bunk again and tried to read, but it was no use and he gave up. "Specs, want to read the book awhile?" he called—"My eyes are tired." He pitched the paperback to Specs Dottweiler who was on the floor in a penny blackjack game. Specs grabbed it out of the air with one hand and stuck it in his hip pocket. Raymond lay down on his back now, fingers laced behind his head, and tried to figure out what was happening. He wondered if Luther was acting up again. Luther was having a bad time of it, and he sometimes felt sorry for him.

He remembered his real father only hazily. What he recalled most vividly was the young man's hairy forearms, which he saw and felt whenever his father picked him up. The hair was coarse and flaxen like his own now. Then somewhere, sometime, in those dim early days, his father's slender, sallow face had swum out of view never to return. He had never really known the man, or loved him. There wasn't time. The memory was distant, static, stirring no ritual emotion. Then sometime later it seemed vaguely that he, Raymond, and Rita had moved somewhere, and in this place he had come to know

Luther. At once Luther was different, and looked very different. He was also warm to the touch, laughed softly, and most of the time smelled deliciously good. But most important of all, he would ride Raymond around on a fiery red motorcycle. Sometimes Rita too went along, making three of them and holding Raymond between them closely against her belly, as some people gawked and a few glowered. It was wonderfully exciting and thrilling and he had never forgotten it. But things weren't invariably so perfect: one time Luther had struck Rita and she had wailed and cried and cursed him. He, Raymond, had cried too, and on such occasions he hated Luther. But it would only last for a half day or so. Then came the time Luther bought the big color television set and unveiled it on Christmas morning. That whole day long, Raymond had loved him extravagantly. In fact it seemed to him now, retrospectively, that he and Luther had always been very good friends. But recently serious trouble had come and Luther was threatening to leave.

The boys' wild fun and games went on. The elongated pine-smelling room, its bunk beds on either side of a long middle aisle, bare rafters overhead, reverberated now with all kinds of weird, hellish sounds. It was manic, as if subliminally the boys considered themselves castoffs, cruelly banished from pleasant city homes to this north-woods experience. There was a happy, fierce hysteria imbuing them. But they were really bored, unhappy, neglected, and, though yelling and laughing all the while, took out their desperation on each other. It was only slightly different when the sun was shining and they were out-of-doors, but today, driven inside by the steady, tedious drizzle, they were out of control.

Finally Cal Staley, a boy big for his age, grabbed up a baseball bat and began swinging it around his head with all his might. The others ducked low, grinning warily at this strangely wanton behavior.

"Look out, Cal!" Francis Flanigan warned. "You're gonna brain somebody in a minute."

"What do I care?" laughed Cal. At full arm's length now he swung the bat viciously, a whirling Appalachian dervish, as the others leaned, then scrambled, back.

"Stop that, you goofy bastard!" Francis yelled menacingly. "Or when you do I'll whip your ass."

Still laughing, Cal finally stopped, but then suddenly, unexpectedly, he tossed the bat to Francis, who caught it just in time. Francis ground his teeth and glared at him, but then stood holding the bat as if not knowing what to do with it, or as if he'd never seen one before. Suddenly he thrust it between his legs, in his crotch, and began making ludicrous masturbatory gestures. Everyone howled with delight now, and for a time at least the bizarre tension was broken.

But slowly Raymond had become miserable. More and more he was dreading Rita's visit. He could not shake the feeling she would bring with her some new, maybe critical, facts he did not want to have to face. Moreover, it could only run the risk once more of resurrecting hints of that most delicate of matters involving his standing with the other boys, who knew who his stepfather was. In the city, neither he nor Rita had ever tried to hide Luther's existence and the boys and their families all knew about him and accepted the fact. Cal and Francis and Specs, and maybe some of the others too, had even seen and talked to Luther. They liked him for his genuineness. And he was friendly most of the time, though at other times a little reserved—they had heard of his erratic temper, although they had never seen it displayed. But his greatest attraction was his ability to do so many things and do them well: he was a natural athlete, a canny fisherman, a wizard at gin rummy and pinochle, and then each year he traded in his motorcycle for a spanking brand-new one—even Francis and Specs had ridden up behind him and hadn't yet forgotten the thrill of the experience. But Raymond knew the boys had discussed every angle of this relationship and in addition had heard it bruited about in their families. He always dreaded the day when one of them, perhaps in sudden hot anger about something else, might blurt out some indignity. He'd never quite been able to make up his mind about what he'd do in such a case. Would he fight, threaten to fight, or just ignore it all and walk away? He couldn't decide. He couldn't predict. He doubted, however, that the situation would ever really arise. It hadn't in all these years. They referred to Luther just as casually, as offhandedly, as he did—as "Luther"—and could surely see how close the two of them had become in the last few years. Still, the possibility of some impulsive, involuntary outburst was always present and made Raymond tense at times, unsure of himself, less outgoing, than he otherwise might have been. A visit to camp by his mother now couldn't possibly be kept secret for long, and could only start the boys to thinking, maybe whispering again, about the family's makeup. He wished *so* she weren't coming. Moreover, he was certain she carried bad news.

The drizzle had slackened but not quite yet stopped, and then a faint rainbow appeared far out over the lake even as the rain still fell. At last Francis said, "Let's get the hell outa here and go catch some bullfrogs—the rain's about stopped. Come on, Ray."

Raymond got up dutifully although he did not want to go. He did not want to lie around in the dorm any longer either, thinking about the mess at home.

"How're you goin' to catch any frogs in the daylight?" Cal challenged. "You haven't got any so far."

But Francis merely went to his bunk, poked around underneath, and brought out a butterfly net. Its opening was a thin circular steel rim about twelve inches in diameter and it had a slender wooden handle about five feet long. It had apparently been left by the contingent of campers preceding them. "You just take this thing," Francis said, thrusting his fist into the net's close mesh, "and go up to a frog sitting on the bank or on a log in the water and wait till he jumps to get away from you. Then with this long handle you poke the net out under him and instead of landing in the water he'll land in it. See? Come on, Ray—come on, Hershel." Little Hershel Reichman quickly got up.

"You still can only catch frogs at night," Cal insisted— "by shining them blind with a flashlight."

"Come on, Ray and Hershel," repeated Francis, ignoring Cal. Then he looked around. "Anybody else wanta go?" But he got no more takers.

The three of them went out into the sunny drizzle and headed down the slope toward the lake and the rainbow, Francis carrying the butterfly net. Raymond went stoically. His mind was on phoning Rita when he returned, to prevail on her not to come tomorrow. He also meant to find out what, if anything, had happened at home. He felt, almost knew, there was something, some new developments, and felt all the more sorry for Luther. Maybe Rita had in fact gone through with it, he thought—gone through with what for weeks she'd been hinting at. Every such hint, inevitably brought Luther, in his solemn, rather prissy, but fierce pride, to vow that he was going to leave. Maybe now Rita had finally come out with it, had told him she wanted her freedom. But Raymond knew it was not freedom she wanted, but another man, another husband. A different husband—Stanley Wosik, by name. She'd said it would mean a better life for them, for Raymond and herself; and that she'd also be able at last to have other married women as friends, some social life. Moreover, Stanley, only forty but a widower, owned and operated a good-sized automobile accessories sales place. While Luther, besides visible disabilities, was a mere clerk in the Veterans Administration. The thought wounded Raymond. He was sick with grief about Luther, and about himself. But he did not condemn Rita for what she was about to do, or had perhaps already done. He was loyal to her against all comers, including Luther. Still, his feelings ran strong for Luther for all the great times they had had together. It was apparently a problem with no solution. Yet he thought hard about it, but couldn't put Luther out of his mind.

When they got down to the lake, Francis began shushing Raymond and Hershel, although neither of them had uttered more than a few words. "We gotta keep quiet now," he warned testily—"real still, to see the frog before he sees us and jumps in the water." They were in a ragged little cove where the water was dark, stagnant, and smelly. There were a few dead tree branches half submerged in the water, and rotten leaves lying flat on the surface. Francis, net in hand, stepped to the muddy edge and peered down hard into his own grotesque reflection, then looked up and down the immediate bank, Raymond and Hershel close behind him. They saw no animate thing. Francis withdrew now and went on a few yards farther down the little lake's jagged rim where in the brackish water he examined a large decayed log bearing splotches of green slime and wet moss. Soon a tiny terrapin surfaced and slowly, laboriously, struggled up on top of it to rest.

"*Shhhh,*" Francis said again to the two already chronically silent boys. "There may be a frog there too in a minute— shhh." Then with his hand he made a motion behind him— "Squat down," he said, and squatted himself, but still watching. The other two did as directed, as Hershel slapped at a mosquito on his elbow.

The drizzle had finally slowed to a stop now. The rainbow, though no more firmly outlined or distinct than before, had grown larger, more embellished, as if arching the very earth. Raymond watched it, but obliviously. He was itching to get to a telephone to talk to Rita. Trying to talk to Luther was fruitless, for he had tried it. Their recent encounters had been solemn occasions for them both, as the trouble had been brewing for weeks. And both understood its serious nature, though neither would volunteer to discuss it. Raymond got his only information from Rita, but in conversations far, far too candid for his comfort, his equanimity. They also made him feel so insecure. But he surmised it was because Rita felt that naked frankness was absolutely necessary, to convince him, her only child, that she was right—right, and not unjust. It was during one of these talks that she had caught a sudden, momentarily horrified expression on his face. "What on earth's the matter with you, Ray?" she had said. After gaping for moments at her he had finally replied, ". . . What . . . what if he should hurt you?" "Oh, heavens, Luther's not that kind of a guy," Rita said. "Besides, he's got far too much pride to try any rough stuff." But ever since then, the specter of Rita's death had intermittently reappeared to him, each time chilling his soul. After all, he thought, full of pride, she was only thirty-four, and still very good to look at.

Soon the little terrapin slid down off the partly submerged log and slowly glided away, leaving a tiny wake. This somehow seemed to nettle Francis. The other two could see his lips moving in whispered exasperation as he stood up and started looking up the bank for another place to which to transfer their vigil.

Then suddenly they heard little Hershel say "*Whoops!*" They saw him pointing down at the tall grass near the water's very edge. Francis and Raymond looked at him, then at the general area receiving his point.

"What *is* it?" Francis said. "Is it a snake?"

"No, no! . . . It's a big frog!" Hershel's eyes were big.

"Where?" Francis brought up his butterfly net to the ready.

"Right there . . . somewhere . . ." Hershel was pointing vaguely now.

Breathing heavily, Francis waited, blue Irish eyes burning, boring into the grass—but where so far nothing moved. Fully a minute passed.

Then suddenly the big bullfrog took a giant leap—right before their eyes—baggy lids bulging, hind legs splayed, and landed, "plunk," in the water. At once it dove out of sight.

Francis, stunned into disbelief, could only gape. "Did you see *that*?" he said at last, hoarsely. "Jesus! . . . wasn't he big!" He brought down his net disconsolately. "Oh, Christ," he moaned—"what a beaut."

"Sure was," Hershel said. "*I* saw him first."

Francis wheeled on him wrathfully. "A lot of difference it makes, you little shit! Right away you lost him in the grass. Or else I woulda caught him. Come on. Let's move down some." They followed him now to a spot under a big beech tree whose great exposed roots extended out into the water, some looping, coiling up to break the surface like random sections of a huge serpent. Francis peered down long and closely at any likely site for a resting frog, but in vain. "Let's be quiet, though," he still told them. "One might be looking at us right now. It's only a matter of seeing him. Let's get down." They all squatted again.

With ever-increasing frequency Raymond caught himself thinking of Rita. Her safety. It was as if his mind had begun to bulge, with anxiety, fear. Maybe she had wanted to come up because she too was afraid, he thought—maybe fear had hit her after all. He thought ahead. . . . So when he talked to her tonight, he should *not* try to prevent her from coming. Maybe she felt that she needed him. If he could only talk to Luther, Raymond agonized now, he perhaps might be able to get some inkling of how the tall, brown, sometimes moody man felt. Had Rita finally told him?—that it was all over. . . . If so, how was he taking it? Luther did not drink, so how *was* he reacting? This was very important, Raymond knew.

The rainbow was finally disappearing. Soon the frog-hunting party was joined by Specs Dottweiler and three other boys. "Oh, Christ," moaned Francis on seeing them. He got up. "This does settle it—we'll never catch anything now. Why don't you ginks go on back and leave us alone?" he said to the newcomers.

Specs sneered. "Are you dumb enough to think you can catch a frog with that thing?" he said, nodding at the net. "You gotta long wait, then."

Raymond and Hershel stood up too now, and Hershel, after scratching in his groin, took a long, back-arching stretch, and yawned. "I'm tired," he said to Raymond, "let's go back."

"We're going back," Raymond finally said to Francis.

"Go ahead then, sissies," Francis said. "I'm still gonna catch me a frog." Then followed by the newcomers, he continued down the bank, looking for another spot.

When Raymond and Hershel returned to the dorm, it was four o'clock. Raymond felt strange and uneasy. It was a feeling made up of many variously obscure premonitions, by which he was confused. The frog hunt, at brief intervals at least, had gently tugged his mind away from these shifting perplexities, but now he was defenseless, a prey to any thought his mind could conjure up. Because the rain had stopped, only a few of the boys were still in the dorm. It was far less noisy than before and Raymond lay down on his back in his bunk again in order to think. He concluded after a time that the most optimistic possibility was that there had been no change at all at home, this despite all his forebodings to the contrary. Anyway, he hoped there had not. There was certainly no evidence, unless it was the sole fact of Rita's phone call to Cavitt, yet this slight evidence was enough to dash his hopes at once. For why would Rita *ever* be going up to Madison? And how could her sister leave a house full of small children to accompany her? He could not possibly bring himself to believe it. None of it made sense. There was only one thing to do—go to Cavitt's hutment and phone her.

He found Cavitt in the company of his assistant, an older man named Rouse, in their nearby hutment. They were drinking beer, and Cavitt was scrubbing a pair of white canvas loafers. The coin telephone was on the wall.

"Can I call home?" Raymond said diffidently, hating it but resigned to talking to Rita in their presence.

"Sure, Ray." And Cavitt turned back to Rouse.

Raymond dropped in a dime, placed the call collect, and waited, his throat dry from tenseness. Soon Rita answered and accepted the call, but sounding as she always did— "Anything wrong, Ray, honey?"

He forced a chuckle. "I'm calling to ask *you* that. Is there?"

"Luther left last night."

"*Yeah?* . . . Was he mad?"

"Oh, sort of, I guess. You can't always figure him out, though."

"What're you going to do now?"

"What do you mean?"

"I mean . . . about Stanley Wosik."

Rita laughed and lowered her voice. "He's here now."

"Gee. . ." Raymond swallowed hard in apprehension. "You sure don't let any grass grow under your feet."

"Don't try to act so old, and so wise, Ray."

Cavitt and Rouse were still talking and Raymond seized the opportunity to say to Rita, "Wouldn't it be better to wait a little . . . till the divorce? Luther might show up there. After all, he's still your husband."

"I don't think he'll show up, ever. We had a pretty friendly, heart-to-heart talk last night, you know. I think he understood everything."

"*Everything?* . . . Did you tell him about Stanley?"

"Of course not. But Luther's no fool."

"Is that why you say he was '*sort of*' mad?—Oh, gee! . . ."

"Now, now, Ray, I only sensed it. Ha, although that may be my vanity."

"Well, be careful, that's all. Gosh . . ."

"You don't mean you're worried about me, Ray. Ha, ha."

" 'Sort of,' as you say."

"Well, don't. And I'll see you tomorrow."

"Tomorrow! I thought you were kidding or something about coming up."

"Of course I wasn't kidding. I did tell Cavitt I'd be with your aunt Irma—that wasn't so. I'm coming up to Madison with Stanley. He's taking me to meet his mother."

"Don't show up here with *him*! . . . Lord!"

"Don't be a ninny, Ray. We'll be driving by within twenty miles of there."

"*Don't come*, Mom! . . . I'm telling you!" Cavitt looked up abruptly and Raymond lowered his voice: "Just do as I say for once, Mom. Don't come. I'll call you again when you get back from Madison. Okay?"

"Ray, you sound like a nervous wreck. What's the matter with you? If it'll make you any happier, then I'll skip it. Yes, call me Friday evening." But Rita sighed now. "I'll be back by then."

"Friday . . . You're staying overnight, eh? . . . Oh, Mom."

". . . That's right, Ray—yes." Again her voice had fallen.

When they had finally hung up, Cavitt smiled. "Talked her out of coming, eh?" he said. "Atta boy. This is no place for mothers." Raymond grinned sheepishly at him and could think of nothing to say. He hurried out and returned to the dorm.

That evening at dinner in the rustic little mess hall, the fare was meatloaf, mashed potatoes, and iced tea. Raymond sat at a table with Cal Staley and two other boys. There were seven tables in all, tonight seating varying numbers, and Francis Flanigan was at one over near the fireplace. In the middle of the meal, Cal, laughing snidely, called across to Francis's table: "I bet Francis is eating frog legs over there." He stood up as if to get a better view—"Hey, no! . . . That looks like meatloaf on his plate!" Everyone laughed, including Cavitt and Rouse. But Francis, who hadn't seen a frog after Raymond and Hershel left him, only grinned and went on eating his second helping of meatloaf and potatoes.

That night Raymond slept fitfully, rolling, tossing, occasionally moaning in his sleep. Then he would awake perspiring and lie perfectly still, thinking, thinking hard. He would raise his hand to his forehead, wondering if he were feverish. His responses were radically varied. One time his head would feel fiery hot, the next clammy and cold. He was convinced he was ill now. But then he would doze off and soon fall into a troubled sleep once more. He would dream, but most of the dreams he could not remember—save possibly those in which Rita was a participant. One such had occurred that night. It seemed in the dream he and Luther had ridden Luther's new red Suzuki motorcycle out to a night aquatic sports show in the suburbs. There they saw the big beautiful turquoise swimming pool, floodlighted, and surrounded by bleacher seats filled, or nearly so, with wealthy-looking people in sleek sports attire. Three wide diving boards, each fixed at a different height, and all reached by an extremely tall steel ladder attached, projected over the water. At the very top, on a platform high above the pool, the entrepreneurs had mounted a powerful spotlight that, after the floodlights during an act were doused, was trained through the darkness relentlessly onto the performers as they went through their routines of high diving, swimming races, water polo, antics by aquatic clowns, water ballet, etc. But the singular (and chilling) feature about the spotlight was the tenacity of its operator, his seeming demonic doggedness. No performer escaped his pitiless, knifing, white pencil beam, which from such a height could make a man or woman below into a puny, insignificant, ridiculous robot, or a group of performers seem wretched little jumping, scurrying june bugs. The light could create some of the weirdest scenes and effects imaginable, and in the dream Luther and Raymond, having paid their admission and now seated in the stands, were fascinated, spellbound. But the spotlight could also create *beautiful* people. It was during one such instance in the water ballet that something very strange and ominous happened. Of all people, the prima ballerina turned out to be Rita. Luther was stunned. He almost fainted. She wore a dazzling white bikini and what seemed a jeweled crown secured on her head by some kind of glittering chin strap. Raymond, gaping, nudged Luther excitedly—"It's *Rita!*" he said. But Luther was already whispering furiously to himself, his eyes popping. As the ballet unfolded, and many of the dancers pirouetted in the shallow end of the pool, Rita's male partner, apparently a handsome prince, now joined her on the wide lower board in a tender, amorous pas de deux. Luther lurched forward in his seat, eyes burning, breathing labored, for the instant the prince appeared the spotlight operator had switched to his kaleidoscopic lenses, producing a startling effect. Instead of having made these two performers into more of his tiny robots, bugs, or beetles, he had transformed Rita and her prince into mythical pastel creatures of the most dazzling beauty. It could only have been a magic spotlight, and its operator an evil (or virtuous) magician. At last, minutes later, in the final throes of their balletic ecstasy, Rita and her prince, still clutching each other in a desperate, passionate embrace, dove gracefully into the water, to the accompaniment of stormy applause. At this, Luther leaped up and pulled out a little blue-steel automatic, flicked off the safety, and, aiming, waited for the pair to surface. Raymond could only remember screaming and grabbing his arm, just as the imminent tragedy broke the dream off. So now he sat bolt upright in his bunk bathed in perspiration. Even some of the boys had been awakened. He was unable to go back to sleep until almost dawn.

Next morning in the mess hall at breakfast he was very tired and glum. The other boys were planning a full-scale, nine-inning softball game to be played later that morning and were noisily speculating on who would be on what team after the two rival captains, Buzz Viverito and Tanny Lyons, had chosen up the sides. It was Thursday, a clear, bright, beautiful July day, and the lake which only yesterday had been such a dark mousy gray was now deeply serene and greenish-blue. Raymond ate in silence as he struggled with the dream. *The dream*—it was now, and would be in the immediate days ahead, his one, total preoccupation. He fought to keep it at bay, clear of his mangled brain. By the time breakfast was over, he had become sullen and distraught, and wanted to be left alone.

But as the boys left the mess hall, Francis Flanigan came up to him and said, "I don't wanta play any damn softball. Let's go frog hunting again. We'll see some this time, I bet, Ray. Come on."

Raymond studied him for a moment. "Okay," he said then, out of habit.

"Then, go on down to the lake to that big beech tree again—now. I'll go get the butterfly net and meet you there in a minute. Don't say anything to anybody. Let 'em play ball if they want to. Hell!''

Like an inert clod Raymond, as directed, went on down to the lake and followed it around to the right, some seventy-five yards, to come again to the great beech tree, its wild, re-bellious roots spiraling high against the blue horizon and into the water. He was already exhausted, and sat down on a large dry root and contemplated his unsightly shoes, caked with the mud of the previous day. He was in a strange, morbid tor-ment. He gazed up at the blue, vivid sky and sighed, emo-tional welts for veins standing out at his temples. He wanted to run away now, to flee the reckoning of the dream. But now the sun already grew hot on his shoulders, partially bringing him back to life.

In a few minutes Francis came with the net, but this time he had wrapped it in a newspaper. Why was this? Raymond wondered, concluding it was his friend's sensitiveness, his re-action to the failures of the day before. Yet Francis was deadly serious today. "Let's go around to the other side of the lake, and work this way," he said. "We've never been over there."

"Okay." Raymond was docile. He was somehow glad to be with Francis now and hoped their efforts would be successful. They set out trudging the half mile around to the opposite side of the lake. It was nine-thirty. The rays of the sun, bright and already harsh, flowed down onto the scrub underbrush through which they passed. Raymond was beginning to feel eager, expectant, as if he were acting in an emergency. They would catch a frog, all right, he thought. Maybe more than one. He was confident. For it was a need, and soon to become a burning necessity. It was a matter of, and *in*, his mind. In some strange, vague way it derived from his own struggles, vexations, over a life at home he was powerless to understand. Torn between these consuming polarities, he was left drained and confused; exhausted, as on a rack. Then, all over again, his fear for Rita would come slamming in. Ah, Luther . . . Luther, don't do it.

Later, when they reached the other side of the lake, they found the terrain far more of a wilderness than the area from which they had come. Here there were enough trees to qualify as woods, if not a forest, plus a melee of dense foliage and bramble thickets all the way down to the water's edge. But the hot sun had dried out everything, including the tall grass underfoot and the wild daisies and marigolds along the way. Both boys were perspiring now and Raymond was already thirsty from the heat and the exertions of the hike. But Francis, still very serious and intent, frequently left him to push forward alone through the weeds to the edge of the water to look for a likely place. Soon he came upon a spot where an ugly, gnarled tree overlooked the water, and the bank was perfectly bare and sloped down gradually from the thicket and grass. It had apparently been used by someone as a fishing site, for there were remnants of the black ashes of a campfire now scattered by rain, a couple of empty pork-and-beans cans, and a small forked piece of tree limb stuck in the earth as a fishing pole support. There were squalid water lilies growing in the stagnant water in the shade of the tree and two giant discarded truck tires lying half submerged in the shallowest water.

Francis stood surveying the site for a moment. "Let's hang out here awhile," he finally said. "It's shady—there's gotta be a frog or two around here." He unwrapped his butterfly net and looked about him for a place to sit down within reach of the two big truck tires half out of the water. "These old tires are a perfect place for some lazy old bullfrog to come up and take a snooze on," he said, passing Raymond a piece of the newspaper the net had been wrapped in and keeping a piece for himself. Soon they were sitting on the newspapers in the shade of the tree, waiting—Francis with net in hand. However, today he was not insistent on silence. He himself talked whenever he wished, although in a more subdued voice. Now Raymond had somehow become spiritless, glum, again.

"What's eatin' you, Ray?" Francis said—his eyes still on the tires, however. "Have you said two words all morning?—I don't think so. What's wrong?"

"Nothing," Raymond said almost inaudibly.

"The hell there ain't—you were havin' nightmares all night long."

Raymond bristled. "I was?" he sneered. "So what?"

"You sick?—don't you feel good?"

". . . Tired, that's all," Raymond finally sighed.

They sat mostly silent now, watching the two old tires for a half hour—in vain. At last Raymond turned on Francis: "Why're you so dead set on catching frogs all the time, Frank?" he said.

Francis looked at him. Then with a curious, solemn grin, almost a grimace, he took his eyes back to the tires. "Damned if I know," he said.

"You're so *nuts* about it," Raymond insisted, frowning. "I don't get it."

Francis said nothing, and only gazed at the water.

"We can sit here all day," Raymond said, "and not catch a single frog. Why do you do it? What would you do with one anyway, if you caught it?!" His voice had risen almost to hysteria.

Francis only gazed at the tires. "Damned if I know."

Raymond stood up in exasperation. "Crimineee! Let's go back and watch the softball game."

Francis turned and looked at him again now. "Naw, you go

ahead, Ray. I'm going to stay. Do you wanta come back out tonight with me? We can shine 'em with a flashlight. I'll bet we'll get some then."

"I'm tired now," Raymond said. "I'll think about it, though." Yet he did not leave, and had soon even sat down again. Also, strangely, his thirst had left him. The two of them then sat there for the remainder of the morning without seeing a frog.

Finally on their way back to the camp in time for lunch, Francis, too, was morose and silent. But just before they reached the dorm, he spoke (almost as if to himself): "My mother sent me up here to get rid of me. So I hunt frogs."

Raymond only gazed straight ahead and made no comment. He well understood.

That night, after both had had afternoon naps, they returned to the same place. Francis had borrowed a flashlight and of course still carried his butterfly net. In the darkness as they approached, even a hundred yards away, they could hear the bullfrogs croaking in the area of the two truck tires. "Hear that?" he said excitedly. "What'd I tell you? Come on." They crept up to the spot where they had sat all morning and Francis put the bright flashlight beam on the two tires. There was a big bullfrog on each. "*Mother of God!*" he breathed, and quickly put out the light. "You saw 'em, didn't you?" They withdrew in the blackness for a whispered strategy conference. "It's too damn bad we can't get both of 'em," he said. "But one'll get away. Here, take the flashlight. When you put it on 'em, I'll go for the one on the left tire, see? He's a little bigger than the other one, I think. Whew! . . . Okay?"

"Yeah . . . I'm ready," Raymond said nervously.

They approached the water's edge again and in the darkness Francis extended and readied his butterfly net. At the brink now, with Raymond standing beside him, he leaned far forward over the two tires and whispered, "Ready?"

"Yeah," Raymond said.

"Okay, turn her on."

The blinding beam went out of the flashlight onto the frog on the left and Francis brought the net opening, the circular steel rim, down over it, as, predictably, the other frog plummeted in the water. "Keep the light on *this* sonofabitch, Ray: keep it on him!" Francis cried. The caught frog was jumping up and down in the mesh net inverted over it and the problem now was to get the net upright again with the frog still in it. Moreover, Francis was pressing the rim of the net down so hard that the tire under it was going deeper into the water. "Keep the light on him, Ray!" Francis breathed, letting up the pressure some. Soon the frog stopped jumping in the net and was quiet. "He ain't fooling me," Francis said. "He wants me to try to bring him in while he's laying still like that, but I ain't about to do that. I'm gonna wait till he jumps again." They waited, Francis pouring sweat. Suddenly the frog leaped. It leaped up into the mesh of the net and Francis swung with all his might, the net coming in toward them with a great *swooosh*. The frog, however, somehow came free of the net and was hurled back some fifty feet or more into the night blackness of the wood. For an instant Francis seemed to have turned to stone. At last he found his voice and began whimpering hysterically—". . . Ooooh, Christ! He got away! He . . . he . . . Oh, no! Oh, no! I can't believe it! Quick, gimme the flashlight! Let's go find him!"

They went up and started a frantic search among the trees, in the tall grass, and the bramble thickets, but of course were unable to find the frog. Soon Francis was crying. Big tears ran down off his cheeks. "Oh, God, he got away," he blubbered. "I had him! . . . I *had* him! Then he got away! Oh,

God!" Suddenly he went into a berserk tantrum, uttering a string of oaths and obscenities, and stomping about wildly in the weeds.

"Oh, cut it out," Raymond finally said, but sadly. "Let's go on down the bank here a little way. We'll see some more."

"Like hell we will!" Francis shouted, choking with rage and despair. "We won't see another one! Oh, Lord! I'm going back! I'm going back to the dorm! *Shit!*" Soon he was crying again—yammering. Raymond led him away, and soon they were on their way back to camp.

The next morning, Friday, was another beautiful day. Raymond had been so exhausted the night before that he'd slept soundly and long and awakened refreshed. But by breakfast time in the mess hall, despite the beauty of the morning and even the noise and raillery of the boys, his old anxieties had returned. He was afraid and had become taciturn again. After the meal and back in the dorm, he tried to talk to Francis, but Francis was sulking. "Let's go back out this morning, Frank," Raymond almost pleaded. "Oh, come on."

Francis curled his lip in disgust. "Are you nuts? Hell no! I brought another book along to read—I'm going outside in the shade and read after 'while." Soon he turned and began talking to another boy.

Raymond went and sat down on his bed and stared out the window. He sat there for a long time, until the other boys had gone out to play. Again he was thinking of Rita. She had stayed the night before in Madison, he found it all too easy to recall. He wondered specifically where? . . . with whom? In Stanley's mother's house? . . . or in some expressway motel? A spasm of agony went through him and he helplessly wrung his hands. Where was Luther? He wished he could go find him and talk to him, try to console him. Maybe he'd even be foolish enough to tell Luther it was all for the best—or as Rita had put it, for a "better life for us" (meaning for Ray-

mond and herself). He would of course make no mention of
Luther's life. Would Luther understand all this? He might
understand it *all too well.* Therein lay the danger. Again Raymond thought of the terrifying dream . . . Ah, Luther, don't
do it.

An hour later he still sat thinking. At last he went over to
Francis's bunk and looked underneath. The butterfly net was
there, and he took it out and left the dorm. The sun was
higher now and the sky a hard bright blue. He went down to
the lake and began examining closely, almost microscopically,
any spot where a frog might be sunning. He must somehow
traverse the interminable time between now and evening—
when he could call Rita. She would have returned home by
then. He went on slowly around the bank of the lake, peering
hard at spot after spot, but in his subconscious well knowing
he would not find a frog. His quest had become a mania. He
would stand and stare for minutes at one lone piece of wet de-
bris at the water's edge, as if he thought he had the power to
raise up a frog on it by some legerdemain or mad magic.
Slowly, methodically, forgoing lunch, he continued around
the lake to the spot where, the night before, the frog had so
disastrously eluded them. He sat staring with hot eyes at the
tire on the left that he had shone with the flashlight in the
darkness. Now the sun was as torrid and bright as it had been
twenty-four hours before when in daylight they had first
found the place. Francis had been so eager, so confident,
then. Raymond understood him and his compulsions, his
frustrations, well.

It was not until four o'clock that afternoon that Raymond
started the half-mile trek back to the dorm, where on arriving
he stowed the butterfly net this time under his own bunk. All
the boys were showering for dinner now. "Here he is!" they
cried on seeing him. "Where have you been all day?" they
catcalled, and Specs Dottweiler answered for him: "He's

been in a haystack with some farmer's daughter, that's where." Then more seriously, almost in awe, they asked him where he had really been, and what he'd been doing. He lied and said he'd been hunting frogs.

Later that evening, around seven-thirty, he went to Cavitt's hutment to call Rita. Cavitt was not there, only his assistant Rouse, a portly, kindly man in his fifties, who looked up from a newspaper and contemplated Raymond for a moment. "Ray," he said in a slightly reproving voice, "we got a little anxious about you this afternoon. Neither Cavitt nor I knew you hadn't come back for lunch, and didn't realize you were gone until Francis mentioned it. When you finally showed up, we were about to go out looking for you. You mustn't do that again—I mean go off by yourself and fool around near the lake. It can be dangerous. I know you can swim, but even so it's not good to be by yourself. Somebody said you were hunting frogs. Heck, you don't find frogs around a lake much. They like old backwoods creeks and swamps. But, anyhow, you mustn't go off like that by yourself anymore, Ray. Cavitt was going to tell you, but now he won't have to. D'you want to use the phone? . . . Okay, go ahead." Considerately, Rouse left the room.

This lecture had strangely angered Raymond. He thought Rouse callous, unfeeling. It was as if he expected Rouse, by some divination, to understand, and therefore make allowances, to commiserate a little. But now he placed the collect call to Rita.

"Hi, Ray, honey," she said on accepting the call, "I've been home almost three hours."

"How'd it go?"

"It went well. It went *very* well, Ray. I was surprised, though, when I met his mother. She's an invalid—part of the time uses a wheelchair. Stanley never told me that. Yet you'd be astounded at how young she looks. She really does. I like her a lot. She's very sweet. She's got class, too—Ray, *real class.*"

Raymond wanted to ask her if she'd stayed the night there, in Stanley's mother's house, but he desisted. "Well, that's—"

"Oh, but listen to this, Ray!" Rita interrupted. "The first thing I saw, in the mail slot, when I got home was an airmail letter from Luther."

"*. . . Yeah?*"

"Ray, Luther's in Los Angeles. Honest to God, he is. He took a plane out there Wednesday—he had only packed and left the house the night before, you know. I was flabbergasted when I read it. He said he's going to get a job out there. He's not coming back here. Ray, he's given up. I'm sure of it. He didn't say so, but it means he won't oppose a divorce. I never thought he would, anyway. You'll never meet a man in life that's got more pride than Luther. He would've amounted to something if he'd been white. I still have a lot of respect for him, a good feeling toward him, really. But it will mean a better life for us, Ray, honey." Rita sighed in the phone.

Raymond was silent. He wanted to ask if Luther had so much as sent him a "hello." Or a "good-bye."

"Ray? . . . are you there?"

"Yes."

"So, that's the way it's shaping up, honey. Golly, things happen fast, don't they? Say, how much longer have you got up there now?"

"Too long. I don't *have* to be up here at all."

"Now, don't say that. Every boy should go to camp. You've got, let's see, almost three weeks yet. That's not long."

"Mom, I want to come home. It's deathly up here."

"Ray, I've already paid for your whole time. You need a little of that rough-and-tumble outdoor life. You were so pale, sallow, when you left. And peevish too—really rude. You don't want to be tagging along hanging onto my apron strings all the time, do you? Besides . . . this is kind of an awkward time for me. . . . Ray, it *is!*"

"I understand, Mom. Forget it."

"But hasn't Luther acted admirably? . . . just admirably. He'll probably do very well out there, too—very well. I'm glad for him."

"Mom, he may get to thinking. And come back."

"Come back? . . . That's ridiculous. Why would he want to come back?"

"To kill you."

"*Ray:* What a terrible thing to say! You're cruel. And impudent." . . . But there was hollow fear in Rita's voice. "Now, you take that back!" she finally exploded.

"Okay, I'll take it back," Raymond said drearily.

They talked for five minutes more, but both hung up unhappy, unsatisfied, still afraid. Raymond was haunted even more now by his premonitions. There was another night of fitful sleep.

He lay there in his bunk in the dark. It was past midnight, and very still. Specs Dottweiler was snoring stertorously and little Hershel Reichman lay with his hand open as if catching raindrops. Raymond counted the days. Seventeen more to go. He hoped to catch at least one lone frog before leaving. Yet *that* wasn't too important. . . . In any event, one would suffice. He would hunt every day, though—*every day*. It was a necessity. And what Rouse had said about not going around the lake alone anymore would only give him, Raymond, the excuse to impress disheartened Francis into service once more. Despite Francis' bitter blustering, this would not be hard. For him, too, it was a necessity. Raymond thought of his times, some happy, some not so happy, with Luther. He had never completely understood them. Some had been simple, others murderously complex. He doubted if Rita had understood them either. Or Luther, for that matter. Or those two, theirs. The complications, in the end, had got them too. So all had been reduced. Luther, perhaps, most of all. That was why no one could foretell his delayed reactions. Raymond's premonitions therefore persisted. Yet he took no inflexible position as to the future. If his forebodings were right, then there would be no future. If they were wrong, there would be none still. He only felt listless now, apathetic, sated, and wanted to shut off his mind. Tomorrow he and Francis would resume their hunting. Maybe some slow, aged, understanding frog would creep forward and cooperate. But failing this, they could always use the net for butterflies.

ABOUT THE AUTHOR

Cyrus Colter is the author of *The Beach Umbrella, The Rivers of Eros, Night Studies, The Hippodrome,* and *A Chocolate Soldier.* He is a lawyer, a former Illinois state official (Commerce Commissioner), and an emeritus professor at Northwestern University, where he chaired the Department of African American Studies and held the Chester D. Tripp Professorship in the Humanities. He lives in Chicago, Illinois.